A Spirited Double

The Midlife is Murder Cozy Mystery Series

Clare Lockhart

APATITE PUBLISHING

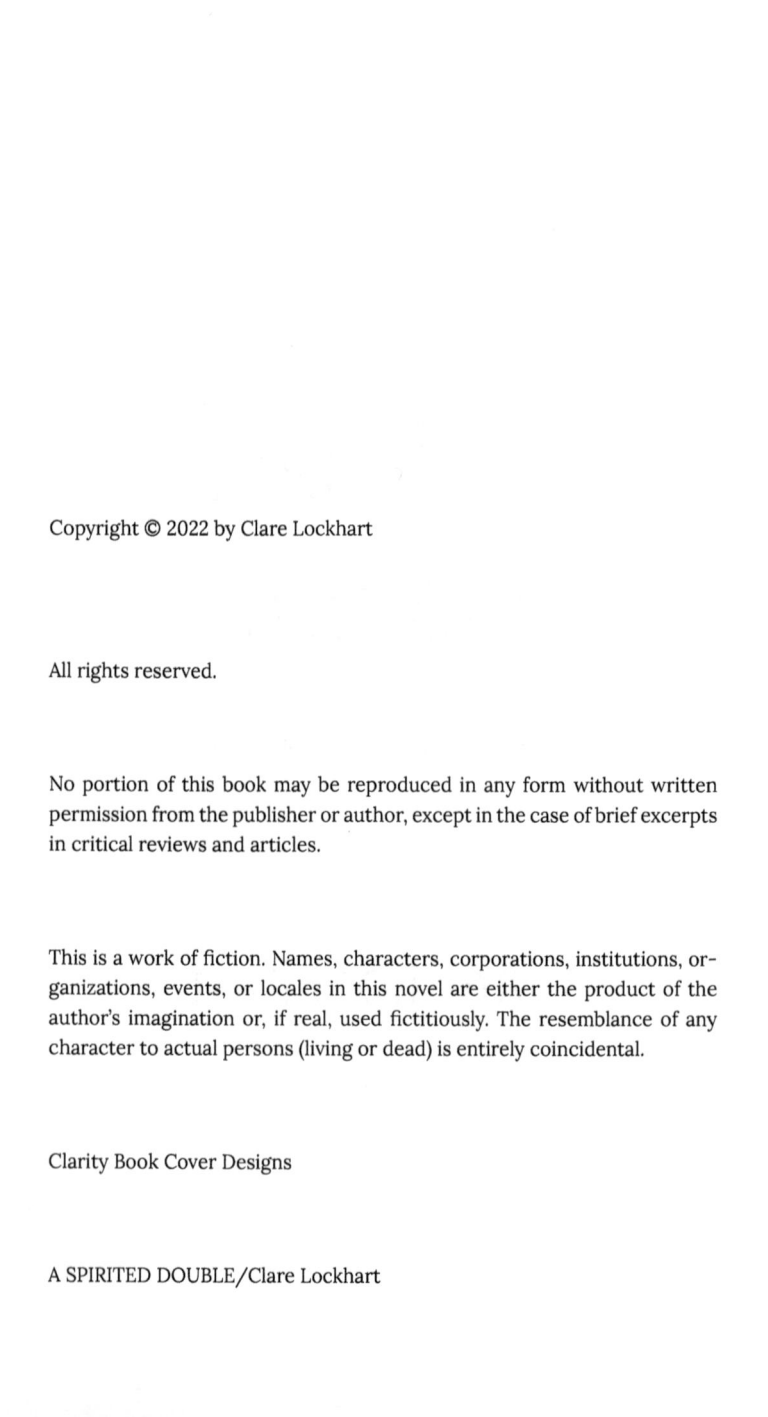

Copyright © 2022 by Clare Lockhart

All rights reserved.

No portion of this book may be reproduced in any form without written permission from the publisher or author, except in the case of brief excerpts in critical reviews and articles.

This is a work of fiction. Names, characters, corporations, institutions, organizations, events, or locales in this novel are either the product of the author's imagination or, if real, used fictitiously. The resemblance of any character to actual persons (living or dead) is entirely coincidental.

Clarity Book Cover Designs

A SPIRITED DOUBLE/Clare Lockhart

To my dad, who was gone too soon.

Also by Clare Lockhart

Midlife is Murder
Paranormal Cozy Mystery Series
A *Spirited Swindler* (Book 1)
A *Spirited Debacle (Novella)* (Book 1.5)
A *Spirited Double* (Book 2)
A *Spirited Vengeance* (Book 3)
A *Spirited Betrayal* (Book 4)
A *Spirited Delusion* (Book 5)
A Spirited Accusation (Book 6)
A Spirited Reckoning (Book 7)

Midlife is Magic
Paranormal Cozy Mystery Series
Visions and Villainy (Novella) (Book 1)
Curses and Consequences (Book 2)
Potions and Plunder (Book 3)
Scandals and Snafus (Short Story in A *Witch of a Scandal* anthology)
Sorcery and Suspects (Book 4)

Magical Matchmaker Romance
(writing as Sharon Clare)
Love of Her Lives
Trick Me Once
In For a Spell

A SPIRITED DOUBLE

Dear Reader,

I want to thank you for reading this book and welcome you back (if you're read other books in the series) to the Midlife is Murder Paranormal Cozy Mystery Series and to the imaginary small town of Bookend Bay nestled on the sandy shore of Lake Superior.

In this series, you'll meet Quinn Delaney, a newly divorced, amateur sleuth who's going through a few changes. Some are welcome (an empty-nest and opening of her dream café) and some not so much (a sudden ability to see ghosts, an OCD twin from a parallel universe, and a rash of murders).

If you like reading about best friends who find themselves in the odd pickle yet persevere until they've caught the bad guys, then you're in the right place.

If you enjoy spending time with Quinn and her friends in Bookend Bay, I invite you to join my newsletter on my website https://clarelockhart.com and get a FREE novella in the series. In my newsletter, I'll let you know about new book releases, book discounts, promotions featuring other cozy mysteries, news about the books I'm working on next, a few personal stories, and fun giveaways.

Or if you'd rather not join the newsletter and just be notified of the next book release, follow me on Amazon and/or Bookbub.

Happy reading!

Love and hugs,

Clare

Chapter One

My kitchen was a cornucopia for the senses—the energizing aroma of rosemary water bubbling on the stove, the heat of the late afternoon sun warming me up, and the murmur of an exorcism taking place somewhere outside the window on the wrap-around deck.

Wait. What was I hearing?

I put down my spoon and cocked my head toward the outdoors.

I swear, this is what I heard through the window: "I command you, phantom spirit, return to the infernal realm whence you came." The plea was from Violet, my tenant. She lived in the guest suite, downstairs on the ground level of my riverside home.

I crossed the kitchen to where Oreo, my black and white Maine Coon cat, had been sleeping on the window seat. Sprawled across the length of the cushion, his thick tail hanging almost to the floor, he lifted his head, gave a disgruntled meow, and eyed me as if the disturbance outside his window was my fault.

"Don't look at me," I said, peering outside. "I would have said no to the exorcism if she'd asked." I scanned the deck for Violet, but she was not in sight.

During the last couple of weeks, she'd complained about a presence in the house. Not that I didn't believe in spirits, I did. But this apparition of Violet's...well, I'd seen no sign of it myself. And if it existed, I was pretty sure her ominous chanting would do nothing to send it packing. It might even make a spirit agitated, but I was no expert.

If she wanted to have an exorcism, that was her business. I had to get my rosemary syrup finished and make the lemon cordial I'd promised to bring to my good friend Toni's tonight, and I was already running late. The drink was a new concoction I planned to feature at Break Thyme, my artisan café here in Bookend Bay. If my rosemary lemon cordial was up to snuff, I was going to enter it, with three other cordials, in the Great Lakes Superior Taste contest. Winning that contest would help put Break Thyme on the map. My brother Craig, the over-achieving, geo-physicist, would not be the only one in the family winning awards. Not that I begrudged him his achievements, but it was hard to always stand in his long shadow. I wanted a few professional accolades of my own.

I gave Oreo's head a scratch and listened for appeals to the otherworld. All was quiet. Hopefully, Violet finished her ritual and believed she'd successfully banished her ghost to the afterlife.

Hooking my long bangs behind my ear, I scooted back to the stove. Two cups of water and one sprig of rosemary. I'd been scribbling measurements and ingredients on a notepad since I'd left my laptop at the café. Now that the water had come to boil, I dropped the rosemary into the pot and would let it sit for ten minutes before I added sugar and honey. I turned off the stove.

On the notepad, a few drops of water beaded over the Gaia Green Earth logo. I swiped them away with my finger. It was a colorful logo of a woman in a starry sky cradling the Earth. I couldn't remember where the pad had come from and had been meaning to look up the organization. It would be nice if I could remember to do that when sitting in front of my computer.

Just as I pulled open the drawer to get the sugar, my front door slammed shut, making me jump.

Oreo vamoosed, hitting the floor with a thump. The cat had no tolerance for sudden interruptions. It was easy to be on his side.

"I consecrate and clear this space!" came Violet's shrill demand from the front of the house. What was she doing now?

Leaving the kitchen, I padded across the glossy wood floor. At the stone fireplace that separated the kitchen and living room, I paused, stupefied by what was happening across the room.

Violet faced the front door, slightly bent over, trailing a line of salt onto the mint-green, painted boards. The ends of a yellow bandanna flapped against her curly brown hair as her flowered skirt swooshed around thick calves.

"Violet! Stop it. What are you doing?" I was beside her in seconds, tugging on her arm to stop the flow of salt she had cupped in her hand. A two-pound bag was crooked in her other arm.

She looked at me. It surprised me to see composure in those brown eyes, but she wasn't fooling me. This could be the calm in the eye of a storm.

"Quinn, shhh," she said, not relenting to my hold on her arm. More salt hit the floor. "We don't want to upset the phantom." She lowered her voice. "Or maybe it's a demon. I'm not exactly sure. But I do know, you must not show any anger. No negativity at all."

She smiled tightly and turned to face the room. "I command you, phantom...or demon of this riverside house, to leave now and never return." She bit her bottom lip and passed me the bag of salt. "Now, go make a circle at the kitchen door."

I took the salt but didn't budge. I knew a thing or two about ghosts. They didn't give a fig about seasonings. "I will not. Violet, this isn't going to help. You're just making a mess. There's salt everywhere."

"I think that's good," she said, admiring her salt circle. "It should be good, right?"

"Definitely not." I tried for a little gallows humor to lighten things up. "Doesn't the salt have to be blessed by a priest to expel a phantom?"

"I don't know," she admitted, seriously. "This is my first exorcism. If you're worried about a little salt, then steer clear, Quinn. I'm doing this for you, you know." Her voice raised in that last sentence.

Well, that was cheeky. "Steer clear? This is my house."

She turned her back to me and reached for a basket that was sitting on the bench beside the door. Good, she was gathering her things and leaving.

Instead of heading out the door, Violet lit a bundle of leaves, blew out the flame, and waved the smoke in a figure eight. I recognized the smell. Sage.

Okay, this was going three steps too far. Any humor I'd harbored capsized. Who did she think she was? Not only would I have to clean up this mess, but I also didn't want her in my part of the house right now.

She came at me with the smoking herbs. "Yes, I know this is your house. I've been patient, but you didn't hang crosses over the doors and windows as I asked. You've done nothing about this phantom, and it's driving me crazy. It pops in and out whenever it feels like it. You scare me half to death."

I scare her? She was the one acting like a maniac. My shoulders tensed. I took a breath to calm down and spoke firmly. "Well, you're the one scaring me, now. Violet, please stop this!"

She waved the sage at my head. I'd been right about the eye of the storm. Her eyes had taken on a cracked look that sent icy bites down my spine. "I call upon you, Phantom. Obey my command and leave the body of Quinn Delaney now." Her shrill voice cut through the room and likely out the open windows.

I was normally a tolerant person, but I'd reached my limit. "You think I'm possessed?"

Violet gave a quick nod. "You will not deter me, demon spirit."

We were both yelling now. I took a step back and put my hand out to stop her. "I've had enough, Violet. Take your burning bush and get out of my home."

"You are an insidious phantom!" she cried, seemingly forgetting not to antagonize the spirits. "I protect this person from all evil!" She pushed the bundle toward me again, lifting and lowering, swooping up and down from my head to my toes. "I will not relent until you return to the infernal realm!"

She was ignoring me! Heat flushed through my body in outrage. If anyone was possessed, it was her!

Wait. Could she be possessed? Was that possible?

Cripes. All this talk of demons and exorcism was freaking me out.

Smoke sucked into my nostrils. I coughed, turned, and hurried back to the kitchen.

Where was my phone? Violet was my brother's work acquaintance. Maybe he could tell me if she had a history of instability or was prone to violent outbursts.

I saw my phone on the counter. I snatched it up and grabbed my purse from the chair. The sound of Violet's creepy demands rang out in the living room.

A ghostly film of sage smoke wafted past me as I ran down the stairs toward my bedroom on the lower level.

"I consecrate and clear this space!" Violet wailed.

At the bottom of the stairs, I found Oreo hiding between the hall tree and my ficus plant. I left him for a moment, took a breath, and flicked through my contacts for my brother.

Hitting the call icon, I hurried into my bedroom at the back of the house. While the phone rang, I riffled through the drawer in the bathroom vanity, grabbing my thyroid medication and toothbrush. I'd already planned to sleep over at Toni's, but I was going to head there sooner than expected. I didn't want to be near Violet right now because I wasn't sure I could hold my temper.

The phone was still ringing. *Pick up, Craig!*

From the closet, I snatched my leather knapsack and stuffed in pajamas and clothes for tomorrow.

I got Craig's voice mail and waited for the beep. "Hey, it's your sister. Hope you arrived at your conference safely. Just to let you know, Violet has gone off the deep end. She's performing an exorcism of my house, burning sage, and throwing salt around. It's creepy. I don't know if I should call the police or just let her wear herself out. Can you let me know what you think? Maybe you could even call her and talk her off the ledge. I'm staying overnight at Toni's. Call me when you can." I disconnected.

Violet's footsteps pranced overhead as if she was doing a do-si-do.

I couldn't remember where I'd put the cat carrier. When was the last time I'd used it? I stood inside my bedroom, facing my mirror. In the reflection, in the upper corner, something moved. Behind me. Quick. Like a shadow dashing by.

A shiver ran down my spine. A cry tripped up my throat, but the rest of me froze.

What if Violet was right, and we did have a ghost? The thought made me shudder as I recalled the terrible time

I'd had last year with a cheating, swindling ghost. It was nerve-wracking to think it could happen again. But if I had a ghost in the house, why didn't it just show itself like the other self-absorbed ghosts I'd met? Not that I wanted dead people to show themselves. Definitely not. I was finally in a good place. I couldn't deal with that kind of havoc in my life. Not again.

I turned and scanned the room from corner to corner. Nothing there.

Get a grip! I was letting Violet's rantings get to me.

Oreo bolted into the room and gave the loudest mewl I'd ever heard. My heart leaped back into my throat.

"Sweet Mother! Did you see something, Oreo?" I asked ridiculously. If we had a ghost, had Violet angered it with her exorcism? Was it irritated now and would take its anger out on me?

I crossed to the French doors and looked outside. To the right. To the left. Nothing moved out there either. I locked the door.

All the hairs on the back of my neck rose. I was not going to talk myself into a state of calm. Not here. I had to get out of this house. Screw the cat carrier.

I stuffed my purse in my backpack, flung it over my shoulder, and scooped up Oreo. He gave a rolling meow to let me know he wasn't happy. "I know. Me neither."

My heart pounded in my ears. *Calm down.* There was no point in letting my imagination run away. Whatever I saw in the bedroom was a shadow from the outside window, probably a bird or a squirrel, that's all.

It wasn't easy maneuvering my way outside with a Maine coon cat in hand, but I kicked the door closed with my foot, and bolted into the carport to my truck, shuffling my beast of a cat into one arm to open the back door. Oreo hated vehicles. It was worse without the carrier. He let out another sharp cry as I set him on the seat and slammed the door just before he smashed his front paws against it. I looked at him through the window. Green eyes pierced me—mad as all get out.

As I ran around to the driver's side, I saw the cat carrier sitting on the lowest shelf at the end of the carport. I couldn't remember storing it there, but I was glad to see it.

I was shaking now as I bent over to grab the carrier.

"Didn't I warn you this would happen?" The harsh reproach from behind was enough to have startled me on a good day. I shrieked.

My neighbor Sandy stood on the property line, tapping her shoe. We were friendly by just a smidgen.

"You scared the daylights out of me, Sandy." My heartbeat was back to thumping in my ears.

"Welcome to the club! How do you think it feels to have that tenant of yours invoking the devil?"

"She's actually doing the exact opposite of that." Although I supposed it was hard to tell with all the demon and infernal realm references.

"I heard you arguing. And now, you're making a run for it. Leaving her here for me to listen to. Well, that just figures, doesn't it? I told you not to go renting your place to strangers. That no-good site is an invitation for hoodlums into good neighborhoods."

I think she said all that in one breath. There was no point telling Sandy I wasn't listed on any website.

"I'm having dinner with a friend tonight," I said. "That's why I'm going out."

"You're taking your cat to dinner? If you don't phone the police on that banshee, I will."

"Please don't, Sandy. I'll talk to the police. I will. And don't worry. Violet is harmless." I may not have sounded convincing, but as I said it, I realized I did believe that. Taking the cat to Toni's was an over-reaction, but he was with me now. I moved toward the truck. "She thinks the house is haunted and is just doing a little smudging."

Sandy shook her head. "You *better* talk to the police because if she disturbs my peace any more tonight, I'll be calling them."

"Gotcha." I climbed into the back seat and worked up a sweat, getting Oreo into the carrier. I smiled in Sandy's direction as I left the house, careful to appear like I wasn't in a panic over Violet's behavior. I hoped leaving Violet in my house with an irate neighbor hovering nearby wasn't a poor decision.

A mile down Harmony Road, I saw Mishka, Violet's dog walker, in a field throwing a ball to Trix, a Golden Shephard mix.

I let out the breath I'd been holding, feeling my heart rate return to normal. Approaching Mishka, I slowed the car.

Oreo let out another cry. I turned to see him licking his paw innocently.

Two other dogs bounded through the field with Trix—a dachshund and a border collie. The dachshund's little legs were pumping at twice the rate of the bigger dogs. Mishka had leashes around her shoulders. She walked over to my car as I pulled over.

Having powered down the window, I called out a hello.

"Hey, Quinn," Mishka said, coming closer to the truck.

Trix bounded over, followed by the other dogs. Mishka threw a ball far into the field and the three dogs took off.

I waited for her to turn back toward me. "You might want to take the dog for a long walk tonight."

"Violet's having a bad day, isn't she?"

That was putting it mildly, but how long could an exorcism take? "Perhaps give her an hour or so, and things will settle down."

She narrowed her eyes. "I doubt that. A thing like this changes your life forever, don't you think?"

I stared back at her, confused by her comment, but I supposed exorcising a demon phantom qualified as a life-changing event. In the rearview mirror, I saw a car coming up behind me.

"I guess it does." This wasn't the time to clarify that Mishka and I were talking about the same thing.

"Car coming. Gotta go. Have a good walk, Mishka!"

As I pulled away, a cloud drew in front of the sun, turning the sky into gloom. I was suddenly cold on a day when the thermometer read 84 degrees.

Chapter Two

I TURNED ON THE satellite radio and continued driving alongside the Manitou River toward Toni's house. As Freddie Mercury beseeched us to find him somebody to love, I relaxed and let my mind wander.

I thought I'd found somebody to love—forever. Two and a half years ago, my husband Bryan and I downsized when our nest emptied. And then, a year later, he downsized further when he hot-footed it out of our marriage and the town of Bookend Bay to teach English in South Korea.

That was only the half of it, and I tried not to ruminate on the other half, the half where he'd had an affair with a woman who was then murdered and came back to haunt me. It was best for my well-being to put that fiasco to bed and leave it there, so to speak.

Bryan said our marriage lacked affection, and sadly, that was true. If I were to sum him up in one word, it would be critical. To him, criticizing was a full-time job—me, our kids, the neighbors, the town, the country. But I had to give him credit where due—he'd been the one to leave. And to my credit, it hadn't taken me long to embrace the gift of his absence.

So, that's how I ended up on my own, after twenty-seven years of marriage. I don't know how I'd have gotten through that period if it wasn't for my best friend Toni.

We'd been friends for thirty-one years. Toni and I connected instantly when we'd first met. We'd gone through a lot together—marriages, kids, travels, the death of her husband, and my divorce. There was nothing I hadn't shared with her.

By the time I pulled into my friend's driveway, my blood pressure was back in the normal zone, and I felt silly for letting Violet's exorcism spook me.

Widowed eleven years ago, Toni had moved to Beach Meadows, a community set on Lake Superior in a neighborhood with plenty of trees, winding roads, colorful gardens, and fountained ponds. At first glance, I knew this was the perfect landing place for the simpler life Toni sought.

Four years older than me, she'd already passed the fifty-year milestone, the one I decided to acknowledge only after Forbes pointed out that over half of the top 100 most powerful women were in their fifties or older. It was time to seize our power, and when I figured out what that meant, I'd do some serious seizing.

Her modular home was just over seven hundred square feet, yet she loved the size. With an eye for design, she'd decorated in a coastal chic style with soothing sea-salt blues and cool ivories. I always felt a spa-like tranquility whenever I visited.

Toni's home was perfect—for her. I couldn't imagine my life reduced and contained to this square-footage. My house wasn't sprawling, but it was nearly three times as big as Toni's, including the suite where my ghostbuster lived.

"I don't think you've ever brought Oreo to dinner," she said, once he'd made himself at home by curling up on the guest bed. Maybe I was giving him more credit than due, but I swear he was giving me the cold shoulder for stuffing him in that carrier.

"I will explain that once we're settled."

"Did you bring a cordial?" she asked.

I thought of the cordial sitting on my stove. "Shoot. No, I didn't get it finished."

"Don't worry about it. Gin and tonic then?"

"Definitely."

She made them just the way I loved them, with a sprig of mint and a squeeze of lime. I took the drink and followed her outside to the patio.

"Okay, what gives?" I said, studying her hair in the sunlight. "You haven't put streaks in your hair in a decade. You look great, by the way."

Toni touched her hair. "Thank you. No more gray. I've gone back to being a blonde."

"Why? You spent a year growing your hair out. I thought you were done with coloring."

"I was." Toni closed the patio door after me. "And then I changed my mind. I have a date on Saturday night."

I open my mouth. Paused. "A date?"

Toni and I talked every day. There'd been no mention of a date in the works. Never. Except.... "No! You didn't."

"She wore me down. When my mother gets a notion in her head...Well, you know, better chance that zombies rule the world before she backs off."

Zombies felt a little too close to home right now. "So, remind me. This man is the son of her friend?"

Toni groaned. "A new friend she met at bridge. The good news is he's a fire chief."

"Well, that's promising. You gotta love firefighters. He's probably in good shape. Have you seen a picture?"

"No. Mom said he's very winsome—*very.*"

"That's bad, isn't it?" At eighty-three years old, Toni's mother spent a year traveling the country in a van with a man who threaded beads into his beard. She once told me a good man should be hairy, *that* was her criteria. I hoped to have her spunk at eighty-three, minus the beaded beard.

"Yep. Pretty much a red flag. Anyway, enough about me. What's going on with you?"

As Toni and I sat in the shade with the sound of waves rolling to shore in the distance, I told her about the exorcism and my irritated neighbor. Talking about it wasn't nearly as unsettling as experiencing it. I felt a lot better about it now.

Toni pulled over a rattan footstool so we could put up our feet. I paused, admiring our toenails. We'd treated ourselves to pedicures last week. I'd chosen a deep purple polish and Toni had gone with aquamarine. Over the last year, even though my lifestyle hadn't changed, I'd been gaining weight. Having pretty toenails helped with that—somehow. Menopause sucked.

"Are you going to go to the police?" she asked.

"I don't know. I don't want to get Violet into trouble." Since I spent most of my time at my café, Violet and I saw little of each other. She'd always been a respectful tenant and her dog was adorable. Sometimes she had a friend over on the weekends. I'd heard them laughing, but things were always quiet by ten p.m.

"Quinn, you showed up here for dinner with your cat. You obviously felt unsafe in your own home. From what you said, Violet didn't listen when you asked her to stop and to leave. And she stunk up your house. Come on, you left without cleaning your kitchen!"

I laughed because she viewed my tidy tendencies as a bit obsessive. She had a point, though. Violet's behavior had rattled me, and rightly so. She'd not only accused me of being possessed, but she also turned a deaf ear on my request that she leave. And, because of her inane conduct, I'd abandoned my cordial.

"Isn't Violet a friend of Craig's?" Toni asked.

"They're work acquaintances. She did something for the mine, I think. Violet broke up with her husband and needed a place to land, and Craig knew I had an empty guest suite. Frankly, the extra money has been nice. I left him a message, but he hasn't called me back."

"Oh? That's not like him."

I felt a little sibling rivalry flare up. Everyone loved Craig. He was a champion for the community. As Senior Vice President of Environment, Health, and Safety at McCourt Mining, he was being honored for five years of responsible environmental practices, the only metal mine to have achieved this standing. Plus, when Craig was fifteen, he'd actually saved a toddler from drowning—gave the little boy mouth-to-mouth resuscitation. Sometimes it seemed everyone in town thought Craig was a superhero.

Even our parents favored him because everything he did turned to gold. Nearly forty years ago, we'd moved here to Bookend Bay, Michigan, when Dad was offered a job in the fisheries industry. After he died of heart failure eight years ago, our mother moved back to Nova Scotia. Mom claimed Craig called her every day. He was a beloved uncle to my kids, Jordan and Samantha. He even seemed to like Jordan's wife Chelsea, a feat I still struggled with.

So, yes. Now and then, I felt a little overshadowed by his greatness and his adoring fans. I could never sustain the feeling, though, because I, too, thought he was a good guy. It was one reason I'd taken on Violet as a tenant: I trusted his opinion.

"He's away at a conference, so I'll cut him some slack," I said.

"Ah. Still, what if Violet causes damage, and you knew she was off the rails and didn't report it?"

"That's a good point. My neighbor was pretty irate. Maybe we should tell the police about the exorcism." I lifted my drink to my lips.

"Stop!" Toni said, reaching for my glass. "You can't have liquor on your breath. We'll finish these drinks *after* we talk to the sheriff. I'll drive."

Fifteen minutes later, we pulled into the sheriff's office on Highway 12, a few miles outside of town. I checked my phone again, just in case I'd missed a message from Craig. Nothing, yet.

The office was at the end of a plaza beside a hardware store. Inside, the smell of garlic and tomato greeted us. "That smells good," I said. It wasn't a smell I associated with the law. A microwave was running behind the deputy's desk. Must be dinner time.

Deputy Cody Wilson, according to the name plate on the desk, was typing away on his computer. He couldn't have been much older than early twenties—a kid—albeit a brawny one. Clean-shaven with bushy, black eyebrows and dark hair, clipped so short, he appeared bald at first glance. After a few moments of us standing at the counter peering down at him, he looked up.

"Good evening, ladies. What can I do for you?" At least he was a polite kid.

"I guess I'd like to make a complaint," I said.

"You guess?"

"I mean, I'd like you to be aware of a potential problem."

"We don't like to work in potentials," he said, frowning.

I supposed not, but wouldn't he want a head's up that Violet could cause more trouble? "I have a tenant in my house who's acting strange. She thinks the house is haunted and is performing an exorcism. It's upsetting the neighbor."

"And you," added Toni.

"Yes, that's true," I agreed.

Toni piped up. "Violet, that's Quinn's tenant, came into the house waving a burning branch and when Quinn asked Violet to leave, she refused. Quinn was scared to death. She had to flee her own home with her cat!"

"I wasn't scared to death, just…er…a bit on edge." Repeating the details one more time made me realize Violet could have done me actual harm. I'd been smart to get myself—and Oreo—out of there before she truly spiraled out of control.

The microwave dinged and Deputy Wilson glanced at it before turning his attention back to us. "Is that so? Where is your husband, Mrs.—?"

"It's Ms. Delaney. I'm divorced."

"I see."

"How well do you know this tenant of yours?" he asked.

"Not well. She's an acquaintance of my brother's—Craig Scott."

"Craig Scott," he repeated, looking thoughtful. "Is that the guy who always wins the Bookend Bay marathon? Mark my words, I'm going to beat him next year."

I rolled my eyes. "Yes, that's him."

"Well then, why don't you let your brother handle this?"

"He really has nothing to do with it, and he's out of town." My spine tightened with indignation. Like I needed a man to fix this?

"Did your tenant threaten you?" he asked.

"Not exactly. I mean, she did wave a smoking bundle of sage at me."

"Sage? Isn't that what you put in turkey dressing?"

I just looked at him. Get your mind off dinner, mister.

"This has nothing to do with turkey dressing," offered Toni.

"But waving the herb around frightened you?" said the deputy, pulling a form out of the paper tray on his desk. "Shall we put it that way on the complaint?"

I let out my breath, loudly. He wasn't taking me seriously. Heat flushed through my mid-section as I got angry. Darn hot flashes. I discretely pulled the bottom of my T-shirt away from my body—fanning myself, so I wouldn't melt in front of this patronizing adolescent.

"The herb isn't the point," I said. "Her behavior was disturbing. And she's been getting worse over the last few weeks, harping on about phantoms. She wanted me to hang crosses over the doors and windows. If truth be told, I don't trust her, and I'd like you to tell her to pack her things and go." There. I said it.

Deputy Wilson scribbled notes. "Did she sign a lease?"

"Yes, but she's crossed a line here. She's...she's disturbing my neighbor. I'm surprised she didn't call you." I shot him a questioning look. Did Sandy call?

"Did you take a video of this disturbance?"

I rarely took photos, let alone videos. "No, I didn't think of that."

"Well, we've had no exorcism complaints today. Listen, Ms. Delaney, it doesn't sound like your tenant has broken any laws. Maybe she's breaking noise ordinances, maybe not. In any case, you must have a lawful reason to evict your tenant and provide adequate notice of eviction." His stomach rumbled. "You know what I think?"

"I do not."

"I think you should wait for your brother to come home and let him deal with it."

Again, with my superior brother. I folded my arms across my chest and narrowed my gaze. Too hot. I dropped my arms, but not my indignation. "And what, exactly, do you expect my brother to do? What could he do that you can't?"

"Now, now," he said, like he was soothing a child having a tantrum. "I can see you're upset, but there's nothing we can do if your tenant hasn't broken the law."

"When that happens, I imagine it'll be too late." I shot him an angry thanks-for-nothing look. "Have a nice dinner."

Toni and I left the station. I pressed the unlock button on my key fob. "I don't mean to sound vindictive, but I hope he gets indigestion from that microwaved meal."

"I don't know about that, Ms. Delaney, but we better get home and iron our tea towels."

I laughed. "We're going to need a lot of gin for that."

Toni gave a soft snort. "Yes. And I'd toss them back with you if having a hangover nowadays wasn't like recovering from a mild brain injury."

"Yay, midlife. We have arrived." I opened the door and slipped in behind the wheel, reminded of that Forbes article on women seizing their power. "I'm taking a stand,

Toni. In the morning, when Violet has calmed down, I'm going to have a talk with her and lay down some rules."

"I think that's a sensible idea."

I didn't need the sheriff or my brother. "I'm taking matters into my own hands."

Chapter Three

The next morning, I woke to a knock on my door. It took me a moment to remember I was at Toni's house.

"There's coffee in the pot," she called. "I'm having mine outside when you're ready to join."

"I'll be right out." I looked at the clock to see I'd slept in, which was unusual for me. It was already 7:00. I washed up, dressed, and stripped the bed.

In the living room, Oreo looked up from the couch.

"Hey, Oreo." As I approached, he angled his head to expose the place on his neck I should scratch. I smiled and did his bidding. Friends again.

Toni called from outside on the front porch. "Come on out. Everything's here." She had the coffee pot, cream, mugs, and muffins set on the table between two chairs.

The coffee smelled strong, just how I liked it. I filled a mug. "I'll be out of your hair after coffee."

"No, you won't. I'm coming with you. Who knows what Violet has been up to? Besides, I want to see if she evicted the ghost." Toni's expression turned serious. "You don't think you're being haunted again, do you? Weren't you warned about another ghost coming?"

That was true, but I had good reasons not to trust the source of the warning—it had come from a ghost who'd lived as a con artist and had targeted my ex-husband. The last I saw of that swindling spirit, she'd warned me something unearthly was coming my way. Sure, odd things had been happening to me over the last year. A few unexplained items had shown up at home and in the café, but I had no proof that an unhuman entity performed these harmless incidents. "Remember, that warning came from a professional swindler. I've wondered what would have happened if I'd acted as if I couldn't see her and had never spoken to her? What if giving a ghost credence is inviting it into my life? I think it's smart to *not* acknowledge anything supernatural." I lowered my voice. I might have already said too much. "I probably shouldn't even talk about it."

"Okay, fair enough. Changing the subject."

"Thank you."

"When does your new trailer arrive?"

I smiled at her reference to the twelve-year-old travel trailer I'd purchased. This was going to enable me and my kids to spend time together on a road trip to Nova Scotia to see my mother. "Tomorrow. It's going to be delivered to a campsite in the park next to Beach Meadows."

Toni brushed a leaf from her shorts. "I hope you're not planning to renovate that thing on your own."

I knew I had a lot on my plate, but I'd couldn't remember a time when I hadn't. So, truth be told, I was hoping to have it completely transformed before our trip. Perhaps it was juvenile, but at this stage in life, I still wanted to impress my mother. I intended to excel at something her "perfect" offspring Craig didn't. And Craig was no handyperson.

"Samantha is going to help," I said. "I imagine she sees her contribution as an investment in future vacation rights." After college, my daughter moved into a small, fixer-upper she'd bought with a girlfriend. They were both good with money and together they'd put a decent down-payment on the house. The two friends had been turning trash into treasure since they were teens.

"Good for her. She always liked our camping trips. She and her friends will have some good times in that trailer." When the kids were younger, we'd often taken week-long camping trips with Toni's daughter. I'd always loved this girlfriend time surrounded by nature and missed it. Our kids no longer wanted to vacation with their moms, although my kids were looking forward to our road trip together.

"What about Jordan?" Toni asked.

My son hadn't offered his services, but things had been a little tense between us lately. I was trying to find things to appreciate about his wife, but so far this was slim pickings. It was no surprise they'd both picked up on my animosity toward Chelsea. She wasn't the woman I'd have chosen for Jordan. It was hard to watch her take advantage of his easy-going nature and behave as if housework was beneath her.

"Jordan doesn't have much free time," I said, not wanting to complain about his wife.

I'd been nearly gulping my coffee as we talked, feeling eager to get to work. I knew I had to clean up the kitchen at home and whatever mess Violet might have left. Now that I'd slept and was away from the panic of yesterday, I was disappointed in how I'd handled Violet, not to mention abandoning a promising cordial creation. Ordinarily, I was the level-headed one and generally able to calm those around me. Something about Violet's chanting landed the wrong way, and I'd let her irrationality get to me. In the clear light of morning, however, I was ready to sort out my house, deal with Violet, and get to my beloved café.

"Do you mind if we get going?" I said. "I've got some tidying up to do at home before I go to work." I hadn't been away from my café for an entire day since I opened it.

"No problem," said Toni. "I'm planning to do a little beach-combing this morning, so I'll follow you to your house."

I cringed when I drove into my driveway and saw Sandy next door in her garden. I was hoping to avoid her. At the same time, it was a relief to see everything looking normal and no signs of an exorcism gone bad. Violet's car sat in the driveway, so she must be home.

Toni, who'd pulled in behind me, hurried to catch up as I bee-lined it into my house to avoid my neighbor. I had my hands full and put down the cat carrier to lift the latch. "Okay, out you go, Oreo."

He gave an indignant meow and bolted ahead of me to the door.

"Did you see the scowl your neighbor sent your way?" Toni asked.

"No. I didn't dare look at her." I unlocked the door and entered, letting Oreo go first. Now he was in no hurry. He planted himself, sniffed the air, and then looked at me as if the house didn't meet with his approval.

Toni leaned forward and sniffed. "He probably smells the sage."

I gave his behind a little nudge with my foot and he sidled over the door frame, then hopped up onto the bench inside. I left my backpack on the floor and walked into the living room. My apprehension diminished when everything looked okay. Not a speck of salt. "Nothing looks out of place here."

I headed into the kitchen and stood still, puzzled by how clean everything was. A chill slithered over my bones. This kitchen was not the way I'd abandoned it. Yesterday, I'd left rosemary syrup on the stove, but now the syrup—at least it looked like my syrup—was in a bottle on the counter. No bits of rosemary strewn about. The pot, knife, and cutting board were in the drying rack. Had I cleaned up before Violet went berserk? Or had she cleaned my kitchen? I wanted to believe it was her, but Violet had never tidied my house before. Then again, she'd never exorcised a phantom before either. I went to the French doors that led out to the deck. They were unlocked.

"I forgot to lock these doors last night." I turned the deadbolt as if there were kitchen-cleaning bandits on the loose.

"I wouldn't be too concerned in this neighborhood," said Toni, picking up the bottle of syrup. "I thought you didn't finish this."

"Me too," I said, straightening the hand towel on the rack.

She gave me a raised eyebrow look, letting me know she thought something was wrong. I didn't know what to say, though. My brain was befuddled, trying to find a reasonable explanation for this.

"I guess the exorcism went well," I said to change the subject, hoping I didn't have menopausal memory loss.

"Wait." Toni squeezed my arm. "Didn't Violet say *you* were possessed? How do I know I'm not talking to a spirit right now, and you've high-jacked Quinn's body for her—"

I poked her other arm, interrupting her joke, thankful for the levity. "For my hot...flashes."

"No! I was going to say your great legs. You've always had killer legs."

"It's a good thing for me and my legs that you suffer from diminishing far-sight."

We were laughing now, heading downstairs in self-disparaging woe. I wanted to check on Violet to be sure she was back to her normal self, and I also wanted to tell her firmly to respect my privacy in the future. No more salting and smudging, and I didn't want her invading my part of the house without an invitation.

"You realize what's next," Toni said.

I knocked on Violet's door. "I've heard stories."

"After hot flashes comes chin hair."

"Life is cruel." I knocked again. "I hate to admit this, but you've got the order wrong."

"Oh no. I'm sorry to hear that."

"Not as sorry as my hairy chin. Violet," I called, knocking louder. "Can you please open up?"

Toni leaned her ear against the door. "It's silent in there."

"I know. Maybe she went out for a walk."

"Do you have a key?"

"Of course I do," I said.

"Should you make sure everything is okay?"

Since I planned to ask her not to invade my privacy, I couldn't invade hers. "I can't barge in on her. She may be sleeping or in the bath."

"Right," Toni said. "But after the way you described her behavior, who knows what she's done. Let's peek in the window to see if the de-phantoming was a success."

I supposed that was okay. We went outside to the patio doors at the back of the house.

"De-phantoming isn't a word." I rapped on the door with my knuckles.

"It probably should be."

"I don't know. It's a mouthful."

"This is true." Toni cupped her hands around her eyes pressed to the window. "Oh no! I can see her. She's fallen. She's on the floor. Get the key, Quinn!"

I looked through the glass and saw Violet lying on the floor by the kitchen counter. "I'll be right back." I ran for the key.

"I hope she hasn't been there all night," Toni said as I unlocked the door. "Hurry!"

Once we were inside, we dashed to where Violet lay. Toni was ahead of me. She stopped suddenly and gave the most horrifying cry I'd ever heard.

My veins turned to ice. Violet was face down on the wood floor—in a pool of blood. She wore the same clothes as last night, but the yellow bandanna was knocked off. A metallic scent hung in the air. Dear Lord, it was the smell of blood.

I looked at Toni. Her face was as white as I'd ever seen.

I couldn't move. Couldn't react. Couldn't speak.

"Quinn!" Toni cried and grabbed my hands. We stood there, clutching each other, eyes locked, too stunned to look down and see more.

"She's dead, right?" Toni finally said.

"I think so." I swallowed and felt tears well up.

"We better check."

"Y-Yes." The neurons in my brain started to fire again. "And phone 911."

Violet was my tenant, so it should be me who checked for a pulse. I blinked away tears and looked down. Poor, poor Violet. I reached for her hand. Her skin was cool, her hand stiff. "Oh!" I dropped it, knowing instantly she was dead.

"How could this happen?" I mumbled, standing up. My tongue felt twice its size.

"I'll call the sheriff." Toni left the room through the patio door, cell phone to her ear. I followed her outside, barely registering her conversation to the police over the buzzing in my ears.

It didn't take long for emergency services to arrive, as well as Sheriff Jansen and Deputy Wilson from last night.

"She's in there, on the floor," I said, pointing toward my guest suite. The EMTs stepped inside.

"You stay here, ladies," said Sheriff Jansen. "You didn't touch anything, did you?"

"No. Other than…I touched Violet's hand. To be sure she was…." I felt a deep sorrow. She was too young to die.

The sheriff nodded and went inside.

I didn't like the look Deputy Wilson shot back at me over his shoulder. There was little sympathy in that look, considering we'd just found a dead body.

"This wasn't an accident," I said to Toni. "Someone hit her on the back of the head." I sat down on a patio chair since my legs still felt shaky. "Someone m-murdered Violet." Had she seen the killer coming and tried to run away? Or had the killer hidden and waited for her to come downstairs? I heard a rubbing sound and realized it was my own hand sliding back and forth across my leg. "Toni, last night, there was a murderer in my house."

Toni was wringing her hands. "It's too horrible to think about. What if you'd been home?"

I shivered at the thought, feeling both relieved and guilty. "If I'd been home, maybe my being here would have discouraged the killer. Instead of getting angry at Violet and then running away like a scaredy-cat, I could have prevented this. But no, I got spooked by a shadow. And then I dismissed the whole thing as a figment of my imagination." What a grave mistake I'd made—a mistake that led to Violet's death. "Toni, maybe the killer was outside my bedroom last night, and I didn't investigate it. I just packed a bag, grabbed my cat, and left Violet alone to face a murderer. What a horrible person I am!"

Toni shook her head. "Oh no, you don't. Don't you dare go blaming yourself. You couldn't possibly have foreseen something like this."

It was easy for her to say, and I sure would try, but at the moment my chest was heavy with guilt. I'd better tell the sheriff about what I thought I saw outside last night, just in case there were footprints.

We sat there without speaking, surely the longest we'd gone without a word, but for once we were too stunned for chit chat.

A little while later, the sheriff came outside with a pen and notebook in his hand.

"While we wait for the coroner, I'd like to ask you a few questions. First, are you two okay?"

I looked at Toni. She nodded. "Yes, we're fine," I said. "Shaken up, but we're okay."

"Good. Now, tell me what happened."

I told him everything I knew from last night's exorcism, including the shadow I might have seen outside my bedroom window, to finding Violet this morning.

"I'll have forensics check for footprints," Sheriff Jansen said. "So, you women were together last night?"

"Yes, that's right. I stayed overnight at Toni's."

"I understand from Deputy Wilson you filed a complaint against the victim."

I figured he knew that, so I hadn't mentioned it. "Yes, I did. I was concerned that Violet might disturb my neighbor."

"Hmm. Which neighbor? Can you give me a name, please?"

I did, but felt uneasy about it. Sandy and I weren't enemies, but we weren't friends, either. I'd always been polite to her, even when she complained about my mint encroaching on her garden, my tree branch leaning over her property, and my cat sleeping on her garden bench. Sandy sure hadn't been happy with me last night, so I didn't know what she might say.

And then another thought occurred to me. Could Sandy have gotten mad enough at Violet to hit her over the head?

I couldn't imagine it. I could, however, imagine her telling the police that Violet and I had been shouting at each other just before I left the house. And would that have been the last anyone saw or heard of Violet? I didn't have time to follow that thought since the sheriff had more questions about Violet's relationships, how she came to live with me and did I know of anyone who bore a grudge. I did not. Violet was a pretty innocuous person. She'd moved to Bookend Bay about a year ago with her husband—ex-husband now—and I knew nothing about him. She was a water quality technician working for the Department of Health and, from what I'd observed of her, liked to read mystery novels. She didn't have children, had a best friend named Josie, and Mishka walked her dog. I relayed all of this to the sheriff and then realized I'd not seen Violet's dog since I got home.

"Where is Trix?" I said, standing up to see if the dog was tied up in the yard. Highly unlikely, I quickly realized. The dog would have made herself known by now. I'd better check to see if Mishka had her.

"Who's Trix?" Sheriff Jansen looked up from the notes he'd been taking.

"Violet's dog is missing. Her dog walker must have kept the dog overnight."

"Oh?" he said. "Do you have the dog walker's name?"

I relayed that information.

"Okay. Thank you. Now, I'd like you to come inside and have a look around to see if anything is missing."

"Do you want me to come with you?" Toni stood, peeling the back of her thighs from the chair. It was already getting hot, and the forecast was for record-breaking temperatures. I couldn't remember having summers with heat like this when I was a kid.

"No. Wait out here, please," the sheriff said to Toni.

I went inside from the patio door entrance. A camera flash reflected off something in the kitchen.

"Take your time." The sheriff and deputy stood watching me—judging, I worried, mostly because I was shaken and feeling guilty for leaving last night. I'd not done anything wrong, I had to remind myself.

"The apartment was furnished when Violet moved in." I scanned the room, starting with the white dining table and four yellow, polka-dotted chairs, trying to remember the things Violet had brought with her. I wasn't thinking straight. In fact, it was hard to think at all.

A cobalt blue fruit bowl dominated the small table—that was hers. Books filled the bookcase—mostly hers. I saw the heavy marble candlestick I'd bought in France. She was using it as a book end. I'd forgotten I'd put it down here. I figured whatever killed Violet had to be heavy, but it wasn't my job to point out potential murder weapons.

I'd put nothing of great value in this suite. What would a thief have taken?

"I don't see her laptop," I said, remembering how I sometimes saw Violet working at the table when I was outside watering the garden.

"We've got that," Deputy Wilson said.

"I've only been down here once or twice since she moved in," I said, feeling pressured to deliver a clue who could have done this. "I really didn't know her well."

"Just take your time," he said again.

I sensed them wanting me to come up with something, and I wanted answers to why this horrible had happened, too. A flush of heat started from my core, and I knew I was about to experience a meltdown. I reached for the magazine on a side table to fan myself.

"Don't touch anything, Ms. Delaney," said the sheriff.

Oh, man. Perspiration sprouted on my forehead, under my hair, and in the middle of my back. I just hated this. I should have turned on the air conditioner, but I always put it off, hating to close the windows.

The gray couch, chair, and coffee table looked normal. Sadness cut through me when I saw the novel with a beaded bookmark sitting on the arm of the chair.

I turned my attention to the kitchen, to the white quartz counter. Coffee maker. Magic bullet. Spice rack. A coffee mug in the sink. What else did Violet keep on her counter? I didn't know.

Don't look down. From the corner of my eye, I saw they'd covered her body with a sheet.

"I don't think anything is missing from the kitchen," I said quickly, wiping my upper lip with the back of my hand. Deputy Wilson's gaze bore into me. "It's a hot flash," I snapped, failing miserably at controlling my nerves.

I spent another minute scanning the bedroom, but it wasn't helpful. Sweat was dripping down my back. I could hardly remember my name at the moment.

Murder. There'd been a murder in my home.

They asked me to look through my part of the house to see if anything was disturbed or missing. I went through my bedroom drawers and my jewelry box. I kept nothing of much value at home and found nothing missing or out of place. At least I didn't think so. I supposed that meant the murder was personal. The killer wasn't a thief who'd been interrupted.

"There's no sign of a forced entry," the sheriff said to the deputy.

"Oh, shoot," I said. "I left the patio door off the kitchen unlocked last night. I locked it when I came home. Just now."

"Is that so?" the deputy said in a tone that seemed accusatory. "You weren't home last night. Do you usually keep your door open when you go out?"

"I'm not vigilant about locking up. This is a safe neighborhood."

"But you locked the door when you came home?"

I didn't know why I'd locked the door. I supposed I'd been on edge. Maybe subconsciously, I sensed something was wrong.

I swallowed. "I was planning to be at work all day, and I usually lock the door when I'm away. I was frazzled last night—with Violet conducting an exorcism and all—and I forgot."

"Huh." Deputy Wilson stared at me a little longer and then scratched a note on his pad.

"Is there anything else?" I asked.

"No. I think we're done, for now," the sheriff said.

I left the house through the front door. As soon as I was outside, I sent a text to Mishka asking if she had Trix. I was heading to the backyard when my phone rang.

It was Craig. Finally. I knew just hearing his voice would soothe my nerves. This was one of the rare times when having a hero for an older brother was a blessing.

Chapter Four

I TOLD CRAIG THE whole gruesome story.

He was quiet for a second, no doubt absorbing the fact he'd lost a work associate. "Are you alright?" he asked.

"Yes. It's...just surreal. The police are here. Investigating."

"What do they think happened?"

"I don't know. Just a minute." I didn't want the police to hear me, so I walked away from the patio, stepping onto the path that wound through the woodland garden. It was cooler in the woods, thankfully. I could recover from my melt-down.

"The deputy is looking at me funny, as if I had something to do with Violet's death."

"What? That's insane. They have no reason to suspect you of anything. You won't kill a fly. Besides, you have an alibi, Quinn. You were at Toni's all night."

"I know. But I don't know what time Violet was killed. What if they think I snuck out of Toni's house last night, came home, murdered Violet, and—"

"Quinn," he interrupted. "Don't go there. You have no reason to have hurt Violet."

I reached the river at the end of the path, stepped onto a smooth stone under a bowed willow, and told him about going to the sheriff's office last night to complain about her.

"Really. You went to the police? I doubt a killer would do that." He paused. I heard a door opening and then laughter in the background. He was still at his conference. "I gotta say, it's hard to picture Violet off her rocker," he said. "She seemed pretty stable to me."

A red kayak glided into view. The guy paddling nodded a greeting, and I waved. Being in the woods by the river, birds singing, talking to Craig, I started to feel less frazzled. "They asked me to look around to see if anything was missing."

"So, they're sure she was murdered?"

"Craig, yes. It's pretty obvious. She didn't hit herself on the back of the head."

"Okay. I guess not."

"I can't get that image of her out of my head."

I heard Craig sigh. "Try not to think about it."

Oh sure, that was easy for him to say. He wasn't the one to find Violet dead.

"Is Toni still with you?" he asked.

"Yes, she is."

"You should stay with her tonight."

I guessed my house was a murder scene now. "I suppose the investigation might take a few days." I worked long hours in the summer, and now I'd be using Break Thyme's kitchen for my cordials, among other things. While Toni's company would be most welcomed, I didn't know how long I'd be out of my house and certainly wouldn't want her to grow tired of me. If I'd finished the trailer renovation, I'd just stay there, but the interior needed work before I'd feel comfortable living in it, even temporarily. I could rent a room at a hotel. Actually, the inn would be nice—I'd probably sleep better in the cozier space. "I think I'd rather stay at the inn."

"Okay. It's too bad you can't stay home."

I hated the thought of leaving my house, but I also couldn't imagine staying even if the police allowed it. Just knowing someone had come inside and...I didn't want to think about that, but it was a reminder Violet's death affected Craig, too. "Craig, I'm sorry for *your* loss. Violet was a friend."

"Yeah," he said. "I didn't know her well, but it's still sad. I guess it's too soon for the police to speculate who might have done it."

I wished I'd seen something more than a shadow that could provide a clue. Then I thought of something. "On my way over to Toni's, I saw Violet's dog-walker with Trix. She must have come back here last night after I left, though she didn't leave the dog. I wonder why? Do you suppose she saw something?"

"You can wonder but, Quinn, don't get involved. Let the police handle the investigation."

"Of course, I will. But aren't you a little curious why she didn't leave the dog?"

"Just because I'm curious doesn't mean I'm going to poke my head in a skunk's hole."

I would never live that down. "That was normal behavior for a four-year-old."

"Stepping on the bottom of the rake to see if it would spring up and hit you in the head like in the cartoons?"

"I was six."

"Pushing open the emergency door at the hospital to see if the alarm would sound?"

I sighed. "I was still a kid."

"It nearly blew our eardrums out, and why were we at the hospital in the first place?"

To stitch up my hand after a knife slipped when I was cutting into a golf ball to see why it was so hard. "Okay, Craig, I'm not a kid anymore." I looked up to my brother, but he always did stuff like this, reminding me of all my goof-ups, even if they happened decades ago. Sometimes it seemed he was just so superior, saving toddlers while I was messing up.

"Well, what about that time—"

"I have to go," I interrupted, saving the venture farther down memory lane. The sheriff's voice drifted toward me like a prickle. "Sheriff Jansen is looking for me."

"Okay, do you want me to come home?"

Not anymore. "Nope. I need no more reminders of my ineptness. Finish your conference, and I'll see you in a few days."

"Sorry, Sis. I was just teasing, trying to lighten things up. Your inquisitiveness has always been charming. Just stay safe, okay."

"I'll do my best. Talk to you later."

Although he could be annoying, the conversation with Craig did ease my trepidations making life feel normal for a few moments. I fixed my gaze on the crystals of light bouncing off the river and breathed in, held my breath, and released slowly. The sunshine lightened the heaviness weighing me down.

When I went to join Toni on the patio, she wasn't there. I walked up the side of the house and saw her and the deputy talking on the driveway beyond the police tape. They'd cordoned my house off with yellow tape. So much for the little solace I'd gained. My home was a crime scene. At that moment, I couldn't imagine this place being the sanctuary it had been for me since my marriage ended.

My phoned chimed—a text message. Mishka had gotten back to me. I glanced up from my phone to see a familiar face walking toward me with a medical bag—Ian Urquhart, our county's medical examiner. Ian was my brother's best friend throughout school. It was Ian's baby sister who Craig had saved from drowning.

"Quinn, this is your house?" he said and opened his arms. Ian was a warm and friendly man. Just above my height of five foot six, he was pudgy and balding, with a closely cropped gray beard and mustache. "Oh no. Oh, geez. What a shock this must have been," he said.

I was surprised by how good it felt to be hugged by someone with authority and a friend. Talking to the police had made me feel like I'd done something wrong.

"Oh, geez," he said again. "How are you doing? I'm sorry for your loss. She was your tenant?"

"I'm okay, and yes, Violet was my tenant. It's pretty awful in there." I indicated my house. "I can't believe this has happened."

"No kidding."

"She was murdered, Ian. Someone hit her on the head."

His expression tightened. Behind him, I saw the teen-deputy talking to Toni. He looked my way and then headed next door toward Sandy's house. My stomach turned over. For all I knew, I was living next door to a murderer. I pushed the thought from my mind. It was too dreadful to entertain.

"I'm glad you're here," I said. "If anyone can find evidence, it's you, so I'll let you do your job."

"Sure thing. You take care of yourself."

We said goodbye, and I joined Toni. She had a strange look on her face.

"What did teen-deputy want?"

"He wanted to know how prone to anger you are."

I gasped. "Seriously?"

"Yup. Don't worry, I didn't tell him about that time you beat up your grandma because she took the remote."

"Very funny." I smiled, appreciating my friend for trying to cheer me up, even if her joke was lame. The sheriff was going to question Sandy and while I'd had that wild thought about living next to a murderer, I didn't truly think Sandy had killed Violet. Besides, she would have an airtight alibi with her house full of kids, a husband, and her mother. Although an alibi might not be airtight when it came from your family.

If alibis were dismissed so easily, in teen-deputy eyes, I could be his prime suspect. It was my house. I filed a complaint—that he refused to take seriously, I might add. Maybe he figured I was angry enough to come back here and shut Violet up for good. As that realization sunk in, I knew I had to get as much information about Violet to the police as I could. That way, I'd be assured they wouldn't land on me as an easy suspect and stop the investigation. I'd start with Mishka's text.

I showed it to Toni. "Want to go check on this? Mishka may have been the last person to see Violet alive, and I'd rather she not hear about her death from the police."

Toni waved a bug away from her face. "What, now? Are we supposed to leave?"

"I'll clear it with the sheriff."

I found Sheriff Jansen and asked if it was okay for us to step away for an hour. He told me not to go far and to keep my cell phone handy in case he had further questions.

We took Toni's car and headed down Harmony Road. One of the most charming things about our town was the names of the streets. Most were named after virtues. The point of these names was to remind people to act virtuously. I'd always appreciated that philosophy, so to know there'd been a murder in our small town felt like a great assault against our values.

Where the Manitou River met Lake Superior, two tall rock formations jutted into the river from the water's edge. The rocks looked like book ends, hence the name of the town—Bookend Bay. I glanced at those majestic rocks as we crossed the bridge over the river to get to Mishka's house.

She was outside when we arrived. Her house was a small, two-story, white Craftsman with a front porch supported by field stone pillars.

Violet's dog Trix was lying under a tree. She bounded over to say hi.

"Hey, Trix, that's a good girl."

I introduced Toni to Mishka and rubbed the pooch behind the ears for a few moments. My chest ached for Violet and now for Trix having lost her owner.

"Do you know where Violet is?" Mishka said. "I've been trying to reach her all morning."

I looked at Toni. There was no easy way to say this. "I have some terrible news." I told her about Violet.

"But no, I just saw her!" Mishka said and then stared at me wide-eyed. "Who would want to hurt Violet? How did it happen?"

"We don't know, but it looks like someone hit her over the head from behind," Toni said.

"Oh my gosh." Mishka blinked a few times. She turned to look behind her at the golden shepherd who'd retreated to the shade

"Do you usually keep her dog overnight?" Toni asked.

"Not usually, but when I heard the arguing, I decided to just keep Trix instead of interrupting. Things sounded pretty heated. Oh no, you don't suppose...."

Holy smokes! Mishka heard me yelling at Violet?

"What?" Toni and I said on top of each other.

Mishka's brown eyes were as wide as the moon. I could see her mind racing as she stood silent. I'd just assumed she'd been in the field for a while when I saw her yesterday, but maybe she'd just gotten there after hearing me yelling at Violet—had it sounded like I was threatening her? And I'd given the sheriff Mishka's name, so now he would hear all about my argument from both Sandy and Mishka.

My mouth went dry. Was this how innocent people ended up in prison? "Wh-What did you hear?"

"Josie," said Mishka. "She sounded furious."

Josie? Violet was arguing with Josie? When had she arrived?

"Who's Josie?" Toni asked.

Self-preservation kicked in, giving me a good dose of relief at the news of this argument. I wouldn't be the only suspect. "Josie is Violet's best friend," I said, swallowing a little easier. "What on earth were they arguing about?"

Mishka pressed her lips together. Why was she hesitating so much?

"Mishka?" I prompted.

"I don't know exactly. They might have been arguing about Derek, but I didn't want to intrude. It felt strange to just open the door and let the dog in without saying anything, so I put Trix in my car and sent Violet a text saying I'd bring her back in the morning, but then my husband took the car and left me stranded."

"Who's Derek?" Toni said, looking confused.

"Derek is Violet's ex-husband." I turned to Mishka. "Are you sure you heard nothing specific? Was Josie really angry? Did it sound like things could have turned violent?"

"I don't know," Mishka said defensively. She crossed her arms over her chest. "I'm not an eavesdropper."

"No, of course not," I said.

I tried another approach. "Mishka, last night when I saw you on the road, you said Violet was having a bad day. She thought my house was haunted and was trying to evict a phantom. That's why I said to take your time walking the dog. You said a thing like this changes a person forever. Were you referring to my house being haunted?"

Her forehead crinkled. "No, I wasn't. And it's not your house that's haunted. Violet said it's you."

Oh man, Violet told her I was possessed. This really showed how she was losing touch with reality. "You know that's ridiculous, right?"

Mishka took a step back and put her hands up as if to calm the demon inside me.

"Oh, for goodness' sake, Mishka." I didn't want to get sidetracked by this nonsense. "Anyway, what did you mean by a thing like this changes a person?"

She hesitated and looked puzzled. "I thought you knew."

"Knew what?"

She opened her mouth. Closed it. "It's not my place to say. I've actually got chickpeas in the oven." She hurried over to the dog. "Come on, girl." Then she turned to us.

"Trix can stay with me. I've got to get my peas out. See you later."

"You better tell the sheriff about that argument," I called after her. I wanted my name cleared from the suspect list ASAP.

"I will." She and the shepherd ran up to her front door and slipped inside.

"Well, that was weird," Toni said. "She sure ended that conversation abruptly."

"No kidding." I opened the passenger door and slid onto the seat. "I don't understand why she'd be concerned about preserving Violet's privacy now."

"Maybe she's worried you'll unleash your demon."

My thoughts turned to the argument Mishka had overheard. "I'd like to know what Josie and Violet were arguing about." I fastened my seatbelt.

"I wonder about that, too," said Toni, starting the car. "I think we should do a little investigating of our own, Quinn. I can't imagine the police suspecting you, but if they ask more questions, it wouldn't hurt to have a better picture of Violet's life."

Toni pulled out of the driveway. The car was too warm for me. I opened the window for fresh air. "You're right, and it worries me that Violet told Mishka I was possessed." This was a little too close to home since I'd started seeing ghosts. "Did you see the way Mishka looked at me—like she wasn't convinced Violet was wrong? You know how fast news travels; I don't want people to start looking at me sideways. What if people think I tried to stop Violet from spreading rumors about me?"

Toni pressed her lips together, a sign she was worried, too.

I knew I'd told Craig I'd let the police handle the investigation, but I couldn't imagine leaving my fate in the hands of someone like teen-deputy Wilson. This was my reputation, my business, and possibly my freedom at stake. If people started making assumptions, I needed to know the facts. I didn't dwell on whether asking a few questions was meddling in a police investigation, I was already considering my next move.

Chapter Five

WHEN I WOKE UP the next morning, I lay in bed for a minute with my eyes closed, remembering an odd dream I'd had. In the dream, I'd woken around two in the morning to use the bathroom. I saw a strip of light shining from under the door and thought it strange that I'd forgotten to turn out the light when I went to bed. As I remembered the next part of the dream, the hairs on the back of my neck stood.

When I'd opened the bathroom door, I saw myself sitting on the edge of the tub reading a pamphlet. My heart hit the roof. The mirror image of myself gasped, and the pamphlet hit the floor. I let out a cry and high-tailed it back to bed.

I couldn't remember having a dream like that where the details were so strikingly vivid—her eyes, so much like mine, popping wide, the pamphlet fluttering to the floor, the sound of her gasp hitting the back of her throat.

Then again, I'd never had a day like yesterday.

It was just a dream, I told myself. I rubbed my neck, pressing the bony vertebrae as if to reassure myself I was awake. The bedcovers felt different, too heavy, so I pushed them off. It took me a second or two to remember where I was.

Yesterday, after the sheriff said my house was off-limits while they conducted their investigation, I'd packed my bags, along with Oreo's bowls and litter box. Needing to maintain my independence—not to mention the restlessness that plagued my nights—and not wanting to disrupt Toni's life, I'd decided checking into Bookend Bay Inn was the best choice, especially since they were happy to have Oreo.

Considering what happened to Violet, it was no wonder I'd had a bizarre dream. It was futile to make sense of it. That, combined with night sweats, meant I wasn't well-rested. Every night lately, it was a dance with the bed sheet—on and off in a constant oscillation between burning and freezing.

Perimenopause was turning out to be a time of life changes second to none. After both my kids left home, there'd been a few months where I'd worried my best years were behind me. With my role as a mother so diminished, I didn't know who I was anymore. A small part of me resented having given up my personal development to make a home for my family, but just a small part. I wouldn't have had it any other way. Then I got excited about remaking myself. Starting over, with the wisdom of forty-odd years. That's when I decided to pursue the dream I'd had of owning an artisan café. And then my marriage fell apart, so I threw myself into my work, and I'd loved every minute.

Single, empty-nested, café owner. So much about my life had changed in the last few years. These physical symptoms of the change would not get me down. I was going to emerge from these darn ashes like an empowered, flourishing phoenix.

I sat up and turned on the bedside lamp, bringing to light two peacock blue chairs adorned with whimsical bird pillows. Not the phoenix image I'd had in my head, but the birds made me smile. I'd never stayed at the inn before and had hardly noticed the rustic and quirky décor last night. It was nice to see artwork by our local artist Aubrey Adams hanging on the wall. Just looking at her Great Lake art, recognizable for the bright colors, cheered me up.

Still lazing at the bottom of the bed, Oreo hardly acknowledged me when I gave his head a little scratch on my way to the bathroom.

As I approached the bathroom, that strange dream popped back into my head, and with it came a flash of doubt. Could Mishka and Violet have been right? Was I experiencing another haunting? I'd had ghosts bud into my life before and didn't like the idea, but at least I knew I could deal with that. But what if it was something worse? Possession. Could some spirit take over my body? How in the world would I manage something like that?

I edged the bathroom door open, slowly, all the way.

The bathroom was empty. No mirror-me in sight. My knees nearly buckled in relief.

Holy cow. Get a grip. It was just a dream.

In the shower, as I massaged my scalp with shampoo, I finally felt a release of tension. Ghosts aside, I wasn't the last person to see Violet alive, and the sheriff could verify that when he talked to Mishka.

Maybe I was taking Mishka's abrupt behavior personally, but it still bothered me she might think I'd done something to Violet to make her believe I was possessed. I wondered if her friend Josie supported these spirited accusations. Or maybe Josie and Violet were arguing about her going all esoteric and dabbling in exorcisms. I couldn't stifle my need to know more about this.

I knew my curiosity sometimes got me into trouble—sometimes. Experts said curiosity was a strength worth nurturing, a way to gain wisdom, live a happier life, and build confidence. I believed this, and I should have reminded my brother about that when he suggested my curious nature was more in line with the kill-the-cat variety.

Of course, the police would handle the investigation. Investigating was their job, but Toni was right. I'd rather know what Violet had been saying about me. My business could suffer if people thought I'd brought about Violet's death.

Toni and I planned to visit Josie later that day because I absolutely had to go into the café. My head barista Poppy had looked after Break Thyme yesterday, but I couldn't leave it to her all day today. And I needed to finish my cordials in time to enter the contest. I was determined to win and prove to myself that I was really good at this—I'd be an award-winning artisan café owner. I already had a spot for the framed certificate to hang—between the two bookcases in the Cozy Nook.

Thinking of business, I had a vague memory of seeing an email from Aubrey asking me to approve her design for Break Thyme. I hadn't responded, so I quickly sent her a thumbs up, then threw on a pair of yellow capris and a black blouse.

To tame my frizzy hair, I applied a dime's worth of my favorite oil blend. With a light application of makeup, I was ready to go. Oreo was still sleeping, so I'd come back in an hour or so and let him out. Mary Carscadden, who owned the inn, loved cats and said it would be no problem for Oreo to hang out in her office and in the fenced garden.

I'd called Bookend Bay home for thirty-seven years and never took this place for granted. Well, except for my teenage years when I'd thought a big city would be more fun. Now, I was happy with small-town life. It wasn't as if we were cut off from the world. In the summer, along with cottagers, we attracted loads of tourists for the fishing, hiking, boating, wildlife, cuisine, and the one-of-a-kind crafts the area provided.

Quaint was the best way to describe Bookend Bay. Many of the old houses were Victorian. Windows, flanked by brightly colored shutters, sat over overflowing flower boxes. The multi-colored shops along Courtesy Boulevard reminded me of the fishing villages on the east coast where I'd spent some of my childhood.

Break Thyme was at the west end of the long row of shops and restaurants along the lake. Close to Moose

Harbor, it got lots of traffic from boaters. My café was two stories, painted cherry red with a cream-colored awning and gingerbread trim. The entrance was centered between two enormous windows that reached the second floor, bringing in tons of light. This was in keeping with my vision for the café to bring the outside inside as much as possible.

My planters were already overflowing with yellow petunias, lemon thyme, and ivy. I might have to trim everything back before the end of the month. As I unlocked my front door, I waved to Mr. & Mrs. Brooks across the street walking their black collie. Their nonchalant smiles meant news of my tenant's murder hadn't reached them. I wasn't looking forward to talking about Violet's death with half the town.

I turned on the lights, came inside, and felt a welcome sense of normalcy. This was my happy place, and it was my goal that my customers feel that way, too. Since I'd been envisioning this café for years before it became a reality, I'd given it a lot of thought. My gaze drew to the left, where an open staircase ran up an exposed brick wall. On the right side sat four booths and beyond these, two steps down, and off to the right was my favorite part of the café—the Cozy Nook—comfy chairs, coffee tables, potted herbs, and bookcases filled with my lending library. The nook opened out onto an outside patio that faced the lake. Picture windows provided a beautiful view of the bay.

My phone rang as I was heading past the counter and into the kitchen. Jordan's picture filled the screen. "Hello, love. It's pretty early to be hearing from my son."

"Yes, well, I've been awake for the last few hours trying to calm down my wife." Jordan's tone of voice was somewhere between hostile and desperate.

I had so little self-control when it came to Chelsea—the princess. I braced for my son's wrath. One day, he'd realize that a side-effect of motherhood was to act in your kid's best interests when said kid wasn't doing such a good job of it.

"She saw your Facebook post," he said.

"Oh? The one about my new cordial?"

He groaned. Okay, not that one. I knew what he meant. Before the cordial, I'd posted an article on the detrimental effects of breast implants.

"You mean the one on breast implants," I said. "I didn't mean for Chelsea to take that personally." But as I denied it, I saw it for the lie that it was. I'd let my displeasure for my daughter-in-law get the better of me.

"Oh, come off it, Mom. You might as well have put her name on it."

I wasn't fooling anybody. But I'd felt like I had to do something. I didn't like the way my son's wife treated him.

"That article was for any young woman considering breast implants. I want to be sure they have all the facts."

"Any young woman? Not once in my life have you mentioned the detriments of breast implants. How did you know Chelsea was getting them? She sure didn't tell you."

This was where I'd crossed a line, but I hadn't meant to. I was doing some dusting for Jordan after dropping off a batch of breaded veal, so he had a decent dinner. The least his wife could do, in between her acting classes and whatever she did on social media, was cook a meal and keep their apartment clean, but no. As the sole breadwinner, Jordan also handled the grocery shopping, cooking, laundry, and, when he had energy for it, house cleaning. Otherwise, it didn't get done. So, I helped when I could by cooking a meal and cleaning things up for my son. Living in a mess made it difficult to concentrate.

Under the dust on their bedside table, I found a brochure for breast implants. Seven thousand dollars! I couldn't believe it. They didn't have the money to replace Jordan's beat-up 2007 Altima, but she was getting breast implants?

"Okay, Jordan, you're right. I saw a brochure for implants at your house and was concerned. Besides the potential complications, they're expensive."

"It's none of your business what we do with our money, and you shouldn't read our stuff."

He was right. I'd acted in the heat of the moment. In doing what I thought was the best thing for my son, I'd actually acted in the worst way. This wasn't the first time I'd tried and failed to keep my judgment of Chelsea to myself. It was really hard for me, but that was no excuse. I just wanted Jordan to know I cared about both of them. "I realize that but—"

"There's no but. No but! Stay out of our business, Mom."

The guilt of over-stepping was heavy in my stomach. "Okay. You're right. I'm sorry. It's your life and I'll bud out."

He was silent for so long, I wondered if he'd hung up.

"Jordan?"

"I've got to go. I'll just say one more thing. A few days ago, I asked you to put together a menu for Chelsea's graduation party, and you've not gotten back to me on that—the one thing I do need from you."

I'd been busy and then a little thrown off course by the murder in my guest suite. I guess he hadn't heard about that. "Right. Okay, I'll send something to you tomorrow."

"Good. Talk to you later." He hung up. No I love you. Just gone, and it was my own fault.

By 9:15, customers filled most of the overstuffed chairs in the Cozy Nook, and because of the heatwave, many were sipping our new drink—Rosemary Lemonade.

Each month, I highlighted an herb by using it in a baked good, a drink, and a jelly. The herb theme was such a hit with my customers that I'd asked my artist friend Aubrey to paint an Herb of the Month design on the wall above my chalkboard menus.

That day, the mood at Break Thyme was somber among the town folk. News of Violet's death had made the rounds although few people knew Violet, but whether she was a friend or a stranger didn't matter to people. It was shocking to know there'd been a murder in our small town.

I'd been accepting condolences and keeping brief with details, which was difficult considering I had a reputation for gab. I told people the truth—Sheriff Jansen asked me not to talk about it.

The bells jingled above the door. I looked up to see Poppy come in.

"Hi, Quinn," she said, softly, like I might break. She came around the counter and hugged me. "Are you okay?"

"Yes, I'm fine. I mean, I'm still a little shaken. I need the distraction of a regular day to get back to normal."

"It'll take some time. You didn't have to come in, you know. I can handle things if you want to take another day." Poppy had that girl-next-door wholesome prettiness, with straight bangs and gleaming mahogany hair that hung just past her shoulders. In her twenties, full of energy and a sunny attitude, she was working on a history degree part-time and dreamed of working in antiquities.

"No, thank you. I'd rather be here. Were things okay yesterday? You called in Melanie to help, right?" I employed five people. Four were part-timers, Melanie, Jetti, Ethan, and Chloe. Poppy was my one full-time employee. When I was hiring for this position, my primary criterion was someone who took initiative and could carry on a conversation. Poppy was a hard worker who made our customers feel not only welcome, but that they mattered. I was lucky to have her.

"I called her, but she had an upset stomach and couldn't come in. Jetti came in and we managed okay.

Everything was fine." Poppy slipped into the back and reappeared a minute later, tying her apron.

All the staff wore aprons to give us a professional look and to protect our clothes from spills. As a bonus, mine hid the extra weight I'd gained, and what I couldn't see, I couldn't bemoan.

Poppy slipped a scone out from under the glass. "Oh, I love these. The icing is lemony deliciousness."

I loved them too—Glazed Blueberry, Lemon-Thyme Scones. They were packed with blueberries and just the right amount of thyme leaves and fresh lemon. I liked my scones with a little extra sweetness, so I sprinkled them with demerara sugar before icing. We served them on a plate with thyme leaves and lemon zest.

I walked over to the shelves to check the stock of jams, jellies, chutneys, and salsas I bought from an artisan near Marquette who made the award-winning products. The ones I sold had an herb or spice in the ingredients in keeping with my theme. I even served a spiced coffee.

I stared at the shelves. Something was different. Someone had rearranged them. I studied them for a second and realized they were now in alphabetical order. Interesting. I supposed it made things easier for people to find what they wanted.

"Thanks for rearranging the stock, Poppy."

"I rearranged nothing on that shelf. I just dusted it."

"That's strange. Maybe it was the other women or an anal-retentive customer."

"Speaking of customers, if anyone comes in looking for a lost notebook, a purple one, I tucked it on the shelf under the cash," she said.

At the counter, I nudged a stool, so it lined up with the others. "Hmm. Did it have a name in it?"

"That's a good question. Jetti found it on the bookshelf and thought it didn't belong there. I was busy and didn't look at it. I just remembered it now."

I retrieved the book and flipped it open. It was actually a day planner. I'd be lost without my calendar, although mine was on my phone. Whoever lost this may not know they left it here.

I grabbed my reading glasses from beside the register and opened the planner, but found no identification. I flipped the pages, looking for the current month of June to see if there was anything written there. If not, the planner may have been on our bookshelf for a while.

There was one notation in June. Brent Lange on June 3rd. I knew most everyone in town, and I'd never heard that name.

I flipped back through May. In the first two weeks, on each day, someone had recorded numbers. The same thing in April and March. I read some of them—98.5, 97.2, 98.4. Maybe they were body temperature readings. Maybe not.

The last few pages were dedicated to contact information, but who filled in those things in the days of cell phones.

As I flipped back, something caught my eye on another page. I'd missed this. The name Craig and a phone number, but the engagement was crossed out.

Huh, weird. I knew my brother was the only Craig in town, but that didn't mean this reference was to him. Anyone in the country could have left this planner here.

Although what I could make of the crossed-out numbers, it looked like his cell phone. The fact I couldn't remember his exact number had nothing to do with perimenopausal brain fog and everything to do with the fact I auto dialed everyone these days. Still, if this notation was him, chances were the planner belonged to someone who knew him. I tucked that information into the back of my mind for later.

The bells on the front door jingled. I looked up to see my friends Aubrey and Colleen come in.

"Holy Hannah," said Aubrey. "What happened to Violet?" For a second, I was distracted by Aubrey's hair—blue streaks through blond. I didn't know anyone who changed hair color as often as Aubrey did.

"I don't know exactly," I said. "She was killed. Someone hit her over the head."

"Oh, dear. What a horrible thing to have happened to the poor lass!" Colleen looked like an Irish hippie with her curly red hair, freckled complexion, flowing skirts, big jewelry, and headscarves. "Violet was in Mystic Garden not less than two days ago. I can't believe she's gone." Mystic Garden was the new-age-like shop Colleen owned down the road. Everything about the store was an embodiment of who Colleen was. I wondered if people would say the same thing about me and Break Thyme. I certainly thought so. The Cozy Nook was the manifestation of my love of reading and the belief that everyone should have access to good books. The locally sourced goods backed up my belief in supporting the local economy and showcasing the talent we had here.

"I know," I said. "I feel terrible for Violet. She was too young to die." As far as I knew, she was in her early forties.

"You found her?" Aubrey said. "That must have been awful. Are you okay, Quinn?"

A small shiver crept up my spine at the memory. "Actually, Toni and I found her. It was shocking to be sure. There are moments it hits me. I'm trying to keep busy, so I don't think about it too much."

Colleen sat on a stool, rested her elbows on the counter, and steepled her fingers. "So, what does the sheriff have to say? Do they know who did it? Was she dead long before you found her?"

"I don't know if they have any suspects. And I don't know the timing. He asked me not to talk about it." I set the planner down, slipped two mugs off the shelf, and poured coffee. Aubrey took one and walked over to the table where I kept the cream and sugar.

Colleen drank her coffee black. She wrapped her hand around her mug and leaned closer. "I don't know if I should tell you this. I mean, I don't want to upset you any further because it's likely nothing."

"Oh? Well, you have to tell me now, or I'll imagine all sorts of things."

Aubrey brought her coffee to the counter and sat beside Colleen.

"I don't know what you do to this coffee, but it's like nectar from the gods," Aubrey said. "What were you whispering about, Colleen?"

"Over the last few weeks, Violet had come into my shop, asking questions about ghosts. You may find this amusing, Quinn. She thought you were possessed."

I might have found some humor in that a few days ago, but now it gave me a foul taste. It seemed Violet had been telling everyone I was possessed. I poured myself a coffee. "I know she said those things, but I don't know why. I did nothing out of the ordinary. I wasn't acting *possessed*. She was trying to exorcise a spirit from our house the night she was killed."

"Maybe the spirit did it," said Aubrey.

I didn't want people to take Violet's claims seriously. "Sure, and next week the sequel will be in a theater near you."

Colleen gave a quick smile. "Violet came into Mystic the other day asking if she left her calendar behind. I looked around but didn't see hide nor hair. Now, I wonder if there'd be a clue in there who could have done this to her?"

My grip tightened around my coffee cup. Did the planner on the shelf below me belong to Violet? If that was true, it didn't look good to have my brother's name written on the day before she was killed. Even if he was away at a conference, this didn't look good at all. I grappled with what to say and realized I was stupidly nodding, my gaze fixed on the brick wall to my right.

"I—I," I cleared my throat. "I sure hope it shows up."

Chapter Six

My days were simpler when I had no reason to believe the dearly departed might show up in my life instead of crossing over to the other side like they were supposed to do. But, last year, after meeting a ghost who threatened to send evil spirits after me if I didn't do her bidding, it was impossible not to be concerned Violet would come back to haunt me. After all, I'd treated her like a crazy person hours before she was killed. A niggling part of me worried it wasn't a coincidence her planner showed up at Break Time and that she was trying to tell me something.

Since, before Violet died, she'd been looking for her planner in Colleen's shop, it stood to reason she didn't think she'd lost it at Break Thyme. So how did the planner get on my bookshelf? I supposed she could have left it behind, and a customer put it on the shelf thinking it was part of the library. That made a lot more sense than to believe Violet had returned from the dead to hound me.

I couldn't remember the last time Violet had been in the cafe, and I didn't want to ask Poppy, not until I talked to Craig about his name being in Violet's planner. If I turned the planner into the police, would they suspect Craig of something nefarious?

When I had a second to digest it, I realized her having his number wasn't unusual. After all, she was an associate of Craig's. They likely had reasons to interact.

But the day before she was killed? Craig hadn't mentioned a canceled meeting with her, although he could have overlooked this detail considering the shock of her death.

"I've got to get back to work," I said to my friends. Besides the usual business and accounting tasks, I needed to get working on another cordial—I wanted to have a few options for my contest submission. I had to relieve Poppy for her breaks and prepare myself for a visit to Josie's later. Plus, we were closing early to give Aubrey time to paint our new sign.

Aubrey picked up her cup. "I'll be back at 3:00 to start your project."

"Great. I really appreciate you squeezing me in before your vacation. I can't wait to see it." I liked to run with my ideas as soon as I made up my mind, so the thought of waiting until Aubrey returned was a little anxiety-provoking. Also, I wanted the sign ready for the beginning of the month.

Aubrey was a talented, creative artist. I loved everything she did. I knew her design would be beautiful, and since she was the professional here, not me, I'd given her free rein.

Colleen stood up and swung her purse over her shoulder. "Now, don't you go forgetting about the psychic readings tomorrow night. Gloria is coming all the way from the Sault."

Shoot. With everything going on, I had forgotten. "I'll be there. Maybe the psychic can see who murdered Violet."

Colleen looked thoughtful. "That would be helpful, although I don't think Sheriff Jansen would want to hear about it."

I agreed with that. When Aubrey and Colleen made their way out the back door to the lakeside patio, I slipped the day planner off the shelf and took it upstairs to my office for safekeeping.

While Poppy looked after the front, I spent the next few hours in the kitchen working on a lemon and rosemary cordial. My first batch wasn't sophisticated enough, lacking depth of flavor after the initial palate encounter. I added another dimension by replacing the caster sugar with vanilla sugar. That batch was a little too sweet, so I made a note to reduce the sugar. I thought my daughter-in-law might like it though, so I put it aside for her.

Poppy stuck her head in the kitchen. "Toni is here."

"Thank you. Are you sure you're okay to work alone until 3:00? I'm going to stick around for a little while upstairs if you need me."

"I'll be fine. Seriously. We all managed yesterday with no fires, right? It's only another couple of hours, and Melanie said she's available if we need her."

"Okay, you're right. I'm sure you'll be fine. Just a reminder, before you leave, be sure to move everything off the counter under the menus, so nothing is in Aubrey's way while she's painting. I gave her the extra key, so she can let herself in and out when she's done."

"I didn't forget."

"And can you check our coffee supply? I think we're getting low on free-trade beans. Maybe I should check—"

"Holy smokes, would you just go already? I can handle ordering beans."

I hesitated, looking for my to-do list to be sure I wasn't forgetting anything. Poppy waited while I ran my finger down the items. These were all things I needed to look after myself.

"Okay, we're good. Thank you, Poppy. By the way, I really appreciate you."

She smiled. "I know you do. And one day you just might trust me to look after things, so you'll take that vacation you mentioned. And don't think I forgot about that."

I sighed. I didn't know why it was so hard for me to let go, but I hadn't forgotten about my road trip either. Since I'd be traveling with my kids, I needed to smooth things over with Jordan because I couldn't stand the thought of him deciding not to come. I loved his company, and I couldn't wait to see my mother's face when we pulled into her driveway and both her grandchildren got out of the truck. I'd start making amends by coming up with a delicious and affordable menu for Chelsea's party.

Since my ex-husband had taken off to South Korea after our divorce, and I'd thrown myself into the opening and running of Break Thyme, our family felt doubly disjointed. At least it did to me. Taking the time to reconnect with my kids and see my mom was essential to me before another year slipped past or the guilt would eat me alive.

I left my competent worker and found Toni chatting with a couple of tourists. I caught her eye and nodded my head toward the stairs to get her to follow me.

"You won't believe what turned up here," I said and told her about Violet's planner.

While Toni looked through the planner, I retrieved my phone and found Craig in the contacts.

I brought the phone back to where Toni was standing. "I see the name Craig in here. Is this your brother's phone number?"

"That's what I wanted to check."

She handed me the planner. I checked the Craig entry against the number on my phone. My heart sank.

Toni looked over my shoulder, took hold of the planner, and pulled it closer. "It's his. Well, they did work together."

"They did, but I don't think they knew each other well." I couldn't remember one time when Craig spoke to Violet when he was at my house. He'd never even asked if she was a good tenant.

"That's the day before she was killed," Toni said in a hush. "But his name is crossed out, so they probably didn't meet or talk or whatever."

Crossed out or not, it still gave me a heavy feeling in the pit of my stomach to see his name there. "Probably. But don't you think the police will be all over that?"

Toni didn't answer. She pressed her fingers against her mouth. "We know he had nothing to do with this."

"I'll ask him about it," I said. "Did you see those numbers written in for the last few months? Do you think she was recording temperatures? She was a water quality technician, so maybe she was recording water temperatures?"

Toni flipped to April. "These are too warm for any water around here. They're more like body temperatures. You know, my daughter records her temperature, so she doesn't get pregnant. Because our temperatures go up—or maybe it's down—when we ovulate, she says she knows if it's safe to have sex."

"The way my temperature jumps, that would never work for me, not that I'm—. Anyway, is that a reliable method of birth control?"

Toni shook her head. "I can't imagine it is and have told her so, but she's a big girl."

I felt a dose of relief that my daughter didn't use this method. At least I didn't think so. I couldn't remember having a conversation with Samantha about her birth control. At twenty-five years old, her sex life was something we didn't talk about.

"Are you going to give the planner to the sheriff?" Toni asked.

Not before I talked to Craig, but then I would. "Yes, I'll do that later."

"I need to use the bathroom before we go," she said. "I've been shopping most of the morning. I can't go an hour without a bathroom—it's ridiculous. Did you get in touch with Josie?"

"Yes, she's expecting us. I'll meet you downstairs."

Toni headed to my private two-piece at the back of the loft.

As I was coming down the stairs, I looked out the front window and saw my good friend Jade Davis coming along the sidewalk toward Break Thyme. I waved as we made eye contact. She looked straight at me, looked away, and crossed the street to the other side.

What was that about?

Did she avoid me on purpose? I hadn't seen Jade for at least a month, which was unusual. Her husband worked with Craig, and the four of us used to get together every Friday night to play cards, but she'd canceled several weeks in a row. When I asked Craig if something was going on with them, he said Jade's mother needed her help, so I stopped bothering her.

Jade might have been in a hurry just now, but why wouldn't she just wave or say a quick hello? Unless I only thought she'd seen me. Or could it be she was hurt that I hadn't asked about her mother? That pricked my conscience. I shouldn't have let her repeated cancelations keep me from being a supportive friend.

"Are you stuck?" Toni came up behind me on the stairs.

I told her about Jade.

"Oh yeah? She probably heard about Violet and thinks you're a killer."

That made me snort. "Me? You and I *were* together. That makes *you* my accomplice. Before you know it, we'll be on a two-woman crime spree like *Thelma and Louise*." We both laughed at the idea of us being anywhere near as bold and rebellious as those characters. Driving over a cliff rather than face arrest? Not Toni and me, that's for sure. "Seriously though, I'm nervous I could be a suspect."

"Oh, go on," Toni said. "Violet's dog walker saw her alive and well after you left, and you were with me all night."

"Says my best friend."

"Alibis must often come from best friends."

"What if the sheriff thinks I was so desperate to get rid of Violet that I snuck back to my house and killed her *because* I knew you'd be my alibi?" Admittedly, saying it out loud like that made the possibility seem remote.

"Okay, well, if you're concerned about being a suspect, then now's the time to do a little snooping. And don't forget, there are other people to consider. For one, you said your neighbor was pretty angry at Violet that night. And the dog walker is hiding something. Not to mention Violet may have been arguing with her friend Josie that night."

I walked down the last two steps. I didn't know if the police considered me a suspect or not. The thought of me or Craig being arrested or spending time in jail was enough to freak me out. Even if one of us were considered a murder suspect, it could ruin both our reputations. Craig could lose his job. People might stop coming to Break Thyme. If my café failed, how would I support myself? My skill set was weak. I'd been out of the workforce for decades. Would I have to leave my home in Bookend Bay to find a job somewhere else?

And what about my house? When I could return home, would a possessive spirit plague me? Or maybe I'd be haunted by an angry Violet because I'd deserted her when she'd needed help. I couldn't have ghosts showing up whenever they pleased. When they popped in abruptly, it was impossible for me not to react. I didn't want that kind of thing happening to me in public. It certainly wouldn't be good for business to be known as the woman who talked to dead people. Getting on top of this was crucial.

"Quinn, you look like you're a million miles away and not in a happy place," Toni said, bringing me back to the moment.

"My brain was throwing several worst possible scenarios at me. Horrible to think about, but this seems to be a situation where being prepared is a better strategy than letting cards fall where they may." I tugged her closer to the wall, out of earshot. "I need to know what Violet and Josie argued about, if it had anything to do with me being possessed, or if the spirit Violet was trying to exorcise made any demands of her. I don't want my life turned upside down again by a pushy ghost."

"Oh, dear. I hadn't thought of the ghost intruding on your life. I was busy wondering if Mishka or Josie or even Sandy had anything to gain from Violet's death."

"That would be good to know, too." It seemed prudent to find out everything we could about Violet's murder. "I guess there's only one way to find out."

"Right." Toni adjusted the collar of her blouse. "We better get over to Josie's and see if she'll admit to arguing with the victim hours before she was killed."

Chapter Seven

I'D LEARNED THAT WHEN you arrive bearing gifts, people are more open to chatting and less likely to show you the door. With that in mind, I packed a jar of lemon jelly and half a dozen blueberry lemon-thyme scones to give to Josie.

The town was bustling with people—tourist season was off to a great start, even with the heat and humidity—so I figured it might take us a bit of time to drive to her place. She lived across the bay near the lighthouse, the sentinel for the dangerous, rocky finger of land that jutted into the lake.

In the passenger seat, Toni pointed the air-conditioning vent toward her. "Didn't you say your travel trailer was being delivered to Beach Meadows Park yesterday?"

"Yes. I better get over there and check it out. I got an email verifying they'd hooked it up to the water and electricity."

"Have you set a date for your holiday with the kids?"

Now I had Poppy and Toni pushing me to carve this vacation in stone. "No, I've solidified nothing yet, but it'll be in September when things slow down. I'll set the dates as soon as I'm sure Poppy and the girls have everything under control."

Toni chuckled. "I'm looking forward to seeing you hand over the reins."

I stifled a sigh. She didn't understand what it had taken to make Break Thyme a success. My life depended on profits, so it wasn't easy to hand over the reins that were my lifeline. "Me, too."

About twenty minutes later, my navigation system led us to 45 Mercy Road, Josie's house. I parked the truck across the street from a white bungalow with a gray porch and aubergine front door. The pop of color saved the house from fading into the streetscape.

"Hi, Josie, it's nice to see you again," I said when she opened the door. Josie co-owned the Moosehead Tavern. She might look like a good wind could blow her over, but I'd seen her easily haul boxes of booze off the back of a truck. Behind tortoise-shell glasses, her usually friendly eyes looked strained today.

"Hi, Quinn. Toni."

I handed her the gift bag with the scones and jam. "Here's a little something for you. We're so sorry for your loss, Josie. It must be hard to lose a good friend."

"It's really sad," she said, pushing the heal of her hand against her chest. "It's hard to believe she's gone."

"I know," I said, still feeling Violet's death was surreal.

"Would you like to sit outside on the patio?" asked Josie, her thumb rubbing the handle of the gift bag. "There's a pleasant breeze, and it's shaded."

"Sure." We followed Josie down the side of her house to the backyard.

"This is pretty back here," Toni said, stopping to admire a small sculpture of a fairy tucked into a hydrangea. The yard was lush, with hedges and trees providing privacy from the neighbors. A potted red petunia sat on a wrought-iron chair beside a pond with a small waterfall. I liked the idea of a pond and the soothing sound of trickling water, but with the river so close to my house, a pond would probably be overkill.

Josie had a pitcher of iced tea and a plate of cookies sitting on the table. She set the gift bag on a chair, filled our glasses with tea, and we all sat down.

"Violet and I talked most days." Josie's lip trembled. "I started texting her this morning and then remembered she's gone."

"That must be hard, Josie," said Toni. "I don't know what I'd do without Quinn."

I patted Toni's hand. "Violet will be missed. I know Mishka, her dog-walker, was sure upset when we talked to her yesterday." Good segue, I thought.

Josie adjusted the plate in front of her, then looked at me. "Oh? You spoke to Mishka?"

"We did. She'd taken Trix overnight."

I hesitated, concerned that Josie may not want to talk about this, but at the same time, I felt vulnerable not knowing what Violet said about me. "Did she tell you why she didn't drop off Trix the night before?"

"Yes. She heard you and Violet arguing and didn't want to intrude."

"It's true. My last words to Violet were pretty horrible." Sitting back, Josie crossed her arms tightly. "I feel awful about it."

Toni leaned forward. "Everybody has moments like that. You couldn't possibly have foreseen...."

"I know. Truly, I was trying to protect her...and Derek."

Protect Derek? Violet's ex-husband. I wondered why.

"I suppose Violet told you she thought there was a spirit in your house," Josie said.

"Yes, she did. When I left my place that night, she was performing an exorcism. Throwing salt on the floor and burning sage. Frankly, she was acting crazy."

Josie looked down for a second. "Yes, I know. I'd never seen Violet so erratic. I arrived around 8:30. I saw the salt and asked her about it. She said it was to ward off the evil spirit. I tried to talk some sense into her, but she wouldn't listen to reason. Quinn, she said the spirit looked like you."

"Quinn has had some bad hair days, but...evil spirit...well, that's just a harsh exaggeration," Toni said.

I would have smiled at her jest, but the demon-Quinn reference only heightened my worry.

"I'm serious," Josie said. "Violet thought Quinn was possessed."

"Over the last few months, I've been working seven days a week," I said, trying not to sound as if I had to defend myself. "I hardly saw Violet. I don't know what made her think I was possessed."

"Honestly, I don't know either," Josie said. "Violet wasn't acting rationally. I wouldn't take it personally. It wasn't your fault."

It was hard not to take this personally, but I was grateful Josie didn't think I'd brought on this craziness. "Violet and I had a bit of an argument over the exorcism. I was trying to calm her down. I suppose you tried to do the same?" I hoped Josie would tell us what had transpired between her and Violet.

Josie touched her hand to her chest. "We also had an argument, but the exorcism was just the precursor to that."

"Oh no, it gets worse?" Toni said.

Josie grimaced and gave a quick nod. "I had a headache that night. When I was in the bathroom, I opened Violet's medicine cabinet for a painkiller. She had prenatal vitamins on the shelf."

"What?" Toni nearly spit out her iced tea.

My jaw dropped. "Violet was pregnant?"

"No, she wasn't," said Josie. "She said she was planning to get pregnant and wanted to be in the best of health."

"I had no idea," I said. "Has she been dating? I never saw a man at her place." I was realizing how little I'd known about the woman living in my home and how potentially dangerous this situation had become considering she'd been murdered.

Josie shook her head. "Not that I knew of. Last year, before she and Derek broke up, they'd been trying to get pregnant, but it wasn't working. I don't think he wanted a baby as much as she did. Anyway, she became obsessive about it. She was even buying baby clothes. Eventually, the stress of it all drove them apart."

"That would be hard," Toni said.

"Yes, and Derek's mother got involved. She wanted a grandchild desperately and was trying to get Derek and Violet back together. At least, that's what Violet told me the night she was killed. She said if she were to have his baby, Derek would come around and be a wonderful father. Violet had no relationship with her own parents and was close to her mother-in-law. When they separated, it wasn't just Derek that Violet lost. She lost his family, too. They were all she had. The break-up was hard on her. She thought a baby would bring it all back."

I looked at Toni, then at Josie. "But they'd split up, and it sounds like a pregnancy wasn't in the cards for them. Besides, babies do not fix marriages."

Josie's gaze pierced the potted impatiens on the table. "I know that. Apparently, they were still hooking up, and Violet was convinced her chances of getting pregnant were better. Her doctor said women often get pregnant when they stop trying so hard." She reached over, snapped off a dead flower, and tossed it on the ground.

Josie's tone was bitter. I wondered why. Maybe she thought Violet and Derek weren't good together, period.

"Considering they were separated, was Derek on board with this?" Toni asked.

"Not that I knew of. I asked her the same question."

"She admitted he didn't want a baby, but she believed it would solve everything between them. She actually admitted to stealing Derek's sperm."

Steal his sperm? This was getting odder by the minute. "That's beyond desperate," I said. "How does someone go about stealing sperm?"

"She had it figured out. She was going to seduce him, and then in the bathroom, take the sperm out of the condom and inject it into herself with a turkey baster."

"Good grief! I've never heard of such a thing," Toni said.

Josie's eyes went cold. "After she said it, I got so angry at her, she changed her story and said she'd been kidding. But I was still angry at her. I left after that. After all, Derek was my friend, too."

I slid a cookie off the plate and took a bite. "Did you tell Derek?"

Josie hesitated and rubbed her nose. Her cheeks flushed pink. "I was going to, but I didn't get a chance. Besides, it's no longer relevant."

Josie wasn't making sense to me. "Not relevant? If Derek thought Violet stole his sperm, I'd say that might be a motive to kill her, don't you think?"

"The police must have questioned you, no?" asked Toni.

"They did. I admitted Violet and I argued. I didn't think a baby was going to help her or Derek. She was already stressed out about the house being haunted. She wasn't thinking rationally. Violet never coped well with stress. How was she going to manage a baby, especially if she'd tricked Derek into it?"

I knew all about the stress and expense of raising children. I flashed back to when Bryan and I learned I was pregnant. Since we'd only been dating a few months, and I was still in my freshman year at college, a baby was not good news. With considerable thought, we got married, but even with my parent's help, it had been a difficult time.

Josie continued. "I want the police to find Violet's killer, but I don't have a lot of faith in that sheriff. Last year, he blamed us at Mooseheads for making him a laughing-stock. Remember when that guy broke out of jail and stopped in for a drink? How were we supposed to know he was a criminal?"

I remembered that. The guy's picture had been all over the news. And then, when the police in Duluth caught him, our sheriff took a lot of ribbing over how a dumb criminal pulled the wool over our police officers' eyes.

I got a bad feeling. This was the sheriff I was counting on to get to the truth about who killed Violet. What if he bungled this investigation? What if he was sure Craig or I had something to do with it? Was I going to leave my fate in this sheriff's hands?

"But doesn't that make you look like a suspect, Josie?" Toni asked.

"The police told me Violet was killed sometime between 11:00 PM and 3:00 AM. I was at Mooseheads with at least five other people during that time, so I have an alibi."

"I see," said Toni. "Well, I imagine the police will talk to Derek about all this."

Josie was running her fingers up and down her necklace. "Yes, I imagine they will. I didn't want to implicate Derek because I don't believe he could have done it. At the same time, I'm not an idiot. If the sheriff found out

I withheld the facts of that argument, he'd be happy to charge me with obstructing justice or something like that."

I nodded.

"I told them everything I've told you." Josie pushed back her chair. "I've got to get to work now."

"Sure," I said. "Me, too. Thank you for being so open with all this."

Toni picked up her empty glass. "Before we go, may I please use your bathroom?"

I stifled a smile. Toni's bladder truly couldn't go longer than thirty minutes. I picked up the plate of cookies and followed Josie and Toni to the patio door.

Inside, I glanced around the small kitchen while Josie tidied up. The walls were the color of rose quartz. Pretty. The focal piece, a yellow-painted hutch, caught my attention. "That's a lovely piece. Did you paint it?"

"My dad did. He's recently retired and likes to keep busy."

A hefty pink salt lamp sat beside a decanter and four stemless glasses. My mouth went dry. A few months ago, when I'd been washing my windows at home, I saw Violet lug a similar salt lamp from her car into her apartment. I remember thinking it looked awfully heavy. I thought back to yesterday when I'd looked over every inch of Violet's suite. I didn't remember seeing the lamp.

I walked over to the hutch. "Violet had one of these salt lamps, no?"

"Yes, we got them at the same time. Why?"

Toni came out of the bathroom and looked at me. "What's going on?"

I gaped at the lamp. "I think I might have figured out the murder weapon."

Chapter Eight

I MAY HAVE BROKEN the speed limit, something I rarely did, rushing along Harmony Road to check on the salt lamp.

"Is it okay to enter your house now?" Toni asked as we reached the spot where the canopy from old trees made a leafy tunnel for us to whiz through.

"No, I don't think so. The sheriff said they'd move as quickly as they could gathering evidence, but he hasn't said I can return home. The salt lamp was on a side table that's close to the patio door, so we'll be able to peek in and see if it's there."

"You don't think you should just go to the police?" Toni asked.

"Not yet. If it's sitting right there, I don't want to make a fool of myself." After my last visit to the station, I didn't want the police looking at me like I was loopy again. It wouldn't take over five minutes to check on the lamp.

It was strange pulling into my driveway, feeling like I was trespassing. I felt like a dark cloud hung over my sanctuary. I parked my pickup on the road and looked at the house. From the exterior, it looked the same, yet I couldn't go in and make myself at home, couldn't relax with my best friend, couldn't enjoy any of the things that made me love this place. I hadn't felt this way since my ex left and the ugly state of our break-up tainted our family home. At least Sandy wasn't out in her garden to witness my hesitation or start in on me again about how misguided it had been to rent to Violet.

Toni and I got out and walked up to the yellow police tape. I ducked under.

"This feels wrong," said Toni, but she followed me. We always followed each other. "We are such badasses," she said, making me smile.

Beside the house were four-tiered steps filled with gravel. It crunched under our feet as we crept down the far side of the house to the back and across the patio.

I'd always thought of my backyard as an oasis. Broad, leafy ferns blanketed the ground along with wild columbine, bluebells, and phlox.

It didn't feel like an oasis today, I thought, as we reached the patio by the guest suite. A latex glove lay on the ground, thoughtlessly disposed of. I stepped around it.

"That's icky," Toni said, her mouth in a grim twist. "Such disrespect for your property. Speaking of, what's going to happen to all your plants?"

"Good question." I checked the potted begonia on the ground and found it damp. The pot on the table was wet too, and my herb garden looked watered. "That's odd. I don't remember it raining."

"It hasn't rained. We're in a five-day drought."

"Everything looks like it's been watered," I said.

"Maybe your neighbor did it?"

I scoffed. "Doubtful." Sandy's house was fairly close, but my other neighbor was a few hundred feet through the woods. "I can't imagine my neighbors creeping under police tape to water my plants."

"Probably not. It must have been the ghost."

"Sure, that makes the most sense. Having a ghost can't just be all rattling chains and slamming doors."

"Exactly," she said. "Who's to say there aren't productive, helpful ghosts out there, too."

I remembered the night Violet was exorcising the phantom, and I thought I saw something move when I was in the bedroom. I wondered again if it could have been the murderer in the backyard?

"You have a funny look on your face," Toni said.

Sweat broke out along my hairline. What if the killer discovered I was asking questions about Violet's murder? What if he came back? Would I ever be able to live in my home in peace again? "I was just thinking about the night when Violet was killed; when I thought I saw something in the bedroom mirror reflection. I've wondered if it could have been the killer in the backyard."

"Not a pleasant thought, Quinn." Toni cleared her throat and scanned the bushes. "Do you think they hid here for hours, waiting for you to leave? Mishka and Josie were here that night, too. Geez, this house was busy."

"There are lots of places to hide in the woods."

Toni jerked. She looked at her arm and brushed off a beetle. "Only if they brought bug spray."

"Yes, the mosquitoes are bad at night."

A trill rang out in the woods, followed by a scrabbling sound.

Toni grabbed my forearm. "Geez Louise, what was that?"

Movement by the white pines gave me a start. I looked over to see a masked face watching us. "Over there—it's a raccoon." I smiled with relief.

Toni let out her breath. "It's huge! Aren't raccoons nocturnal?"

"Yes. It should be sleeping, instead of watching us. I understand. I can't sleep through the night either."

"You think the raccoon is menopausal?"

"I don't know. Maybe."

"Well, those beady eyes are giving me the creeps." Toni took a few steps closer to the tree and clapped her hands. "Go on. Back to bed." The raccoon scrabbled down farther instead of up. Toni stepped back. "Let's get a move on. I'm not a fan of menopausal raccoons at a murder scene."

I was okay with that since goosebumps were running up my arms. I stuck my face against the patio door and cupped my hands around my eyes to reduce the glare. The side table where I'd seen the salt lamp was empty. "The lamp's not there."

Toni nudged me over. "Are you sure?"

I scanned the room from wall to wall. I could see almost the entire living space except for the bedroom and bathroom. "Well, I don't see it."

"Keep an eye on that raccoon. Let me have a look." Toni peered inside. "Are you sure Violet had a salt lamp?"

The masked mammal hadn't moved. "Josie said she did. And I remember seeing it on that table right there because I considered selling them in my shop."

"Really? Isn't that more Colleen's thing?"

"Yes. I came to that conclusion, but that's why I'm sure it was there. I wish I noticed when the police were here. Maybe we should have a quick look inside to be sure she didn't move it."

Toni glanced over at the raccoon. "I don't think so. I have a bad feeling about this. We should get out of here." She turned to go back the way we'd come, but Violet's bedroom window was on the other side of the house.

"Okay, but not that way. Her bedroom is over here. We'll just peek in the window quickly."

I was ahead of Toni as we started around the corner of the house. That's why it was me who nearly smashed into a big, hulking guy.

With a gun!

The scream that ripped through my lungs would have terrorized the un-dead. Especially when Toni did a great job as my echo.

My heart was somewhere near Mars as I realized the man with the gun was the teen deputy.

Toni was clutching her chest. "I just aged a decade."

I had to give Deputy Wilson credit. Other than a few eye blinks, he was pretty calm, considering our banshee impersonations.

"All right. Calm down, ladies. What are you two doing here?" Wilson's lips pressed into a slash as he put his gun away.

"I was...We were...looking for...the salt lamp." I caught my breath and then explained about the missing lamp.

"You should have called the sheriff's office, not come to the crime scene," he said sharply. "I could charge you with criminal trespassing."

"At my own house?" I tried to sound confused, like I didn't know I shouldn't be there.

"Yes. Take this as a warning to stay clear of these premises."

"Okay. I will. You'll have a look for the lamp then? It could be in the bedroom."

"Yes, I'll look. You two, leave the investigating to the police."

Toni gave me snake eyes and then marched toward my truck.

I understood that, but it was difficult to leave my fate to the deputy who was looking at me with more suspicion now. After all, if I'd left the investigating to the police, they'd never have known about the salt lamp. What else would they miss? The teen deputy would never admit it, but I'd unearthed a pretty good clue today.

I started to follow Toni, but then stopped and turned back to Wilson. It couldn't just be my bad luck he showed up at this moment. "Did my neighbor tell you we were here?" Sandy was one of those people who was always watching, always complaining. If it wasn't my groundcover creeping into her grass, she was mad because I lit my chiminea or I'd laughed too loud on my patio when I had friends over at dinnertime.

"We got a call. That's all I'm saying. Goodbye, Ms. Delaney."

I looked over at Sandy's house. Everything was still and quiet. Too quiet. She had called the police on me. I was sure of it. That dillweed was trying to make me look guilty.

The next morning, after a restless night, I got out of bed at 5:00 a.m. Even without a million thoughts in my head, I rarely slept in. According to many of my friends, this habit seemed to be a by-product of midlife.

Oreo was snoring softly, tucked against the pillow on the peacock chair, lying on his back, spread-eagled, one paw over his eyes. I smiled at the look of him. Cats so often appeared more comfortable and cozier than I'd ever been. He didn't stir as I padded into the bathroom.

I turned on the shower and stepped into the claw-foot tub, sliding the curtain closed. The inn was at least a century old, but everything had been updated. This was my preferred style, keeping the character of an older aesthetic without the headaches of old pipes, wiring, and heating.

My thoughts drifted from charming old houses to what I'd learned yesterday from Josie. As I stood under the rainfall showerhead, I wondered if Derek West had killed his ex-wife with a salt lamp in my guest suite. I wasn't convinced Josie hadn't told Derek that Violet intended to violate his...person by stealing his sperm.

Oh, Violet. What had you been thinking?

Whatever she'd been thinking, she sounded desperate. Surely, the sheriff would have interrogated Derek by now, and they'd now be looking for that salt lamp. If it was the murder weapon, hopefully, the killer left some identifying evidence behind.

I finished my shower and dried off. I wished I could have washed away my rambling thoughts. I'd hardly spent a moment on my cordials, and I had a constant anxious feeling in my stomach. I just wanted this resolved and for things to return to normal.

Violet's daytimer was still at Break Thyme. I intended to hand it over to the police today. No more delay, regardless of my reluctance to compromise Craig. He still hadn't called me back.

I tried him again, got his voice mail, and left another message. Where was he?

I realized I was gnawing on my fingernail. I dropped my hand. I'd given up that habit years ago.

Okay, get a grip. Worrying about things I had no control over was not helpful. It was time to focus on the many other things I had to do. Life marched on with all its responsibilities, and I'd agreed to meet my daughter at the campground to figure out a renovation plan for the trailer. I needed to do something physical to ground myself and getting the trailer finished would enable me to set a date for our trip—something tangible I could work toward.

Twenty minutes later, dressed in old clothes, I filled a thermos with coffee and added it to a bag of supplies I was bringing to the trailer.

"Come on, Oreo." He meowed a complaint as I fixed an old harness I'd brought from home on him. I didn't want Mary, the inn owner, to feel like my cat was her responsibility all day long. "Don't get ornery on me. I'll bring you back here for the afternoon."

Another meow. He gave me a forlorn look. A vocal cat, Oreo responded to comments directed his way. Not to be outdone by Mary, who'd been feeding him treats, I looked at him and said, "Hey, I'm bringing cat treats."

He meowed his response. I leaned down and scratched behind his ears, feeling love for the big guy. My kids, mom, and ex-husband had moved on or away. Oreo was the one constant in the sea of change.

In the sky to the east, a brilliant orange was washing up over the horizon. Nothing like a sunrise to clear the mind, at least for a few minutes. I glanced at the sky and vowed not to think of murder and demon spirits.

I passed the marina, where a slew of boats moored in the finger docks and a few sailboats bobbed peacefully in the bay. I felt a pull but drove straight past Break Thyme, and all the other shops, wishing Henrietta's bakery was open because I could go for a treat right now. The emotional stress of the past few days had me craving carbs to calm my nerves, even though I knew indulging would pack pounds on my hips. Luckily for my shaky willpower, I also wouldn't be tempted by a fresh-from-the-oven scone at Break Thyme. Poppy and Jetti were making the scones this morning—a massive transfer of responsibility on my part. We were all proud of me for relinquishing the task.

I entered Beach Meadows Park, driving past the dark office and along the winding dirt road to spot 110, where my recreational trailer was parked. There it was: our mobile adventure in a thirty-one-foot white box with black and red decals. At twelve years old, the interior showed its age but had been within my budget. The makeover would bring it up to date and transform it into a place I'd want to spend time in, which might lure me away from the café occasionally.

I was grateful to have this distraction. Keeping busy was the best way for me to deal with stress. And better for my waistline.

The humid air carried the aromatic scent of evergreens. I stood still for a moment and listened to Lake Superior, the rumble of waves rolling into the shore. That sound took me back to the beaches of my childhood on the east coast, to when my mom encouraged my inquisitive nature by buying me a metal detector to search for treasures buried in the sand. I stood still, appreciating the dewy glisten on the leaves and grasses as a sunray filtered through the trees. Taking this moment immediately helped me to feel restored, better balanced, and blessed to live so close to nature. Now I was ready to get to work.

The guy who'd delivered the trailer had leveled it, hooked up the water and electricity, and extended the pop-outs to give it more floor space. I opened the door and had a look around. The kitchen was on the left side, facing a couch and dinette. A three-piece bathroom and bunk beds were at the far end. To the right was my bedroom behind sliding doors, a queen bed, and two small closets—minuscule, really. I chose this trailer because of its light weight, solid structure, and it had been well looked after. I also liked the layout, and the fridge was new. Because of their compact dimensions, fridges for these things were expensive.

It was musty inside, so I opened the windows and let the breeze in. When I turned on the tap, the water sputtered, then flowed. I wasn't sure about the water quality or the cleanliness of the lines, so I'd brought bottled water to drink. I retrieved Oreo and let him explore inside while I filled his water bowl.

"What do you think, boy?"

He paused to tell me and looked up with indifference. While he continued his cautious sniffing, I got my box of supplies from the truck. No time like the present. I planned to install blackout shades later, so I got to work removing the window valances and blinds. I was taking down the ones in the bedroom when my phone rang. Craig. Finally.

"Hey, Quinn, what's going on. Why all the messages?"

"I need to tell you something that may be important." I told him about finding Violet's day planner with his name and number in there the day before she was killed.

He was quiet.

"Craig? Did you contact her or vice versa?"

"No. I hadn't spoken to her in months." There was something off in his conviction that worried me.

"So, you don't know why your name is in there?"

"No, I don't, Quinn. No idea at all. Sorry, things are pretty busy right now. I have to go."

"Okay. I just wanted to talk to you before I gave the planner to the police."

"Sure." This came out sounding skeptical. "Quinn, you don't think I had something to do with Violet's death."

"No. No, of course not." I was absolutely sure of this. The night Violet had been killed, he'd been away, although the police might consider he hadn't been that far from Bookend Bay—an hour or so. "Now, you have a head's up, if the police ask you about it."

"Great. Thanks. I'll talk to you later."

As I hung up, I heard a car approach and looked out the window to see Samantha pull in beside my truck.

"Hey, Mom." She hugged me as I met her at the door. My sunny-dispositioned daughter was the bubbly one of my two kids. She and I had the same hair color, at least some of mine were still natural brown. I had highlights to hide the gray. Samantha had her dad's eyes, narrower than mine, and her grandmother's smile, which warmed my heart and made me miss my mom.

"Hello, my love," I said, stepping aside for her to come up the stairs and enter. "Well, what do you think?"

"Hmm, let me see." She gave it the once over, pulling open most of the cupboard doors. "I like it. It's got potential."

She sat on the bench and Oreo climbed onto her lap for attention. As she scratched under his chin, his purring motor engaged. "By the way, how's Oreo taking the change in scenery?"

"Oh, he's fine. He thinks he's the boss of the inn."

"Of course he does. You know the old saying—dogs have owners, cats have staff."

I laughed. "When I came home last night, he was sitting on the lap of a guest in the garden at the inn. Apparently, the cook gave him salmon for dinner."

"Is that so? Lucky cat. He's never going to leave." She shifted Oreo onto the bench and stood. "So, what's the plan?"

On my iPad, I showed her pictures of renovated trailers and shared the research I'd done on how to paint the papered walls.

"Wow, what a difference it makes to paint everything white," Samantha said. "Really brightens things up."

"No kidding. For our trip, I'd like to get the painting done. If there's time, we'll rip up the carpet and lay down vinyl flooring. Eventually, I'll replace the counters and bathroom vanity and get Sue to recover the bolsters."

She stared at me for a second. "Seriously? Do you think that's enough, or are you going to overhaul the engine too?" Samantha blamed me for giving her the over-achiever gene every time she bit off more than she could chew.

"You're hilarious. It doesn't have an engine. It's a trailer. We have to pull it."

She gave me a cheeky smile. "What do you want me to do first?"

"You can help remove the blinds and then get the mattresses out. I'm going to replace them."

"Okay." She narrowed her gaze, scrutinizing the brown decor. "I think a gray floor would look nice with white walls." Her expression then turned to one of concern. "How are you doing, Mom? You know, after finding your tenant like that."

"I'm okay. I mean, it was a shock, but you know me—I'm keeping busy." I wanted to tell her about the sleuthing Toni and I were doing, but I didn't want Samantha to worry I might put myself in any danger. And, frankly, I wanted a break from the whole thing.

"Grandma is going to go nuts when she sees us," Samantha said as she rifled through my toolbox. "I'm glad Jordan is coming."

My relationship with Samantha often came easier than with my son, especially since he married Chelsea. I hoped that three weeks together would help Jordan and me find our way back to the easy rapport we used to have. I knew my disapproval of his wife had negatively affected our relationship. From now on, I was going to keep quiet and allow him to live his life even when it meant making mistakes.

"Me too," I said. "So, do you think we should have a name for the trailer?"

"Definitely."

I took a moment to think of possible names while Sam pulled out her phone, fingers flying over the keyboard. "Since its first trip will be to Nova Scotia to see Gramma, I think something Scottish." She looked up. "Oh! Remember that Acadian story Gramma used to read to us when we were kids?"

"Evangeline?"

"Yes. Longfellow wrote it. Don't you think this thing looks like a long fellow?"

"It's the longest thing I'll ever tow. Longfellow is perfect."

"We're going to need a bottle of champagne to christen it," she said.

"That's a great idea. We'll have a toast before we start our voyage."

"Guess that's better than breaking the bottle over the front window."

"Indeed." That settled, we started removing the rest of Longfellow's window coverings and stripping off the wallpaper border.

"I think I heard my phone," Samantha said a little while later.

I grabbed my water bottle and stood by the door, taking in our progress. We'd accomplished a respectable amount and would be ready to prime the walls on the weekend.

"It's from Jordan," she said with an exasperated expression.

"What's up?"

"He's canceling on me. Again. I swear it's Chelsea's doing. Mom, I don't know if it's my imagination, but I think she's jealous of the relationship I have with Jordan."

"What? Why do you think that?"

"Every time the three of us get together, she inserts herself between me and Jordan as if she has to know everything we talk about. I honestly can't remember just the two of us having a conversation since he met her. And now, he was supposed to come hang out at my place tomorrow, but instead, he's going to Chelsea's parents'. Why can't she go on her own?" She tugged the elastic from her ponytail and worked her fingers through her hair. "It's like he doesn't even care about having a relationship with me anymore." Her brow wrinkled in anger. "If that's what he wants, he can have it."

It was upsetting to hear that Chelsea was coming between my kids. I wanted to rile against her, but I stopped myself. How would that help? Samantha's anger was a lightbulb moment for me. Sure, I was mad about Jordan and Chelsea too, and I'd been taking it out on him in some rather passive-aggressive ways. I never liked this quality in myself and could see I hadn't conquered it. I didn't want to lose my son, and I didn't want Samantha to lose her brother. "I hear you, but please, Samantha, we can't give up on him. Ask him to set another date. Let's keep reminding him how much he means to us. And Chelsea, too. I'm going to make a point of being nicer to her. Maybe she's feeling threatened for some reason, and that's not very nice for her."

She had her lips pressed tight together. Slowly, the wrinkles in her forehead smoothed out. "Okay, fine. I'll try again."

I felt a small dose of relief, but this was only one step toward saving our relationship with Jordan. I made a mental note to call him later and start making things better between us.

Thinking of relationships reminded me of my friend Jade, and if she'd truly snubbed me the other day. I'd racked my memory for anything I'd done to cause friction between us. The last time we'd seen each other, we'd played euchre with her husband Edward and Craig. Jade and I had won, and from what I remembered, we'd parted on happy terms. The most reasonable explanation was that I'd misinterpreted her behavior, and all was well between us. Despite my rather busy life, there was only one to find out.

Chapter Nine

IT WAS NEARLY NOON before I dropped Oreo back at the inn. I'd worked on the trailer longer than expected, giving the cabinets and walls a light sanding. Time often slipped away on me when I got into a project where there was lots of work to do.

It was another beautiful day. A light breeze sent leaves fluttering overhead as I exited my truck on Honesty Street. I always enjoyed walking to my café under the canopy of ancient trees. One day, I'd love to live on one of these streets in a big old Victorian, close to the lake, but these homes were out of my budget.

I crossed the boulevard and slipped down the lane between Break Thyme and my neighbor, May Flowers. The back of my café faced the lake. I skirted the patio off the Cozy Nook and entered through the private entrance into the kitchen. I couldn't wait to see the new Herb of the Month sign Aubrey had finished yesterday.

Our first herb would be thyme, to celebrate the name of the café. In keeping with this theme, we were serving citrus thyme, iced tea and glazed blueberry lemon-thyme scones. I planned to put the apple thyme jelly on sale.

As I tied on my apron, I heard Poppy laughing with the customers, and it made me smile to know my café was cheery. I came out of the kitchen and saw Mr. and Mrs. Brooks sitting on stools at the counter. They owned one of those big, old houses in the neighborhood across the street.

"I think muddled is a great verb," said Mr. Brooks. "How about this: last night, I got a wee bit muddled after Edna served muddled mint juleps!"

Two women sitting next to the Brooks laughed. "I love this!" the redhead said. "Okay, my turn. This morning, I left my room in a muddle because nothing stands in the way of my caffeine."

"Good one!" said Poppy.

From across the room, in a booth, a dad called out: "We managed to muddle through the morning despite being up half the night feeding the baby."

A cheer sounded as a couple came in the front door and instantly laughed. "Now, that's the kind of greeting we deserve, don't you think?" The young woman said to her partner.

"What's going on?" I whispered to Poppy.

"Hi, Quinn. Everyone just loves Aubrey's sign. What a unique idea. We took a vote and decided the first verb of the month should be muddle. Everyone wants their mint tea muddled today!"

I had completely missed the context of this conversation. "What are you talking about?" I looked up at our new sign. It looked great. Bundles of herbs in a curve around a chalkboard oval with a flowing script font that said: Verb of the Month.

Wait. What? The first word was taking a second to register. I blinked, but the word still said Verb instead of Herb.

Good grief!

I didn't know what to say. I plastered on a smile and turned to Poppy. "Can I see you in the back, please?"

She followed me into the kitchen. "There's a spelling error in the sign. It was supposed to say herb, not verb."

Poppy opened her mouth, then closed it. "I wondered about that, but then everyone was having so much fun with it. I thought I must have heard you wrong."

I paced five steps and then came back. "Who has a verb of the month?"

"The Lexicon Society?"

I rolled my eyes. "Does this look like grammar headquarters?"

"It does now," Poppy said, failing at hiding her smile.

I put my hands down flat on the counter and hung my head—thinking. Should I call Aubrey and ask her to change it?

I turned to my assistant. "I don't know how this happened. Aubrey sent a sketch two days ago. It looked good to me."

Poppy had a way of pushing her lips over to one side when she was thinking. "Didn't you have a bad day two days ago?"

I sucked in my breath. "Oh no. Probably the worst day of my life." I had a sudden, horrible recollection of getting to the inn after finding Violet and feeling exhaustion like I'd never known. I'd seen the email from Aubrey with an attachment. Did I look at it? Or did I fall asleep and then approve it the next morning without checking?

"Verb of the month is weird," I said.

"My two cents: it's weird in a good way and people remember weird in a good way." Poppy removed a bag of peppermint leaves from the fridge and headed to the front. "We're going to get short of things to muddle."

"My brain is about two verbs short of muddled."

"Whatever that means." Poppy's laugh followed her out the door.

"I don't know what it means," I called after her. "My brain is muddled!"

I took twenty seconds and did nothing but breathe. I'd figure out what to do about the verb of the month later. It was well after noon and I needed to create another cordial, so I had time to get the portions right and the flavors balanced. With each iteration, I was often inspired to alter or add ingredients.

Munching on a tuna sandwich, I retrieved my folder full of inspirational recipes I planned to try. As I lifted the folder off the shelf, one note fell out and fluttered to the ground. As I bent to pick it up, I recognized the colorful Gaia Green logo at the top of the page. Written underneath was Elderflower, Mint, and Rhubarb Cordial. I didn't recognize the handwriting.

I stared at the next line: Start by muddling fresh mint.

Muddle. No way!

Whose recipe was this? I read through and thought it sounded like a good starting point, but I'd try adding a touch of lemon juice.

The front of the café got busy, so I put the recipe aside and helped Poppy for the rest of the afternoon. In this heat, everyone wanted a cool drink. I was happy with the revenue, but I was also feeling anxious about developing my cordial recipe.

Toni showed up at six o'clock just when things finally slowed down. I was happy to see her, but I would never get to that cordial, especially now that I couldn't sneak away to my own house and work in peace.

"I brought sushi from Atami's," Toni said. "There's a breeze. I figured we can eat on the patio and then head over to Colleen's for the psychic readings."

I pretended like I hadn't forgotten about that and tamped down the slight resentment I felt at having to attend a psychic reading I didn't believe in. Still, my friends were important to me, so I cast aside my hard feelings.

After pouring iced teas, I grabbed a couple of paper plates to take outside to the staff table. The vast expanse of Lake Superior, calm as glass, reached as far I could see, meeting the cloudless sky in illusion. The expansiveness often gave me a sense of possibility. Just the sight of it was restorative.

"Have you heard from the sheriff yet?" Toni opened the box of sushi.

"No. I have no idea where they're at in their investigation and don't know when I can go back home." I didn't know if I'd ever get the vision of Violet out of my head. I wondered if every time I entered the guest suite, I'd see her in my mind's eye.

"You still think Derek did it?" I asked, nabbing a thin scrap of ginger.

Toni dabbed her chopsticks in the little mound of wasabi and brushed the green paste on a roll. "He's a pretty viable suspect. I don't think we can rule out Josie, though. The more I thought about it, the more I realized she didn't seem all that upset at the loss of her best friend."

"Hmm, I guess you're right. Although everyone grieves differently. It would have been hard to justify Violet's behavior if she admitted she wanted to steal Derek's sperm."

"True. I know I'd be upset if you were sneaking around stealing sperm."

I laughed. "That's an image I don't want in my head."

"I know. Gross. What about Mishka and your neighbor?"

As I finished chewing my nigiri, a realization dawned. "Considering the stress Violet was under, maybe she told Mishka she was trying to get pregnant. That could have been what she meant by Violet having a life-changing event. I guess Mishka thought I knew about it."

"That makes sense. Mishka didn't have a reason to want Violet dead."

"Not that we know of. And it's a stretch to think Sandy's annoyance led to murder. I think it's going to turn out to be Derek."

Toni checked her watch. "We better finish up and get going."

"I'll be right back." I popped a roll into my mouth and hurried upstairs to grab the planner. I'd drop it off at the sheriff's office after the psychic reading. I had no good reason to think Craig would lie about speaking to Violet before her death. As I thought about it, I couldn't imagine my brother as anything but a hero. He'd never broken the law, he rarely broke the speed limit. People like Craig don't suddenly commit murder.

Since the café wasn't too busy, I told Poppy to go home and asked Melanie and Jetti to stay until closing. I didn't have official closing hours, although the time on the door said ten o'clock. Because our busy summer season was short, we stayed open as long as there were customers.

Toni and I headed down the boulevard toward Colleen's. A group of people were gathered in front of Ollie's Outfits.

"What's going on at Ollie's?" Toni said. "Is that the deputy?"

"I think it is," I said, noticing Deputy Wilson standing on the sidewalk, facing Ollie's revolving door, with his hands on his hips, looking intimidating. The subject of this intimidation remained to be seen. "I was going to drop off Violet's planner. I can save a trip if I give it to him now."

"What did Craig say about his name being in it?" Toni asked.

"He said he doesn't know why it's there. He hadn't talked to Violet for months."

"Okay, well then, there's nothing to worry about."

"Exactly."

"I've seen nothing like it," said a woman staring into Ollie's. "Where did it come from?"

I peered into the shop and did a double-take. Lying at the foot of a mannequin, chewing on the hem of a summer dress, was a brown and white, curly-horned animal. "Is that a goat?"

Deputy Wilson flashed a dirty look my way. At least it felt like a dirty look. Perhaps I'd asked a dumb question, but still.

"I'm pretty sure that's Jeffrey's goat," said Bill, a regular customer of mine.

Ollie was standing beside the deputy. "It came right through the revolving door. And it won't budge. Not a bit."

"It probably likes the air conditioning," said Toni. Everyone thought that made sense.

Seeing a goat making itself at home in Ollie's store was amusing, but it also gave me a bit of the willies. While I loved the quirkiness of this small town, I was starting to wonder what on earth was happening lately. It was like I'd stepped into an alternate reality where exorcisms, murders, and shopping goats were the norm.

"You could spray it with water," said Bill. "They don't like water."

"Not in my store!" Ollie lifted his cell phone. "I'm going to give Jeffrey a call. If he's got a missing goat, he can come and get it. Do you have his number, Bill?"

Bill did. While they took care of the phone call, I removed Violet's planner from my bag and sidled up to the deputy.

"Can I speak to you for a moment?" I said.

He looked relieved at the distraction. Not a goat man, I guessed. We stepped away from the crowd.

"What is it?"

I held up the planner. "I found this in my café. I'm pretty sure it belonged to Violet."

He took it from me and leafed through it. "Is that right? What makes you *pretty* sure?"

I realized I had to admit that yesterday Colleen said Violet had come looking for a planner. "Colleen Cole, who owns Mystic Garden, mentioned that Violet came into her shop last week looking for a planner she'd left behind. Since a planner turned up on one of my bookshelves, I'm assuming it's hers."

Teen deputy frowned skeptically. "You just happened to find Violet's planner on a bookshelf in your store?"

"Actually, one of my employees found it."

"Is that so?" He stared at me for so long I caved and looked at Toni, feeling his gaze penetrating the side of my head.

"Yes, that is so," I said finally, guessing he wanted me to confirm I'd said what I'd said.

Toni shrugged.

"Listen, you're lucky I don't charge you with interference. Do you think I didn't see you back at your house when I told you to stay away? I don't find you amusing, Ms. Delaney."

I didn't find him amusing either. Was he off his rocker? Of course, I knew he saw me. We'd had a conversation, and I certainly hadn't been back there since. If this was any example of the brain power going into their investigation, it was a good thing I'd interfered. I was pretty confident I'd already uncovered more information about Violet and possible suspects than they had, and I was an amateur! He should thank me for discovering the murder weapon and finding Violet's planner. "Of course, I know you saw me. And on that note, do you know when you'll be finished with the investigation?" I imagined the police suspected Violet's ex-husband, and they'd surely have checked for his fingerprints. At the same time, I couldn't remember seeing Derek West at my house, but that didn't mean he hadn't been there visiting with Violet at some point, which could explain a fingerprint. I wondered why the sheriff hadn't asked me about this.

"I do not," he said, brusquely. "We are being thorough, Ms. Delaney."

I seemed to have gotten on his bad side. The vibes coming from him were not pleasant.

The feelings might be mutual, but it wasn't smart to be on the bad side of the police. I gave him a small smile of support. "Good luck with the goat."

I had a psychic to meet.

Chapter Ten

Toni and I left the ruminant spectacle and continued down the road to Mystic Garden for the psychic readings. This evening would be a couple of hours of entertainment that I wouldn't take seriously. I couldn't. As a matter of fact, I was a little nervous about tonight since I didn't want to give the occult my attention and end up manifesting things I didn't want in my life. At the same time, I wanted to support my friend's event.

"I wish I believed in psychics enough to think this woman will tell us who killed Violet," I said to Toni.

She gave a soft snort. "I want to be there when you tell the deputy a psychic told you who the killer is."

"Or I could tell him the goat figured it out and told me telepathically."

We were laughing as we walked past the community hall. I waved to a neighbor of Toni's who I recognized from the park. Joking about the goat, seeing familiar faces, and walking a route I'd walked thousands of times helped disperse the weird feeling I'd had earlier. It was time to get back to my normal, mundane life.

I looked up to see a white drape fluttering in the Mystic Garden's second-floor window. All the shops along the lake had second stories. While some of the top floors were rented out as apartments, Colleen used her second floor as an extension of her gift shop, which had been the inspiration behind my plans for the loft space in Break Thyme.

Mystic Garden always smelled like a spa. Inside the front door, a diffuser dispersed a soothing blend of lavender and sweet orange into the air. I loved scents and paused to breathe in this one. Throughout the store, wooden shelves held trays of every imaginable stone. Glass shelves held a variety of colorful crystals. Colleen also sold incense, oils, diffusers, books, jewelry, healing teas, and plaques with inspiring messages.

Colleen ushered Toni and me into a sitting room upstairs to join three other women. I recognized Delores, a seasonal cottager, while the other two were strangers. We introduced ourselves to Caitlyn and Siobhan, who it turned out, were also seasonals with places just outside of town.

Colleen wore an ankle-length, green paisley dress and copper jewelry set with amethyst. Her curly red hair was held back by a headband allowing the sparkle in her earrings to catch the light. I'd not taken time to put in earrings, let alone match them to my clothes, and the rest of my jewelry was gathering dust. I'd never felt as put together as some of my friends, but now that I was in my forties, I'd finally stopped thinking of my casual style as some kind of fashion defect.

"There's water in the cooler, my lovies, and tea and coffee if you fancy some." Colleen then introduced Gloria, the psychic from Sault Ste. Marie. I guess I was expecting someone who looked like a gypsy—or at least as bohemian as Colleen—but Gloria was a petite, plain-looking woman with short brown hair, dressed more like me in denim capris and a sleeveless blouse. I wondered if she'd dressed this way on purpose to give her more credibility than if she'd been wearing a headscarf and an armful of bangles.

Gloria sat on a chair across from Toni and me on the couch. "I hope you've thought about what you'd like to learn from our reading today. If anyone wants a private session, I'm happy to do that as well."

I figured Gloria would offer vague, generalized statements that could apply to anyone. Heck, she'd probably googled us all, but that was part of the entertainment.

For the first fifteen minutes, Gloria focused on Siobhan who had career questions and wanted to know if she should go back to school. The conversation turned to her deceased grandmother, who'd always encouraged Siobhan to follow her dreams.

"Was your grandmother someone who told jokes?" Gloria asked.

"Yes!" said Siobhan. "She didn't just tell jokes, she played practical jokes on us all the time."

"That, I believe," said Gloria. "She's here, now, but she says she doesn't want you to think she's kidding around."

I'd not been expecting Gloria to commune with the dead, and this got my nerves on edge. What had I been thinking about coming to this event?

My hands clenched as I glanced around the room for a ghostly presence.

Thankfully, I saw nothing unusual. I exhaled slowly and reminded myself Gloria was probably making this stuff up. Or, I realized with excitement, if she was communicating with the dead, it could mean I was cured of whatever midlife affliction had given me a sixth sense. Maybe my life would be forever normal again. I relaxed my shoulders and leaned back into the couch cushion.

"Your grandmother wants all your family to know she harbors no resentment over being placed in a nursing home during her last years," Gloria said to Siobhan. "She understands she had dementia and needed full-time care. She was well looked after. She knows you love her and wants you to let go of any guilt you hold."

Sensible advice, but I imagined there were very few people who didn't feel guilty over a relative ending their life in a nursing home.

Siobhan wiped a tear from her eye. "Thank you. This means a lot to me. I'm glad she understands."

"This is...odd," Gloria said, squeezing her eyes closed. I couldn't tell if she was puzzled or in pain. We all sat quietly, waiting. I looked at Colleen, whose gaze was glued to the psychic.

Gloria's eyes popped open. She stared at me. "I've never experienced an energy like this. I don't know what it is."

I didn't like that she was looking at me. I shook my head, since I didn't know what to say.

"Quinn? Have you had a shock lately?"

"Well, just the murdered tenant in my guest suite." As soon as I said it, I realized I'd sounded crass. Her question struck me as obvious. Violet's death was in the news, so Gloria could have known this. "Sorry, that came out the wrong way."

"That might account for it," Gloria said.

"Unless you saw me with bed head," said Toni.

Everyone laughed, except Gloria, who was looking a little pale.

"Son of a biscuit!" Gloria jumped out of her chair. "Who was that?"

Siobhan stood up, too. "What—who? Where?"

Gloria was staring at something behind me.

The hairs on my arm rose as I cemented myself in denial. *There is no ghost. No ghost is standing behind me.*

I braced and looked back to the alcove where Colleen had a few tables of tiffany lamps for sale. No ghostly presence. Nothing out of the ordinary. Thankfully, I released my breath.

"The death of your tenant—was she your twin?" Gloria asked.

I wasn't expecting that. "No, I hardly knew her. I don't have a twin, just one brother."

Gloria shook her head. "I don't think so. You have a twin."

She said it with such conviction; I believed her. What the heck had my parents kept from me? I actually thought about confronting my mother before common sense prevailed and reason resumed. I had to give Gloria props: she had her schtick down pat.

Gloria crossed the room and made a big show of peeking in the corner and around the furniture, a hand outstretched as if going by feel, but there was nothing to see. "She's hiding now, but she was here, plain as day."

If a ghost had come to call, it certainly wouldn't be my non-existent twin.

"It was probably Violet's ," said Toni.

I hadn't thought of that, and I didn't like the idea being raised. "That phantom wasn't real," I said, meaning it.

Siobhan sat back down. "What are you talking about? What phantom?"

Toni wiped her nose with a Kleenex, possibly to hide a smile. She was always the cool cucumber in the group. "The tenant who was killed thought Quinn was possessed by a phantom, or maybe it was a demon," she said matter-of-factly.

"It was a spirit, not a demon," I said defensively. As if it was more of a sleight to be possessed by a demon in the hierarchy of the supernatural.

I heard Gloria suck in her breath and looked to see her shaking her head. "I think you're right. It's not a demon. I don't think she's evil. I get the sense she's confused about where she is, and she's trying to help you."

"That makes two confused Quinns," Toni said, and one confused psychic by the look on her face.

"Is there something we can do to help with the transmission?" Siobhan whispered.

Gloria shook her head. "I'm sorry. I've never encountered a spirit like this. She doesn't feel like she's on the other side. I get a sense, this twin of yours is a little OCD, as in constantly cleaning, tidying things, putting them in their places."

"Can you send her to my house?" Toni said.

I could always count on Toni for levity when needed. She was probably thinking I might be a little freaked out by this twin-spirit talk, and she was right. On top of seeing ghosts, I'd had a few unexplained instances over the past year. Innocuous things like finding a painted rock on my café counter, full coffee pots, plants being watered. Some of these things I'd explained away to my peri-menopausal memory. Frankly, I wasn't sure why it felt better to think my brain was failing instead of relegating these strange occurrences to the supernatural. Then again, it was a toss-up between which was worse.

No one else in the room had cracked a smile. Toni's joke aside, I was getting spooked by all this talk of demons and twins. A change of subject would be nice.

"I've taken enough of your time—" I didn't get to finish my sentence because a crumpled sheet of paper flew past my shoulder onto the table in front of us all.

Caitlin screamed.

Toni grabbed my arm.

Gloria let go an expletive a little stronger than son of a biscuit.

"That came out of nowhere," Colleen said as she hurried over to the alcove and looked around. "There's no one here. We're the only people upstairs."

My heart pounded like a military tattoo in my ears. I reached over and picked up the ball of paper. As I uncrumpled it, the first thing I recognized was the Gaia Green logo. What was this doing here? This was the second time I'd seen this logo today.

Toni was leaning into me. "Elderflower, Mint and Rhubarb Cordial," she read from the top of the paper and then looked at me. "What in the world is this?" Now Toni looked rattled. This unsettled me the most. If she was losing her composure, something was really wrong here.

"That's a recipe I found in my café today," I said. To make matters worse, I felt a hot flash coming on. A sign, in case I had any doubt, of stress.

"You brought it here?" asked Siobhan.

"No, I didn't." My hairline was instantly damp. Again, I scanned the room for a ghostly presence, but whatever this was, it wasn't showing itself to me. I didn't know if that was good or bad, but whatever it was, it was unnatural.

Gloria came around her chair to look at the recipe. "This twin of yours is trying to tell you something, but her message isn't clear to me. I'm sorry, I've lost her."

Good. May she stay lost forever.

A horrible thought occurred to me. Had what I feared just happened? Had Gloria now unleashed a ghostly entity that was going to start haunting me? "Please stop calling it my twin."

Toni touched my arm. "We should get some fresh air, Quinn."

"Yes. Good idea." I didn't want to run out on Colleen's event, but this invisible twin talk was being made doubly worse by my melt-down. "I'm sorry, Gloria, Colleen. I'm not feeling well. We'll leave quietly, so you can continue." I turned to Siobhan and Caitlin. "Nice to meet you both."

We made our way out of there, with me mopping my brow as I went. I was confused and disoriented, hot and cold at the same time.

Gloria was not acting. She hadn't snuck into Break Thyme, stole that recipe, and tossed it onto the table. So, did this mean she was right about my ghost twin?

I couldn't get my head around that one.

Why was this happening to me? One book I'd read over the last year said asking that question made you a victim, so take control. It's your choice how you react. Find a way to fix it.

I'd repeated those words to a customer only two weeks ago. It was much easier to give advice than to take it.

Chapter Eleven

AFTER TONI AND I bolted from the Mystic Garden, we high-tailed it back to Break Thyme to see if the crumpled recipe had disappeared from my folder.

"I would know if I was possessed, right?" I asked Toni.

"You're sometimes obsessed, but you're not possessed. I would notice if your head was on backward."

I smiled. "You're sure?"

"Absolutely."

Once again, I appreciated Toni's levity. Honestly, I didn't think I was possessed, but after that recipe appeared in front of everyone, I couldn't brush it off to a midlife memory glitch. However, that didn't mean this was the work of an OCD ghost twin, either. "Okay good. Maybe I'm mistaken. Maybe that recipe didn't come from thin air, but just blew into the room at Colleen's. Her window was open. Maybe it's not the one I saw in my kitchen."

"Son of a biscuit. That's a lot of maybes," Toni said as I unlocked the back door and turned on the light.

I looked at her. "Son of a biscuit?"

"It's fun to say."

"Yeah, it's a real humdinger." My recipe folder was sitting where I'd left it. I took it off the shelf, set it on the counter, and rifled through it. Twice.

My heart picked up its pace again. "It's not here."

"You've been under a lot of stress, Quinn. There's a reasonable explanation for all of this. I don't know what that is at the moment, but I guarantee you, it has nothing to do with demons or spirit twins. There's no such thing."

I swallowed and gave her a look. I wanted to believe that, but how could we know with any certainty. This thing with Violet had brought the paranormal into my thoughts again, as well as my house. "So ghosts are real, but demons and spirit twins are not. Got it." Saying it out loud didn't strengthen my confidence, but there was one thing I believed without doubt. "It's not possible I have a twin sister on this green Earth or any other place. My mother wasn't the kind of woman to have kept a secret like that. If I'd been a twin, we'd have known it."

"You're right about that, Quinn. We'll figure this out. Everything will look better in daylight." Tony leafed through the recipes in my folder. "Do you want to sleep over at my place tonight?"

"For your sake or mine?"

"Mine."

I gave a soft snort. "How's your gin supply?"

"Well stocked." We often had sleepovers, so we could have a few drinks and not worry about driving. Not that I liked to get drunk. I didn't. As soon as I felt the least bit tipsy, I stopped drinking. Losing control was not my thing, go figure.

"Perfect. I'll stop at the inn and pick up my cat if I can pry him away from all the good loving." Getting tipsy in the company of my good friend was exactly what I needed to put all this crazy-making business down for a bit. I'd be better in the morning when my rational side was strong again.

Animals had a way of detecting when their people were upset. Oreo, who usually liked his space, slept close to me all night. At least I think he stayed with me all night. I woke to see him, no more than ten inches away, casually preening himself. I rubbed him under his chin and his motor started. A soothing sound.

On the chair sat a pillow with an ostrich on it and the saying: One day you're an ostrich and the next you're a feather duster. This brought a smile to my face. The circle of life.

I wanted my normal life back. The routine of waking before sunrise and driving into Bookend Bay when everything was still and quiet. Making my morning coffee at Break Thyme and starting the scones for the day. Pouring iced ginger teas for Mr. and Mrs. Brooks, two of our regulars. I loved these simple, ordinary things in my life.

After breakfast with Toni, I headed to the inn to drop off Oreo. Luckily, he was adapting to the car rides.

As much as I wanted normalcy, I was still feeling the effects of Gloria's revelation last night and couldn't help wonder if Violet's ghost was trying to tell me something.

Then, as soon as I had that thought, I dismissed it. Even if there was no reasonable explanation for that recipe showing up at Colleen's—*it didn't just show up, it came from nowhere!*—I couldn't imagine what Violet's death had to do with a cordial recipe. I'd never spoken to her about cordials. Those two things were not connected.

I desperately wanted to call the sheriff and ask them if they'd caught the killer, but logically, I knew murder investigations took more than a few days.

There was nothing I could do about the investigation, spirit twins, disappearing recipes, or even Craig's evasiveness, but I did have one problem I could solve. Instead of calling Jade to find out what was going on in her life, I was going to visit her. I'd rather see her in person.

At the inn, Mary Carscadden's mom was sitting on the patio in the garden chatting with guests. My cat bee-lined it to his new best friend. I didn't want to interrupt, so I waved hello from the gate and then left.

As I walked across the sidewalk toward my truck, Mary came out the back door, looking cool in a sleeveless sundress, her purse over her shoulder. "Hello there, Quinn. How goes it today? Are you keeping cool enough?"

"Just barely. There's no point running the AC in my truck. I hardly go far enough for it to cool down."

"I hear ya. I'm being sent on an avocado run. Gotta keep my cook happy."

"Speaking of your cook, please thank her for treating my cat so well."

"Oh, we all love Oreo. Especially my mother. See for yourself." Mary pointed to the shaded patio in the garden where people were having coffee. Oreo was already perched on Mary's mother's lap. "I can't keep my mother inside no matter the heat, and your cat doesn't seem to mind it either."

"He thinks he's the center of the world, so it's no surprise he goes where the attention is."

"She's always loved cats and has had one most of her life, but after her last one died, she didn't want to get another. Said it wouldn't be fair to the cat if it outlived her. So, the fact Oreo comes running the second she sits down thrills her. All the attention and none of the work."

I was relieved to hear Oreo was so well received. At least one of us had loyal friends. I gave myself a mental shake at the thought. For all I knew, Jade hadn't seen me, and I was making a mountain out of a molehill. I wouldn't know until I talked to her directly.

"I better get to the market. See you later, Quinn."

I said goodbye and headed to my truck, pondering what I'd say to Jade that wouldn't put her on the defensive. After the way I'd handled my son and his wife, I was concerned that I might have done something to offend Jade. If she was upset with me, then I needed to know if I was in the wrong, or if there was something I could do to help because she was one friend I didn't want to lose.

Jade and her husband Edward lived on the river, south of my place, in a much bigger house. It wasn't far, so when I pulled into their driveway about ten minutes later, I still hadn't worked out the best way to approach this. They had a three-car garage and didn't park in the driveway, so I couldn't tell if Jade was home.

I grabbed the gift bag from the passenger seat—I'd made a quick stop at Break Thyme to pick up a jar of pear and ginger jelly. It was delicious baked on brie. I wondered if this would be a conciliatory gift or a goodbye one. *No. No negative thoughts.* I had to believe there was a good reason she hadn't acknowledged me.

I rang the doorbell and waited. A few moments later, I was surprised to see Edward open the door. Since it was after nine, I'd assumed he'd be up at the mine, minimizing health and safety hazards or whatever he and my brother did at McCourt's.

Edward had a ruddy complexion—he'd always reminded me of a jolly Santa Claus with his rosy cheeks and generally pleasant disposition. His face was redder than usual, as if he'd been exerting himself.

"Hi," I said. "I didn't expect you to be home. No work today?" *Smooth, Quinn.* I'd been so focused on what to say to Jade, niceties escaped me.

"I'm going in late. What can I do for you?" Edward wasn't his usual jovial self, so now I was more concerned something was wrong. He was never abrupt and to the point. More the type to shoot the breeze at any moment. So, if he didn't have time for me, did that mean I'd somehow crossed a line with Jade? I decided not to beat around the bush.

"I'm looking for Jade. I think she snubbed me the other day, so I want to be sure there's nothing wrong." Again, not my smoothest delivery, so I smiled, as if Jade snubbing me was a misperception.

Edward's expression remained flat. "She's been busy. Her mom's taking a lot of her time lately."

"Oh, I see." I handed him the gift bag because things were going from awkward to downright arctic. "Can you give this to her, please? I think she'll like it." I was about to turn away, but thought it would bug me later if I didn't ask again. "Is everything okay between us, I mean?"

He took the bag. "Quinn, I have to go. Thanks for stopping by." He stepped back and closed the door, leaving me standing there with my mouth open. Something was definitely wrong. As I walked back to my truck, my heart sinking, I vowed to sort this out, do something before this situation festered and became worse.

After leaving Jade's, I'd come straight to Break Thyme. Not only did I have a bunch of tasks to cross off my list, but also it was the one place I had right now where I felt secure and where I could lose myself in busyness so my mind could mull over the problems that suddenly abounded in my life.

Around eleven, Poppy burst in the front door. "Quinn! Did you hear the news?"

I closed the cooler where I'd been restocking drinks and looked her way. "I don't think so. What news?"

"The sheriff brought in Derek West to question him about Violet's murder."

Something inside me gave way—like a balloon full of tension deflating. I'd not realized how much I wanted the murderer caught. Since this had happened in my home, I felt vulnerable as long as the murderer was still out there. "How do *you* know?"

Poppy set her purse on a bar stool. "My cousin lives on the same street as Derek. She called and said the sheriff just picked up Derek. All the neighbors are in shock. Everyone liked the guy and couldn't imagine him doing such a horrible thing."

"Doesn't everyone say that? It's always a shock to the neighbors, but people have a dark side, and if they're pushed too far…." As I kid, I once came upon my uncle yelling at his son. I'd never seen Uncle Randy spitting mad like that. I didn't know he was capable of such language and fury. He never knew I witnessed that scene, and I never saw him lose his temper again, but that moment made me wary of him forever. "In fairness, Derek's not been charged, right? But the sheriff must have a good reason for questioning him. It would be nice if he confessed. I wonder if the police found the murder weapon, maybe a salt lamp with Derek's fingerprints on it?"

"I have no idea. I'll ask Cody. I think he likes me." She opened a tube of lip gloss and swiped her lips.

"Cody?"

"Deputy Wilson. I knew him in school. You must have talked to him, no?"

I couldn't picture Poppy and the teen deputy as friends. Where she was bubbly, easy-going, and friendly as can be, he was serious, judgmental, and not a great people person. Or maybe that wasn't fair since I'd never been around the deputy off duty. "I have talked to him, yes. I don't think he likes me."

"Oh, that's nonsense. Everyone likes you, Quinn. I'll definitely call him. He asked me out once, but I had my eyes on someone else back then. Cody sure has filled out nicely, though." A dreamy expression came over her face.

I kept my mouth shut and wiped the counter.

"I guess you'll be getting your house back now," she said.

"I guess so, although I can't say I'm eager to go back there." After the event with Gloria, it was harder to believe I'd been imagining things when I'd seen something in the mirror the night Violet was killed. I wondered if my house would ever feel like my sanctuary again.

"That's understandable. I'd find it spooky to sleep in a house where.... Never mind. Maybe one of your kids could come and stay with you for a while when you move back in."

That was an interesting idea. Maybe it would help to have Samantha at home for a couple of nights. "That's a good idea, Poppy. Thanks." If the investigation was over, then I'd have to get my head around moving back home. I'd better confirm with the sheriff, settle my bill at the inn, and pick up a gift for Mary for being so good to Oreo.

With the lip gloss put away, Poppy plucked her purse from the stool. "I'll get my apron and brew a new pot of coffee."

It surprised me to feel uncomfortable at the thought of the investigation ending. Perhaps this was because I didn't have the answers I needed. I wished I'd taken

Violet's phantom seriously enough to ask questions like what did it look like, what did it want, and why did she think I was possessed?

Gloria said the spirit thing she'd seen at Mystic Garden was hiding, yet the ghosts I'd met didn't hide. They capitalized on the fact I could see them and asked for favors. So, if there was a spirit thing following me around, why was it hiding?

I stopped my thoughts right there because I was going in circles.

Would I ever get my normal life back? Whatever was going on, I was sure it was tied to Violet, and it hadn't ended with the exorcism or her death. If I wanted to understand this thing, I couldn't stop digging, and there were a few stones I planned to turn.

Chapter Twelve

When I was a kid, my greatest joy was unraveling mysteries with Nancy Drew. It was my first experience being someone else. With Nancy, I went to haunted houses, archaeological expeditions, and seaside towns. I uncovered treasures, phantoms, charms, and truths. These girl-power stories gave me more than adventure. When solving mysteries, often with the help of Nancy's dad, I imagined the relationship I'd always wanted with my father.

One time, I so wanted him to solve a mystery with me. I told my father that one of our neighbors was hiding someone in their cellar. That hadn't turned out to be the bonding experience I'd envisioned.

He'd been gone eight years and the bitterness inside me for the way he'd favored my brother used to nag me like an old witch. And as if that wasn't self-punishing enough, I'd been ashamed of myself for that bitterness.

As a forty-nine-year-old woman, I'd figured out my father's disinterest in me wasn't my fault. It had never been my job to be a better child, so he'd notice me, so I'd matter to him. It would have been nice to know this forty years ago, but at least I knew it now. This was one upside to getting older, but I wasn't kidding myself. I still wanted to win that cordial contest.

As I was returning *The Secret in the Old Attic* to the shelf in the Cozy Nook, I heard a man at the counter asking to speak to the owner. Heavy-set with short, brown hair, his substantial beard reached his sternum.

I walked over to where he was leafing through his satchel. "Hello. I'm the owner, Quinn Delaney. Can I help you?"

He handed me a brochure. "Brent Lange, Superior Water Filtration Systems. Are you aware that recent testing showed your drinking water is contaminated with sulfate concentrations that exceed the WHO's recommended levels for safety? I don't know if you're familiar with the metal mine on the Manitou River?"

Having a brother who was winning environmental excellence awards for that mine meant yes, I was. "I'm quite familiar, and I doubt very much our drinking water is contaminated. My brother works for McCourt Mining. The mine has an outstanding record for responsible environmental practice."

"*Had* an outstanding record. Not anymore, and that's why you must have the absolute best water filtration system. At Superior Filters, there's nothing more important to us than your health, and that's why we use a deionization system to give you water of the highest purity. Our process safely removes not just sulfate ions, but iron, sodium, and copper. After all the work you've put into your business here at...Break Thyme, you don't want to make your customers sick and lose everything you've worked hard to achieve."

Wasn't he slick? As if not only the health of the community was at risk, but my business, too. "Nice try, Brent. Our water is tested regularly, so please don't scare my neighbors, trying to make a buck with your filtration systems."

"I'm not trying to scare anyone. Just educate you. Maybe your brother hasn't told you about what's happening to the wild rice growing downriver of McCourt. Did you know wild rice is highly sensitive to elevated levels of sulfates? It's like a canary in the mine, so to speak, a warning there's a problem with the watershed. The rice is showing evidence of destruction and that's a sign of sulfate pollution."

It was probably a sign of many other things, too. "My brother is a geo-physicist and the vice-president of Environment, Health and Safety at McCourt. There's no one more committed to clean water than him." I handed Brent Lange back his brochure. "Have a nice day." I turned my back on him and joined Poppy behind the counter.

"You should ask your brother about the latest water quality report," he said, not deterred by my dismissal. "Ask him why the numbers don't jibe with the testing Gaia Green is doing. Ask him why someone murdered the person who submitted those numbers—Violet West. Or maybe, since he's a VP, he's part of the cover-up."

At the mention of Violet's name, gooseflesh turned me cold. I suddenly remembered Violet's day planner had Brent Lange's name in it. Had he contacted her about the water quality? Could Violet have told Craig there were discrepancies in the tests? Or in the reports? Or whatever signified a problem?

I wanted to believe Brent Lange was full of malarkey. I found my voice. "Sure, it's all part of a big conspiracy to make everyone sick and stop you from selling water filters. As I said, have a nice day." I turned my back on him again and ran the water to rinse out a mug for the dishwasher.

As Brent left the café, Poppy waved at his back and then turned to me. "You sure made a muddle of that guy's sales pitch, boss." Poppy always saw the upside in everything.

I forced a smile. "He's going to have to try a lot harder to make me into a muddling, filter buying fool."

I'd heard about salespeople using scare tactics to sell their goods, but lies like this could worry people who didn't have inside information on the mine. They had to be lying. I knew McCourt would once again win an award for its dedication to the environment and responsible mining. The official announcement was in two weeks.

Just in case Craig hadn't heard about the guy in town besmirching the mine's record of excellence, I called him.

He answered on the third ring. "Hey, Quinn, what's up?"

"A couple of things. First, I don't know if you heard Derek West is being questioned about Violet's murder this morning."

"What? No. I didn't. Do you know the details? Are they sure they got the right guy?"

That was a strange question. "I don't know the details."

"Right. Sorry, I'm a bit distracted. You know…work."

Yep, work seemed to take most of his attention lately. "I'll be quick." I told him what Brent said about the water.

I expected Craig to shoot down the blatant, self-serving lies, but he hesitated. "Where was he from?"

I was getting an uneasy feeling. "Superior Water Filtration Systems, I think."

"What else did he say?"

"He said wild rice is dying. Shoot, Craig, is there a problem with the water?"

"No," he answered quickly. Too quickly? As if he was on the defensive. "Just a sec."

In the background, I heard someone interrupt my brother. I recognized the voice of Edward Davis and wondered if his wife, Jade, would acknowledge my visit to their house. Was her mother taking so much of her time that she couldn't even send a text?

"Sorry, Quinn. I've got a meeting. Gotta go."

"Okay, Craig, let's have dinner next week. I'll invite the kids."

I disconnected, but as the hours passed, the unease I felt grew stronger. Why would Craig ask if the sheriff had the right guy unless he knew something about Violet's death? And what about the water? I tried to convince myself I was imagining things, that Brent Lange was a smarmy swindler. My brother's work had him distracted, and he wasn't hiding anything at all.

I swallowed hard. I may have wanted life to return to normal, but that wouldn't happen now. I didn't know what to do next, but when Toni and I put our heads together, we'd figure it out because I wasn't letting this go until I was sure there wasn't a sliver of truth in the salesman's accusations.

Chapter Thirteen

To take my mind off Craig, I made a new cordial—blackberry and star anise. When I finished, I poured about half an ounce to taste. It was good—good enough to be added to the menu. The star anise, with its licorice undertone, was a great compliment to the blackberries.

"Good job on the clean-up last night, Jetti," I said as I came out of the kitchen. I wanted to be sure to compliment Jetti for a job well done. Sometimes when she closed, she forgot to wipe the counter or put out the garbage. She was good with customers and often upsold the baked goods or an extra takeout drink, which was one reason I'd kept her on after the trial period. The downside to her work was the cleaning and tidying. When she was on shift, the behind-the-counter area quickly became messy with utensils, dirty dishes in the sink, and spills littering the counter beside the blenders.

Poppy was pouring ginger beer into copper glasses. We called the drink a Malia Mule after the river, a non-alcohol version of a Moscow Mule, with fresh lime, mint, sparkling water, and our secret ingredient—cardamom syrup. I noticed, on our blackboard menu, Poppy had written the word muddled in front of the mule.

"Umm...thanks, but it wasn't me." Jetti scratched her nose with her shoulder.

Poppy looked up after slicing a lime. "That's strange. I had to leave in a hurry last night to log into my class."

I wondered if Poppy was carrying so much weight here that she cleaned up on auto-pilot. Maybe I needed another staff member to help when I went on vacation. I'd have to discuss this later with Poppy.

Jetti shrugged. "Weird. I thought you'd cleaned up before you left. Oh well, Poppy, don't forget to muddle that mint. By the way, Quinn, I love the new sign. It sure is original."

"That, it is," I admitted. I was still undecided about keeping the sign. Aubrey was on vacation with her family, so I'd decided this was one detail I could put on the back burner until she returned and could fix it.

I was pouring myself a glass of citrus water when I heard a familiar laugh and looked across the café to see my daughter-in-law in a booth with two of her friends. I could count the number of times Chelsea had come into Break Thyme. Always with Jordan.

When Jordan first brought Chelsea home to meet our family, I figured the attraction on his part was purely physical because they seemed to have little in common. Jordan loved nature, white-water kayaking, and camping, whereas Chelsea seemed to love social media, fashion, and swimming pools. Jordan hadn't had his kayak in the water once this season. I didn't want to see him neglect this healthy activity.

Chelsea was bewitchingly pretty, blond, and too thin. At least I thought so. Her parents had paid for her to have nose surgery to perfect what I thought was a lovely nose. She'd had cosmetic fillers to smooth and plump her facial features. Imagine a twenty-something needing to smooth and plump! All in the name of launching an acting career that was going nowhere because, as far as I could tell, Chelsea either was fearful of big cities or refused to leave her mother and sister. They were close to the point of all-consuming. Sometimes I worried they'd consume my son, but he said he was happy with his life, so I would keep quiet.

I kept reminding myself we'd have our road trip together. I couldn't say it disappointed me that Chelsea had turned down my invitation to join us.

That day, she wore a red calico dress with spaghetti straps. I glanced at her chest. I couldn't help myself. Everything looked normal there, to my relief.

I picked up a tea towel to dry a glass pitcher. My feelings were a little hurt that she'd not come over to say hello. Then the small voice inside my head piped up and said I was supposed to be the more mature one in our relationship.

"I have exciting news," Chelsea said, loud enough for me to hear. "Jordan and I are trying to get pregnant."

As her two friends squealed, my heart sank. Not that I wouldn't love a grandchild. I would, of course. But not yet. Jordan was already financially stressed, and babies were expensive. In the eighteen months they'd been together, Chelsea hadn't kept a job longer than three months. I hoped a baby wasn't her way to stay out of the workforce. I didn't think it would help in her quest to become an actor.

"I wish we were ready to have children," her friend said. "But we agreed to build up our savings after buying the house, and I just got a promotion. I want to stay in this position for a couple of years before taking a mat leave."

A voice of reason. My ears perked up. I listened for Chelsea's response to sensible planning.

"If I can't get any acting or modeling jobs, I'm going to be a stay-at-home mom," she said.

There it was.

I struggled with my place in this, with wanting to talk to my son. Or I could do as I'd promised and let them figure out their own lives. I knew it was the right thing to do, but this was going to be hard.

Why had Chelsea chosen Break Thyme, within earshot, for this announcement? It was almost as if she were challenging me to stay out of their lives as I'd promised Jordan I'd do. If that was the case, it wasn't nice of her to taunt me like this. She wasn't talking about getting a new sofa. This would be my grandchild.

I walked over to their table. "Hello, ladies. I'm Quinn, Chelsea's mother-in-law. It's nice to see you here at Break Thyme."

Chelsea's cool greeting was lost in the warmth of her friends. We chatted for a few minutes, just small talk.

"I overheard your talk of babies," I said, looking at Chelsea's friend. "I think you're smart to build some financial stability before starting a family. Things didn't go that way for me, and it made my life very difficult. Chelsea, I know you're a smart cookie and will think this through with Jordan and do the right thing for any children you bring into the world." I'd said my piece with kindness and hoped she'd taken it that way.

Her friends were nodding. Chelsea's cheeks were pink. "Sure. Thanks, Quinn," she said.

"You're welcome. I've got to get back to work," I said, remembering that my accountant had asked me to email her the month-end figures. "Nice meeting you."

As I headed toward the staircase, I looked through the window and saw Toni struggling to open the door with a white box in her hand.

I took a step back and opened the door for her. "Whatcha got there?" I asked.

"I think I've got sticky buns, but I'm not sure. I was standing at Henrietta's counter, about to order, when I saw your text about Derek West."

"Come on upstairs," I said, and let Toni go first.

"You must be relieved the sheriff picked up Derek." Toni set the bakery box on my desk upstairs and opened it. "Yep, sticky buns. Would you like one?"

I was suddenly aware of the breadth of my tummy hiding under my apron. Toni could eat anything and never gain an ounce. "I will not be happy with myself, but you know it's impossible to say no to Henrietta's sticky buns."

"Let's split one," she said. "Is that okay?"

"Absolutely…to start." I was hopeless. "I'll grab us a knife." I was back in a flash and had the bun cut.

I peeled off a sticky piece of heaven and took a bite. The cinnamon exuded just a touch of heat on the tongue and the crystals of sugar gave a crunch of sweetness. Yum! The joy was worth the calories.

"So, give me the details," Toni said.

I told her everything I knew about Derek as a suspect, which wasn't much. "Deputy Wilson has a thing for Poppy, so she's going to grill him. She thinks he's hot."

"I don't see it," said Toni. "But then again, I don't pay attention to men that age."

"Same here." And then it hit me. "Cripes. I forgot to ask you about your date with—what was his name? The firefighter."

Toni laughed. "I've been waiting for you to ask."

"I can't believe I forgot."

"I'd say it's a menopausal moment, but you've had a wee distraction in your life over the last five days. His name is Harry and things went better than I will ever admit to my mother."

"Oh? That's great. Where'd you go?"

"We met for coffee and talked for hours. He was easy to talk to, which was a pleasant surprise."

"Tell me more. What does he look like?"

"He's not as fit as I would have thought, for a firefighter. He has a bit of a paunch. Dark brown hair and a kind smile. Actually, he has a gentle way about him. He seemed genuinely interested in me, despite my boring life."

Toni was a confident woman who believed in her worth. Still, she hadn't been on a date in over twenty-five years, not since she'd married Norman and not since his death eleven years ago. I felt the need to reassure her. "What do you mean? Your speech therapy business is thriving. You've lived abroad. You've traveled to the Far East. You raised a beautiful, successful daughter, and you make the best Beef Wellington I've ever tasted."

"Oh, don't get me wrong, I'm happy with my life. It's just not as exciting as saving people from burning buildings. We agreed to have dinner in a couple of weeks, so we'll see how it goes."

I squeezed her hand. "I'm happy for you."

Toni stared at me. "It's been one date, and I'm not looking for a relationship. He's a good man, but he's not Norman."

"No one will be Norman," I said, pointing out the obvious. By the way Toni talked about her husband sometimes, it seemed she missed him as much today as she did when he'd died. It was a wonder she didn't rage at the unfairness of his death, but Toni was always the pillar of control.

"Okay, enough about me," she said. "What's wrong with you? You have worry creases in your forehead."

In the twenty-seven years of my marriage. Bryan never knew me as well as my friend did. Bryan didn't have deep conversations. He didn't have a great awareness of people's feelings. Maybe that was why my friends had always been so important to me. I told Toni about the visit from the water filter guy and my conversation with Craig.

"You don't think Violet's murder had anything to do with the mine, do you? With Craig?"

"Craig's name was in Violet's planner, remember?"

"He didn't know why his name was there. He wouldn't lie about that. Not Craig."

"Yes, of course," I agreed. "It's ridiculous to think he's part of some conspiracy to put our water at risk." I knew my worry lines weren't smoothing over, so I reminded myself who my brother was. Craig was extremely proud of the environmental excellence awards the mine won. His team had been the first to achieve these standards. It was a tremendous deal. Just because I'd long grown tired of his adoring public, I still believed him to be one of the most upright people on the planet.

Another thought occurred to me. "What if Violet told Craig the water was showing those signs of toxicity that Brent Lange talked about?"

"That would mean Craig lied about talking to her." Toni turned away from me for a second, shook her head, and turned back. "This is our water. There's no way McCourt would risk the community's health. That water filter salesman doesn't make money if our water is clean. I'd say that fear monger is the one with everything to gain by spreading false rumors."

I so wanted to believe that. "True. And the sheriff brought in Violet's ex-husband for her murder. He must have the evidence to support that." I felt better with this realization. Again, I told myself it was silly of me to suspect my brother of wrongdoing. Integrity was crucial to Craig. He had a demanding job and many reasons to be distracted.

So why, with everything I knew to be true about my brother and McCourt Mining, did I have even a speck of doubt that Violet's death had anything to do with a vengeful ex-husband?

Chapter Fourteen

THE NEXT DAY, I'D arranged the shifts, so Poppy opened the café with Melinda's help. Jetti would come in at noon to give Poppy a break. This gave me time to work on Longfellow.

I brought Oreo with me to give Mrs. Carscadden a break from cat sitting, although she wasn't complaining. I was starting to appreciate Oreo's adaptability. The car ride didn't freak him out like it had the day of the exorcism. Maybe he'd been on edge from Violet's behavior.

When we arrived, he sniffed his way through the trailer and settled onto the back cushion of the dinette to look out the window.

I set up my blue tooth speaker, found a Motown station, and to get my energy up, danced to Marvin Gaye's Ain't No Mountain High Enough. I was never going to win awards with my dance moves, nor for hitting high notes. I was just happy to dance where no one could see me.

Shoot, I had that wrong. I'd spun a hundred and eighty degrees and saw a guy walking along the trail past Longfellow. And what a guy.

I couldn't remember the last time I'd even noticed a man. I'd been single for nearly two years and hadn't thought to change that. I lived my life as if I were unavailable, still monogamous. This mindset was habitual, and I'd put no effort into changing it. Probably because I'd been focused on Break Thyme.

I don't know why the man walking by my trailer stunned me into silence. I could guess it had something to do with his swagger and his smile. Had he slowed down? He'd not looked away. He was cool, dark, lean, sexy, woodsy, and...I was probably making all this up. He could be a peeping Tom for all I knew. Anyway, he was past my trailer now, and I had work to do.

I found my magnets and stuck the picture I'd printed from an RV transformation blog to the fridge. This was my inspiration—the cloud-white walls and slate gray cupboards. Fabrics would be black, white, and caramel. Brushed bronze hardware. I'd found a stick-on white subway tile I planned to use for a backsplash in the kitchen and bathroom.

First, I'd set up the dining tent our family had used when camping. Next, I'd remove all the cabinet doors in the trailer. I'd brought two party tables. With the doors on tables in the tent, they'd be out of the way and easy to paint. Samantha preferred to work on Longfellow in the evening, so she'd agreed to prime the doors that night. I needed to get them lightly sanded, cleaned, and ready for her.

The sheriff's office had given me the okay to move back into my house, but I was still living at the inn. I'd only gone home to water my plants—that was it. My house gave me chills and not the good kind. I needed more time to stamp out the vision of Violet's dead body on my floor, but this wasn't the only reason I wasn't eager to return.

A movement reflected in my bedroom mirror spooked me. And Gloria, the psychic, hadn't eased my trepidation one bit. Typically, I didn't let my imagination wander, but with paranormal stuff, I knew it existed, and I knew it was trouble. I didn't need trouble.

I needed a distraction. I started removing door hinges and sang with the music. "How sweet it is to be loved by you." Time passed and my mood improved.

I was carrying the last cupboard door into the dining tent when I felt a change in humidity. I looked up to see a blanket of gloom. That just figured. No rain for two weeks and now the sky turned dark when we wanted to paint. It would be a good idea to check the satellite weather to see what the chances were of this storm blowing over.

I went into the trailer to get my phone. To my left, Oreo let out a strong hiss, his back arched in defense.

"What's the matter, boy?" He fixed his gaze behind me.

I turned to the bedroom and yelped at the person I saw. Then I calmed down, realizing I was looking at myself in the mirror.

Geez! I was on edge. I shook my head and reached for my phone on the counter when I realized something terrifying. I froze and felt a wave of nausea.

There was no freakin' mirror in the bedroom. Holy smokes! I'd hallucinated myself!

My heart pounded. A part of me wanted to run, but I was braver than that. *It wasn't real. Just a figment of my stressed imagination.*

I turned back to the bedroom and nearly peed my pants.

Beside the bed stood a woman, looking equally horrified. Equally horrified because she was equally me. Except for the clothes, a midi dress that looked fantastic on her, she could be my exact twin. We even had the same haircut.

"Oh shoot," she said. "You can see me."

I blinked. It was a bizarre thing to say. Of course, I could see her. She was standing right there by the edge of the bed.

"Who the heck are you?" I said. "How did you get in here?"

"Um, well…" She even sounded like me, and the way she pressed her lips together and wrinkled her forehead reminded me of Samantha. I knew that look. This woman was stressed.

"I'm still trying to figure that out," she said finally.

"What are you talking about? Do you have some kind of amnesia? Where did you come from? Who are you?"

"I'm pretty sure I'm you, Quinn."

Chapter Fifteen

SHE KNEW MY NAME. My knees turned to jelly, so I squeezed my calf muscles, supported myself with a hand on the counter, and reached for my phone.

"I'm calling the police," I said. This woman was probably mentally ill and maybe I should be understanding and patient. But I'd had a bad week, and she was freaking me out—

"I wouldn't do that," she said.

I punched in my password and flicked through my recent calls to find the sheriff's number. "I'm going to step outside and call the sheriff, or you can get out of here and never sneak into my trailer again." Behind me, Oreo was still hissing.

"I can't do that."

"Okay, then. Your choice." I had my hand on the door.

"Quinn, it's *not* my choice to be here. I'd rather stay in my own life, but I'm getting pulled into yours every time I take a nap or go to bed at night. I just want a good night's sleep. If you bring the police here, they won't be able to see me, and they'll think you're the one who's lost your grip on reality, not me. And besides, I'll be—"

I didn't hear the rest of what she said because I was out of there, having scooped up Oreo. I nearly tripped down the two stairs and hit the ground with a thump. And if that wasn't drama enough for the morning, lightning flashed across the sky, followed by a crash of thunder.

It startled Oreo and he let out a wail and nearly jumped out of my arms. I dropped my phone in trying to hold on to him and suffered a scratch from his claws.

"It's okay. It's okay," I cooed and scratched behind his ear, awkwardly, since I was trying to get my truck door open and not lose my cat.

With Oreo safely trapped, I picked up my phone. With all the shuffling, I'd lost the call-the-sheriff window. I found the number again and hit it.

I might be a curious person, but I wasn't a woman who went into the basement alone to see if a killer was hiding behind the furnace. The police were there for a reason.

As the phone rang, I heard the squeal of kids nearby. The next campsite was only thirty feet away but hidden behind trees. Knowing people were close took my nerves down a notch.

Was this a police matter?

Gloria's warning of a spirit look-alike popped into my head, but that woman in my trailer hadn't looked like a ghost. Her face had been flushed with color. The ghosts I'd seen were quite pale.

I had to believe she was a real person. I couldn't be haunted again. I couldn't deal with an unexplained—

"Sheriff's office. How can I help you?"

"Hello, this is Quinn Delaney. I'd like to report an intruder in my trailer."

"Are you inside your trailer?"

"No, I'm standing outside."

"What's the address, Ms. Delaney?"

I hurried over to the post with the campsite number on it. "I'm in Beach Meadows Park. Campsite number 110."

"Is the intruder a man or a woman?"

"A woman."

"Has she threatened you?"

"No." This was starting to feel familiar. "She didn't threaten me, but she wouldn't leave when I asked her."

"Is she familiar to you?"

That was a loaded question. As familiar as the nose on my face. "I've never met this woman before." True, even if, technically, I recognized her.

The wind howled, sending leaves scuttling across the ground.

"She's inside your trailer now?" the policewoman asked.

I took a few steps to peer in the bedroom window. I looked closer and didn't see my twin. There was no place to hide in there.

"Ms. Delaney?"

"I'm checking. Just a moment, please." Because the sky had turned dark, it was difficult to see inside without opening the door. Feeling safer now, I stepped up, opened the door, and peered inside.

The intruder wasn't in the bedroom, or bathroom, or hiding in a bunk. I even opened the skinny closet. How in the world did she get out? Maybe when I'd been looking for the campsite number? That had to be it, and the wind had covered the sound of her leaving.

Sure, blame it on the wind.

"She's gone," I said into the phone. Whatever I'd seen, I now felt like I'd over-reacted in calling the police. If I described the woman, I'd probably sound unbalanced. She hadn't threatened me and had appeared to be as upset about our coming face-to-face as I'd been. Maybe I'd misunderstood her when she'd said she was me. "I'm sorry to have bothered you. Everything is okay here."

"Are you sure?"

"Yes, I'm positive. It's a small trailer. There's nowhere to hide."

"It's understandable to be jittery after what you've been through." This policewoman had recognized my name. "Be sure to lock your door and be safe."

"I will." I disconnected as the first raindrops fell.

Had the woman I'd seen been real or had she been something else? How could she be a ghost and look exactly like me? Didn't people have to be dead to be ghosts? If she wasn't a ghost, what was she? I'd read everyone has a doppelgänger. Could that be it?

I'd rather think I'd imagined this episode, but I couldn't make up stuff like this in a million years. I wondered what Toni would say about my trailer twin. I wondered if Gloria made house calls.

I sent Samantha a text asking her to call me when she had a minute. Now, I was worried Samantha might think, if that woman came back, she was me. I wanted my daughter to have a friend with her tonight if the rain stopped and she came to paint.

I thought back to the warning I'd received from the first ghost I'd ever encountered. She'd said I had twin auras, which meant nothing to me, and that something ominous was coming my way. The word twin seemed to be a consistent theme. Her last words to me hung in my mind.

Your life is not going to get easier, so you're going to have to get smarter to handle who's coming your way. You're not going to believe it. Not in a million years.

I didn't have a million years to figure this out, but I would not panic. Not again. Falling apart wasn't an option. I was strong and resilient. I could handle whatever came my way.

Did other people have to handle ghosts and spirit look-alikes?

Whatever it was, the next time it appeared, I wouldn't run. I didn't need the police to solve this for me. I would draw on my inner Nancy Drew and get the answers I needed to figure this out.

Chapter Sixteen

"Guess what I found out about Violet's murder," Poppy said the next morning when she came into the kitchen where I was unpacking pastry boxes.

I put down my box cutter. "What? And how did you get information about her murder?"

Poppy fluffed her hair and smiled coquettishly. "I had a date with the deputy last night."

"You did? I hope you're not dating the man to fish for information." She could do better than teen deputy, who in my opinion, wasn't nearly upbeat enough for Poppy's sunny disposition. I'd hate to see him bringing her down.

"Quinn! Of course not. I like Cody."

I moved a stack of boxes into our storage cupboard. In fairness, I didn't know the deputy very well, and just because he'd been demeaning to me didn't mean he'd treat Poppy unkindly. Besides, she wouldn't put up with behavior like that. "I'm sorry, that wasn't kind to suggest you had ulterior motives. Of course, you wouldn't. So, want did you find out?"

"Well, two things. Two *big* things." Poppy smiled like she was enjoying keeping me in suspense.

"Are you going to tell me?"

"Violet had sex the night she was killed, but not with Derek. The medical examiner found sperm inside her, but it wasn't his."

"What?" This news stunned me, given Josie's depiction of Violet's pregnancy plan. "Josie was adamant Violet wanted to reconcile her marriage to Derek, so who was she sleeping with?"

"Don't know, but that's only half of it. Derek and Josie were seeing each other."

I'd thought Josie was a good friend to Violet. "Seriously? Wow. Sleeping with her best friend's ex when she thought Violet wanted to reconcile with Derek. Josie mentioned nothing about this to Toni or me, but I guess I can understand why. I wonder if Violet knew?"

"I don't know. Cody thinks Derek is trying to deflect suspicion away from himself and onto Josie. Apparently, the night Violet was killed, Josie found out Violet and Derek were seeing each other. Josie wasn't happy about it."

Boy, Cody sure had spilled the beans. My mind was racing. Josie wouldn't have been happy to learn Violet was trying desperately to get pregnant. How invested was Josie in her relationship with Derek? Enough to want Violet out of the picture? "I wonder if Josie and Derek were seeing each other while he was still married to Violet?"

"That's a good question," Poppy said, flattening the empty box and setting it beside the back door. "Either way, Josie has a motive for wanting Violet dead, so she could have Derek all to herself."

"Yes, I suppose that makes sense, and it wouldn't be the first time a love triangle ended in murder." I remembered the missing salt lamp and thought Josie was certainly familiar with the lamp. She'd have known it was heavy enough to kill someone. "What about the murder weapon? Did the police find it?"

"Oh, I forgot about that. I don't know. Cody didn't mention it, so maybe not."

"Are they going to charge Josie or Derek?" I asked.

"I don't know. There's a witness who said she saw Derek at your house that night."

"There is?" I asked. "Who?"

"A neighbor."

Must have been Sandy. "She identified Derek, huh? Well, that's pretty incriminating."

"She did, but Cody didn't feel one hundred percent confident in the identification. The neighbor wasn't very close, and it was dark."

The doorbell chimed, indicating a customer had come in.

"I'll get it," Poppy said.

I hoped a love triangle *was* responsible for Violet's death but wondered how accurate all this information was. And why had Cody shared these details with Poppy? Had he been trying to impress her and appear more important to the case than he really was? In that case, had he embellished the facts because he'd only heard bits and pieces second-hand from the sheriff?

I wanted to believe he had the story straight because it would be a relief if Violet's death had nothing to do with McCourt Mine and our water quality. Unfortunately, this concern still niggled at the back of my mind, but I wasn't sure what to do about it.

Poppy leaned into the kitchen. "I almost forgot. Colleen dropped off this cordial recipe. She said it was yours."

I took the wrinkled paper, the one that had appeared out of nowhere at the Mystic Garden, a reminder that the murder in my guest suite was just one distressing situation going on in my life. I also had a spirit double and a teleporting recipe to deal with.

I had to admit, though, I was intrigued. Elderflower and Rhubarb Cordial. It sounded unique enough to win the contest. For some reason, this recipe kept showing up. I supposed I could use it for inspiration and put my touch on it by adding an herb, maybe mint. First, I'd have to find elderflowers and do a little reading on how to use them.

Despite my best efforts to lose myself in the sensory experience of creating a new cordial, questions of what that spirit twin was all about wouldn't leave my mind. So, when Toni showed up after lunch, I was more than ready to spill my thoughts.

I didn't want to be overheard, so we grabbed the folding camping chairs I kept at the café and we went down to the lakeshore to stick our feet in the water. Lake Superior was cold enough to make me suck in my breath when the water hit my toes, but my body acclimatized quickly. It had been so hot lately, the chill felt good, and we had a shallow, protected beach here in Bookend Bay.

I looked at my friend and told her what I'd seen in my trailer. Toni and I had been through some crazy adventures together, but this was the first time I'd admitted to seeing a ghost who could be my twin.

She opened her mouth, then closed it again.

"I know," I said.

"Do you really think she was some kind of spirit?" Toni asked.

I let out a sigh. "I don't know. Oreo hissed like crazy when she appeared. He doesn't do that to regular people. I could fool myself into thinking she slipped in and out of the trailer without me noticing, but that seems even more far-fetched than her being a ghost."

"Okay." Toni hesitated. "So, let's be the devil's advocate and assume she is a ghost. She could be the phantom Violet was trying to exorcise. And then remember what Gloria said—she called it a confused twin that was trying to help you. Right?"

"Yes, I remember. The twin isn't the only one confused. I don't get any of this. I can't, for the life of me, comprehend where she came from."

Toni was quiet for a moment. "You're sure your mother would have told you if you'd been a twin?"

"Yes, and I can't imagine asking her a question like that—it would sound like an accusation. She'd want to know why I was suddenly asking. What would I say?"

"Maybe there was a twin in utero that died and no one knew about her?"

"I suppose, but if that was the case, how did it become a grownup version of me. The "ghost" was my age."

Toni stretched her legs out. "What did she say again?"

"Well, at first, she was surprised I could see her."

"Okay, so it sounds like she knows she's not human."

A soft snort escaped me. "And I thought *my* life was weird."

"Yeah, it sucks being your spirit double."

"When I asked who she was, she said she was pretty sure she was me, and she was tired of getting sucked into my life every time she goes to sleep."

Toni furrowed her brow. "Goes to sleep? I don't know what to say to that."

"No kidding. That's when I grabbed Oreo and beat it out of there."

"Speaking of beating it out of there, when are you moving back home?"

My stomach sank. "I have no desire to sleep in my own bed—at least not yet. Maybe I'm being too sensitive about the murder in my guest suite, but I'm still creeped out over it."

"I'm not surprised, and I don't think you're being too sensitive."

Speaking of sensitive, I tilted the brim of my hat to block the sun from damaging my skin. "Oreo likes it at the inn. I could see myself staying there indefinitely, but since I'm not independently wealthy, I'll have to go home soon."

"You're always welcome at my house, you know."

"I know. Thanks." I still didn't want to encroach on my friend's space. I might feel better about going home if the police had apprehended the killer. I told Toni what Poppy said about Derek and Josie.

"That sure points a finger at Josie," Toni said. "She was arguing with Violet that night, and she was sleeping with her best friend's ex. Can you imagine how upset she must have been when Violet admitted she was trying to get pregnant?"

"Yes, I can. And Derek, too, since someone saw him at my house that night."

"Maybe they were in it together."

"Maybe, but I can't help wondering if Violet's death had anything to do with what that filtration salesman said about the water quality. He suggested that Violet may have submitted a false report."

"Do the police know that?"

"They must. If Brent Lange told me, he must have gone to the police. He said Gaia Green did their own testing and proved the mine was polluting the water, but the water quality report said otherwise." The Gaia Green logo from the recipe popped into my head. Why had I not made this connection before?

"Toni! The recipe for Elderflower Rhubarb Cordial, that keeps appearing out of nowhere, was written on Gaia Green notepaper. Their logo is at the top. You don't suppose it's a sign?"

My friend's blue eyes opened wide to the possibility. "You know I believe in signs, and if ever there was a sign, a recipe tossed in from the other world would have to qualify. Not to mention, a recipe from your ghost twin, the one that Gloria said was trying to be helpful. It makes perfect sense." And then she laughed. Because none of this made perfect sense.

"As perfect as flying over the rainbow and landing in Oz." It seemed to me, these things were connected, somehow. Violet's phantom, my ghost twin, Gaia Green, the water quality, and possibly Violet's murder. By the thoughts swirling around in my head, I knew I was going to have a hard time concentrating on anything else if I didn't get answers to some of these unknowns. As I stared at a seagull dipping into the wind, an idea popped into my head.

"I wasn't going to tell anyone else about my ghost twin, but there's one person I think I should confide in—someone who could help."

Melanie and Jetti were on the closing shift. They were handling things well, and the café wasn't busy at that moment, so I called Colleen to see if she was available to chat. She agreed to meet Toni and me on the beach, so I grabbed another camp chair and made up a thermos of Blackberry Anise Spritzer. I also plated a few of the lemon-thyme shortbread cookies from Henrietta's Bakery made exclusively for Break Thyme.

We moved our chairs so we could see each other. When everyone had a drink in hand, I told Colleen about the look-alike I'd met in my trailer.

She listened to my bizarre story with rapt attention. "I believe you've had an experience with an extra-physical consciousness. How exciting is that!"

"A what? And I don't think I'd use the word exciting to describe it."

Colleen leaned back and beamed at me. "I prefer the phrase extra-physical consciousness or non-physical realities to the word ghost because when people hear the word ghost, all sorts of fearful images come into play, mainly from television or movies. The fact is, people do interact with other dimensions and a visit like you've had doesn't have to be scary."

"I've had one of those experiences," Toni said, brushing away a strand of hair caught in her lipstick. There was a nice breeze ruffling the lake. "When I was a little girl, about five or six, I woke up one night and saw my grandfather in my bedroom. He was standing at the doorway, looking in on me. He said hello and told me to get my mother to finish reading Tom Sawyer. He'd been reading it to me when I visited him. I said I would and went back to sleep. The next morning, I learned he'd died in the night, in his bed. He certainly hadn't been at my house."

"You never told me that," I said.

"My parents convinced me I was dreaming, but it hadn't felt like a dream. I hardly ever woke up in the night, so it stood out to me."

"Many people have similar experiences when a loved one dies," said Colleen. "You know, a census carried out in the nineteenth century showed that ghostly visions, just like the one you described, were remarkably widespread and accepted. Many people reported seeing an apparition of a loved one suffering an accident. These visions turned out to be true."

"Things changed in the late twentieth century," Colleen continued. "Science explains experiences like yours, Toni, as hallucinations due to the stress of losing a loved one. These experiences are even seen as healthy coping mechanisms to help in the bereavement process."

"I can see how that makes sense, but I didn't know my grandfather was dying," said Toni. "I wasn't worried about him at all."

"That doesn't explain what happened to me either," I said. "I didn't see a loved one. Not that I don't love myself, but...."

"You have been under unusual stress lately," said Toni.

That was true, but I wasn't feeling terribly stressed. Yes, I'd had moments, but overall, I was grounded in my everyday life. "You were with me when we found Violet, and you're not seeing your ghost twin."

"People react to stress in different ways," said Colleen. "It doesn't matter to me whether your experience was due to stress. To me, what's important is whether or not the experience was helpful."

I thought about that for a moment. "I didn't allow the apparition, if that's what it was, to do anything that might have been helpful. I was freaked out and told her to leave. Wouldn't you be wary of someone who showed up out of nowhere and said they were you?"

Colleen laughed. "Yes, I imagine that would rattle the gutsiest ghost-buster. I have a thought about that, though. If she comes back, perhaps you can ask her some questions. Ask her why she's visiting you."

As strange as this conversation was, it felt good to have Colleen's support and to be taken seriously. I'd had many stressful moments in my life, yet I'd never projected myself into a talking hallucination before. Colleen was the perfect person to reason this out.

"I can try. If she comes back. I'm not going to lie—I hope she doesn't."

"That's understandable," said Toni, and then turned to Colleen. "Is there anything else this could be?"

Colleen wiped away a drip of condensation from the bottom of her glass. "Some people believe we live parallel lives. When we reincarnate into a new life, we leave part of our soul energy in another realm—a higher realm. This part of us acts as a spirit guide to help us live our lives here on Earth. This guide has a better understanding of our journeys through life than we do."

The old me would have scoffed at this, but Colleen had taken me seriously, so I was going to give her the same respect. I marveled at not just how my life had changed, but at how my perspective was changing. I'd hardly been inside Colleen's shop because I'd thought it revolved around mystical things that I didn't believe in. I'd thought she was a bit woo woo. How ignorant I'd been to judge others when I'd never had their experiences. Still, I was feeling a bit rattled by all this and needed time to absorb it. "That sure would be handy. Maybe my higher self is sending me a winning cordial recipe."

Colleen smiled, and I got the sense she knew I had to take this in small doses. "So, tell me more about the Superior Taste contest you want to enter. I think you should use Toni and me as guinea pigs for your recipes."

I told them about my plan to use the ghostly recipe and find elderberry flowers. They both thought this would make a fun adventure. It was nice to talk about simple, normal things for a while, even though in the back of my mind, the next task I was planning could thrust me into uncomfortable territory where life may never return to normal again.

Chapter Seventeen

I WAS IN MY office at Break Thyme when my phone rang. When I saw my son's face on the screen, I smiled with peace of mind because I'd nearly finished Chelsea's party menu that morning. "Hello, my love."

"Hi, Mom. How are you? Is life back to normal?" His tone was less aggressive than in our last conversation, and that made my smile grow.

I thought about my ghost twin in the trailer. That was not a conversation we'd be having. He was not open-minded when it came to ghosts or elements from alternate realities unless they were part of his video games. "Not quite normal, but I'm getting there. You'll be happy to know I'll be emailing Chelsea's menu to you this afternoon."

"That's why I'm calling. I'm sorry, Mom, but I decided to have the party catered. You've got enough going on, and my work has picked up, so I don't have time to shop and prepare things."

I was a little disappointed to hear I'd wasted my time, but since I'd dropped the ball on this, I couldn't complain. I also wouldn't share that I didn't like the idea of Jordan paying for catered food. It felt good to follow through with my promise to let him make his own decisions. "I'm going to supply the refreshments, okay?"

"That'd be great. You can still bring over the dishes and glasses, right?"

"Yes, for sure." Before I opened Break Thyme, in my old life where I was still married to Bryan, we threw parties a couple of times a year. Stored in the furnace room at my house, I had enough dishes, glasses, and cutlery for a party of sixty.

"So, work is picking up. That's great." I was relieved Jordan's income would increase. He'd started a business a couple of years ago. I didn't quite understand what he did, something to do with ethical hacking where he broke into his customer's computer systems to find where they were vulnerable.

"Yeah, things are good. I may have to work remotely while we travel out to see Grammy, though. And on that topic, I need to know the dates we'll be away. I have a project that's finishing up mid-September, so if we could leave after that, it'd be good for me."

He was right. I had to make this decision for myself, too, so I knew exactly how much time I had to get the trailer ready and be sure I'd trained my staff well enough to keep things running smoothly at Break Thyme. "Okay. Let's set the dates right now." I pulled up my calendar on my phone. "Does September 20th work for you?"

I waited for him to check. "That's perfect. Okay, it's in my calendar."

"Yay!" I said. "I hope you'll also be able to relax."

He laughed. "You, too."

"I will if you will. I'm so looking forward to us having this time together with Samantha. It's been a long time since we had a family holiday."

"I have good news on that. Chelsea has changed her mind and is going to come with us."

I was stunned for a second and tried to keep the disappointment from my voice. I knew Samantha was looking forward to having her brother to herself, and I'd been looking forward to that, too. I hoped this didn't mean Chelsea would monopolize Jordan's attention.

"Mom? You're okay with that, right?"

"Yes. Of course. I was just envisioning the four of us in tight quarters, but we'll manage. That's great news."

He gave a clipped laugh. "You don't have to pretend it's great news. I know how you feel about Chelsea. This will be an opportunity for you two to spend some time together. I want you to get to know her and see her good qualities."

All I could envision was her dislike of nature and their messy house. Things could devolve quickly if we didn't keep the trailer organized. But Jordan had a point. I didn't know Chelsea very well. This would give me time to discover the mysterious qualities he was talking about. Who knew? We could both end up liking each other by the end.

"I will try, Jordan."

"Thanks. I've gotta get back to work. Love you."

"Love you, too."

Since my calendar was open, I entered the task of retrieving dishes next week, as well as our departure date. As much as I tried to keep positive, I could feel resentment rising in me over Chelsea joining our family holiday. This wasn't good. She was family, too.

Should I give up my bedroom to the two of them? That would leave Samantha and me in the bunk beds, which I didn't want. But not offering them the bigger space might add more fuel to Chelsea's anti-Quinn campaign. If Jordan and Chelsea took the bunks, where would Samantha sleep? I supposed she could share my bed.

She certainly deserved to be comfortable considering all the work she was putting into Longfellow. Over the last two nights, she'd primed and painted the cupboards. I'd said I'd get the walls done later that day.

I didn't have to determine our sleeping arrangements at the moment, but I needed to keep things on track, so I spent twenty minutes ordering new mattresses for the beds. Then, I found a place in Traverse City that sold elderflowers. I planned to try that cordial, so I placed an order to be shipped.

With those tasks complete, I came downstairs and checked the Cozy Nook to see everything was in good order. As I glanced out the window, I saw a couple of young mothers leave their table on the patio. I should clean up their dishes and save Poppy the job.

I grabbed a wet dishcloth and headed outside. The longest heatwave I could remember had finally relented. There was a beautiful breeze off the water. This was the perfect temperature for me until my next hot flash.

"Get away!" I called to a seagull as I approached the empty table. The gull had claimed a piece of pastry left behind. Bird poop was always a challenge, so we tried to keep things food-free and uninviting to wildlife.

When I finished wiping up, I took a moment to look out over the lake and watch a two-masted sailboat motor into Manitou Harbor. The breeze was perfect for sailing. Seeing a sailboat was like hitting a pause button on my constant thoughts. My father had owned a thirty-two-foot Navigator. My fondest family memories revolved around that sailboat, especially when I'd been allowed to crank the winch to hoist the mainsail. I could do it as well as my brother.

As the boat backed into its slip, I saw a woman walking from the pier in the direction of the parking lot. She looked like my friend, Jade Davis. She and Edward had a sailboat, so she was often at the harbor. I squinted and took a few steps forward. From where I stood, it sure looked like her. I dropped the dishcloth on a table and hurried to reach her as she entered the parking lot.

"Jade!" I called.

She didn't smile when she saw me, but she slowed down for me to catch up. Something was definitely wrong.

"Hey," I said, deciding her body language didn't welcome a hug. "How are you? I haven't seen you in ages. You didn't return my last email." I'd invited Jade and Edward for a games night with Craig, something we used to do regularly before Violet's murder.

"We've been busy," she said, glancing away for a second. "I'm kind of in a hurry. I was just dropping new seat cushions off on the boat."

"Edward said your mom's been needing you lately. Is she okay?"

"She's fine." She'd said it too quickly.

"Well, that's good news. Listen, I'd love to have you and Edward over for dinner. It's been a long time, and I miss you guys."

Her frosty demeanor warmed a degree. "I'll have to check with Edward. He's pretty busy these days."

"Yes, I know. I'll check with Craig—"

"Quinn, why don't just the two of us have lunch one day."

"Lunch would be great. We'll do dinner with Craig and Edward later."

Jade's expression hardened again. "I don't think it's a good idea if they see each other socially right now."

Suddenly, I had heartburn. "Is there something wrong? Did Craig do something?" I couldn't imagine what. Craig's middle name was diplomacy.

"From what I understand from Edward, it's what Craig's *not* doing that's the problem. He's been ignoring warnings about the rising temperature of the lake. This has some kind of impact on sulfur reactions and will greatly affect the mine, Quinn, just because he didn't get on board with climate change protocol. People's jobs are at stake. Our ecosystem is at stake. I'm sorry, I know he's your brother, but I think it's shameful what he's allowed to happen. We're only as healthy as our environment."

The accusation shocked me, but ten times worse, I could reconcile what she was saying with what Brent Lange had said. But that didn't mean any of it was Craig's doing. Sure, I'd had the uneasy thought that something wasn't right with him, but I could be wrong, or it could be for many other reasons. "This doesn't sound like Craig at all. You know him. He wouldn't jeopardize our drinking water."

"It always shocks people when a loved one is accused of wrongdoing. It's time to take the blinders off. No one enjoys his status as a hero of Bookend Bay more than Craig." Jade started walking. "I'll call you when life settles down. See ya later."

I stood there with my mouth open, watching her walk away. I'd concede her one small point. Craig could be pompous at times. There'd been moments when I would have paid to knock him down a notch or two. He'd always been an impossible act to follow as a big brother. But I'd never known him to be negligent.

I walked back to Break Thyme, reassuring myself that Jade was wrong and just because he'd been acting strange lately, it didn't mean my brother had willfully ignored warnings that would have a detrimental effect on our water.

I grabbed the dishcloth from the table where I'd left it and went inside.

"Verb of the month—muddle. What a hoot," a customer was saying to Poppy. "I'll try the Lemon Cordial with Muddled Rosemary, please."

At least my muddled sign was a hit. The positive way customers had been responding to the sign meant I was going to keep it and would not have to confront Aubrey about the mistake. I wished I didn't have to confront Craig either, but he needed to explain why Edward was saying these things about him.

I dialed his number. Jade couldn't have the facts straight. That Craig had neglected any facet of his job was incongruent with the brother I'd known all my life. I knew there was a reasonable explanation, but until I heard it from him, my stomach would be in knots. When I got his voicemail, I left a brusque message, telling him to call me back as soon as possible.

I headed upstairs to my office. When I opened the door, I froze.

Leaning over my desk was a woman. It was her! My mirror image. I couldn't stop the screech that escaped my throat.

Chapter Eighteen

THE WOMAN STRAIGHTENED WITH a jerk. Her hand went to her throat, and then her startled expression relaxed into a sheepish smile. "Hi," she said, as if she hadn't meant to scare the bejeebers out of me again.

My galloping heart slowed to a canter. "What are you doing up here? Where did you come from?"

"I'm tidying up. You write a lot of notes. They're everywhere, and they're not very well organized. I don't know how you find anything. I keep color-coded notebooks for the different facets of my day."

That was cheeky of her to go through my stuff. How would I find anything? "I have my own system, thank you very much." Maybe it was a stretch to call it a system, but I didn't appreciate her criticism.

My lookalike came around the desk. This time, I studied her more closely. It was almost like looking in a mirror. Except, and I hated to admit this, she looked like she hadn't gained the ten pounds I'd picked up in the last couple of years. Her hair was shorter than mine, shoulder-length, same chestnut brown, tapered bangs, parted at the side just like me. *Should I cut my hair?*

At least I'd put on a dress that morning, so I didn't feel like the hobo I'd been last time when I'd been working on Longfellow. Briefly, I wondered about my self-esteem as I compared myself unfavorably to an apparition. If that's what she was.

She appeared to be giving me a close inspection, too, coming to stand about four feet from me. Her royal blue blouse was a shade of blue I wore often. It was a good color for my complexion. *Our complexion?*

"At first I thought you were in my dream," she said, finally. "Now, I'm not sure."

"I am not in your dream. This is the real world, has been for about four billion years. How did you get up here?"

"I...I don't know. I never know. I remember going to bed, and now I'm here talking to you."

She didn't look like she was sleepwalking. I was starting to feel sorry for her. She sure was muddled. "Did you move to Bookend Bay recently?"

"I've never heard of Bookend Bay. I live in Sidmouth, England."

She didn't have an English accent; one more thing that didn't make sense. "Do you have family here? What's your name?"

I heard Poppy humming to herself, coming up the stairs, and was grateful to have her help with this. "I didn't want to bother you." Poppy glanced around. "Oh, I thought I heard you talking to someone up here."

I laughed. "Seriously. I'm talking to this woman—the one who looks like me, standing right here." I pointed since, for some reason, Poppy had a blind spot.

Poppy gave a skeptical laugh. "You're joking, right?"

"Quinn," said my twin. "She can't see me. Most people in this dream world can't see me. I don't know why this is the case. I haven't figured it out yet."

I felt my jaw drop. Actually, it was worse than that. It was more like the floor dropped out from under me, and the world turned upside down, or maybe it was even worse than that.

"Quinn, you're scaring me." Poppy said. "There's no one here."

The mirror-me was shaking her head. "Tell her you were kidding."

I swallowed. "Never mind," I said to Poppy. "I was just kidding around. Can I help you with something?"

Poppy just stood there looking at me, her face all screwed up with a mix of confusion and concern.

I could relate. I scrambled to think of something reasonable to say.

"I'm considering taking improv lessons," I improvised. "To better relate to my daughter-in-law, who wants to be an actress. I was practicing on you. Sorry, I can see I'm lousy at this."

Poppy relaxed her shoulders. "Yup. You sure are. Anyway, I had an idea. I think we should start a loyalty program. You know, like buy ten drinks and get one free. I thought it might be a nice thing to do for our regulars."

"That is a good idea. Let's talk about it later, okay?" I walked around the opposite side of my desk away from the mirror-me, who Poppy couldn't see, amazed that I could walk and talk at the same time. "I have a little work to do."

"Sounds like a plan." Poppy narrowed her vision to have another look around, settling on me. "You're sure you're okay?"

"Of course, I am. Thanks, Poppy." I looked down at my computer as if I was about to work on something. Geez, my desk looked great. The picture of my kids, my pencil holder, and a small dish of candies were in a perfect triangle. I *was* a constant note taker and always had scraps of paper lying about. My scraps were now in three neat piles topped with sticky notes labeled: Potential Recipes, Orders, Staff. Okay, so maybe she hadn't messed up my *system.*

With Poppy gone, I turned my attention to the someone who was now sitting down holding her head in her hands. The invisible someone who I could clearly see. The ghost?

Physically, she looked more solid than any ghost I'd met, yet she wasn't visible to everyone. She'd been moving papers around on my desk, so she could interact with physical things. Emotionally, she didn't look well, and I felt a wave of compassion for her. Just because I understood nothing about who or what she was, I was no longer worried she was a threat. It seemed apparent she was impossibly displaced.

"Excuse me," I said softly, coming closer to her.

She lifted her head, looking at me with an expression I understood completely. She was trying to keep it together.

"Listen, I don't know what's happening to you, but I will help you figure it out." I didn't know why I'd developed an ability to see paranormal entities, but one thing was clear. I hadn't been able to turn off this ability. Maybe it was time to stop trying to deny my new reality. If this was going to be part of my life, I had to believe there was some purpose in it, something that would better my life and theirs. Maybe I was meant to help.

"Thank you," she said with notable relief. "Trust me, I don't enjoy invading your life like this, and it's horrible to not be seen."

"I can understand that," I said, but then realized I really couldn't. "Let's see..." I was at a loss. I didn't know where to start. "You called me Quinn, so you know my name. What's your name?"

She hesitated. "I'm Brielle. Quinn Brielle Scott. Sound familiar?"

That was my name before I married Bryan and became Quinn Brielle Delaney. "Good grief." I took a chair from my stack of extras and plunked it on the floor beside her. I no longer trusted my legs to hold me. I was struggling not to feel creeped out by her, but to remain empathetic.

"You go by Brielle," I said, wondering why I never took Brielle as my given name. My father named me Quinn after his maternal grandfather, Duncan MacQuinn, a frontiersman, who my father admired for the stories he told of hunting grizzlies in the west. I'd always said I had no plans to live up to my name.

If we had the same name, then she wasn't my twin. That made things even more confusing, if that was possible.

Besides our name, another thing we had in common was that we both wanted to understand what the heck was going on. "You said something about your appearance here being a dream, and you can't get a good night's sleep," I said.

"Yes, that's right. I go to bed in my life and the next thing I know, I'm in your life where no one can see me. Well, nearly no one. There was a woman—"

I gasped, remembering Violet's phantom. "Did my tenant see you? She lived in the suite at my house. Do you know my house?"

"Yes, I know your house. She's the one with the curly brown hair?"

"Yes, that's her."

"I don't know how many times she saw me. At first, I didn't know she could, so I wasn't trying to hide."

"Oh, she saw you alright. She thought you were a phantom."

Distress showed in her eyes. "She may have seen me vanish. At least I believe I must disappear from this world when I wake up in my life. I don't think I'm still walking around here when I'm awake, but who the heck knows." She looked into my eyes like I might have the answers. I shook my head.

Before I could speculate on what life Brielle was waking up in, whatever that meant, I had other pressing questions. The foremost being, who or what was she? "You said you think you're me. For obvious reasons, this is a bizarre belief, Brielle, so let's try to figure that one out. Who are your parents? Do you have parents?"

"Of course, I do. Well, did. My father, Arthur Scott, died of a heart attack nine years ago. My mother, Carrol Scott, is alive and well. She lives on the east coast in Nova Scotia. Like yours, Quinn. I've looked through your things, so I know our parents are the same people."

She'd looked through my things? Okay, on top of that violation of my privacy, it also made me feel vulnerable. I had no control over this situation. I didn't even know if she was telling the truth. If she'd looked through my things, she could be lying about us having the same parents. Time to throw her a curve ball, if I could. "What about siblings? Do you have a younger sister like me?"

"We don't have a sister, Quinn. We have one brother, and he's older—Craig." She then rattled off his major achievements and the fact that she also felt inferior to her big brother. These weren't things she could have learned from snooping around my house.

I remembered what Colleen said I should do if my apparition came back. "Brielle, why are you coming here? What do you want?"

"What do I want? Nothing. I want nothing from you. I'd be happy to stay out of your life," she said, sounding offended that I'd asked.

"Hey, I'm just trying to make some sense of this."

"I understand that. Me, too, but don't think I'm doing any of this on purpose."

I let out my breath in more of a huff than I'd meant to. We might look the same, but it was really hard to put myself in her place. Maybe Toni's theory was more on the mark. Was it possible Brielle was the ghost of a twin that had died in utero? "Okay, I want you to consider what I think might have happened. My mother didn't have an ultrasound when she was pregnant with me. Maybe she was carrying twins. Tragically, one twin died before its presence was detected. Could you have been this twin?"

Brielle blinked and shook her head. She stood and took a few steps toward the back wall. I wondered if she planned to walk through it, or even if she could, but she stopped short.

"I know this is difficult," I continued, feeling badly that I'd upset her, "but you may be holding onto this life. You need to leave this world and go to the other side." I didn't know where the other side was but thought it a concept that didn't need explaining. Rationale was kind of out the window here.

She turned to face me. Again, strangely, her expression was one I'd made many times. She thought I was nuts. "You think I'm some kind of ghost who needs a push out of the land of the living."

"Well, I—I think it's possible. How do you explain the fact that no one can see you? If you don't think you're a ghost, what's your bright idea?"

"I do have an idea. I just don't know if you're ready to hear it, Quinn."

"Really. Well, why don't you try me?"

"Okay. This is what I think happened. You and I have the same parents and the same brother. I believe we lived the same childhood, even our teenage years. Then, there came a time when we had to make a choice, a monumental, life-changing choice. You went in one direction. I chose another. From what I've determined, I'm living the life you were too afraid to live."

"Wha—" I didn't finish my word because Brielle vanished. As in disappeared. Gone. I stood there for a moment, stunned, staring into my empty office. What the heck did she mean by that?

Chapter Nineteen

Brielle would rattle anyone of sound mind, I told myself. That boded well for my sanity, even though seeing someone vanish into nothing made me feel like I'd lost touch with reality.

She was living the life I was too afraid to live? The nerve. Me, afraid? What about her? She couldn't even go to the other side like she was supposed to.

So, maybe I'd not lived as adventurous a life as my namesake, but that didn't mean I'd been afraid to live. It didn't mean I'd only made safe choices. Come on. I'd taken risks. Opening Break Thyme was a risk. I'd been a mother at age nineteen—that was pretty adventurous, if you asked me. I'd even solved two murders. Two! How many murders had she solved?

A groan escaped my throat. Why was I letting an apparition get me all riled up?

I wasn't going to figure any of this out on my own, so I called Toni. She knew I wasn't timid. She, like Craig, thought I often followed my curiosity into trouble. I was courageous, not fearful.

Like the good friend she was, Toni said, to come on over, pronto. It took me less than ten minutes to knock on her door.

"Holy smokes, you saw her again," Toni said, pulling me inside. "Did you speak to her? Who is she?"

I dropped my purse on the floor by the side of the couch and sat down. Toni had drinks and a bowl of candied nuts sitting on the table. "Yes, I talked to her. She said her name is Brielle."

"What? She's using your middle name?"

"I know! She thinks she's me. At first, I felt sorry for her, and in all fairness, she's not happy with whatever has happened to her. Poppy came upstairs, and she couldn't see Brielle, as in Brielle is the invisible woman!"

Toni raised her brow. "Okay, well, I suppose that's in keeping with the other ghosts you've seen, right? Or should we call her a spirit instead of a ghost? It seems more dignified."

I picked up the drink and took a gulp. "It does?"

"I think so. Does she look like a ghost?"

I'd already thought about this. "Not exactly, no. The ghosts I've seen are quite pale and somewhat translucent. Brielle looks solid to me and she's got good color. Excellent color, actually. Rosy. The picture of health. Still, I asked her if she could be the ghost of a deceased twin."

"Did that make sense to her?"

"No. She didn't like that idea. You were right. It doesn't make sense." I guess I'd wanted her to be a twin ghost, and then I could enlighten her and give her the nudge she needed to leave the land of the living, but maybe Brielle wouldn't be so easy to banish.

"If you're the only person who can see her, she must realize something is off. Do you think she's a spirit guide like Colleen suggested?"

"She's too distressed to be a guide to anyone. Oh! I forgot. She said Violet could see her, which is probably why Violet thought I was possessed. She might have seen Brielle disappear into thin air."

Toni cocked her head. I could see her wheels turning. "Quinn, did Brielle see Violet the night she was killed?"

My pulse raced at this possibility. "Good question. I didn't even think to ask her. I was trying to figure out who or what she was." I sucked in my breath as a possibility occurred to me. "Brielle said she tidies up, compulsively, which explains a few things that have been going on in my life. When we found Violet, my kitchen had been cleaned up from the night before. I couldn't figure that out. Brielle must have done it. She must have been there that night!"

"Son of a biscuit. Do you think she could have seen the killer?"

"She didn't act like she'd seen a murder, but who knows how any of this works. I'll remember to ask her the next time she appears. Toni, she did say a rather strange thing."

Toni gave a soft snort. "Strange should be her middle name. What did she say?"

"She said she's living the life I was too afraid to live." It couldn't be true. Toni would confirm that. She'd known me for decades.

"What the heck does that mean?"

"I don't know. After she said it, she just vanished."

"After saying a thing like that?"

"Yes! I know. Where'd she get that idea from? I'm not afraid to live my life—that's nuts. Right?"

Toni hesitated.

What? Didn't she think so? "Toni, I'm not walking around like a mouse, afraid to live my life. Come on. I'm not."

"Of course not, Quinn. I was just wondering what she gains by saying such a thing. You are not a fearful person. If anything, you've got more courage than what's good for you—no offense. And besides that, you're perfect just the way you are, so don't go doubting yourself."

That was a relief to hear. "Thank you. If I was a big chicken, I wouldn't be trying to figure out if my brother had something to do with a murder. I wouldn't get involved. I'd back off, let the cards fall, and the sheriff could turn them over, or not."

"Wait. Are you talking about Craig? Violet's murder? What cards?"

I was still feeling disjointed, but certainly not afraid. I was even more determined to get to the bottom of this thing with Craig and Jade. "Sorry, the cards were just a metaphor. As for Craig, remember I told you Jade was avoiding me? Well, I ran into her."

"Oh. *Was* she avoiding you?"

"In a way, yes. She's avoiding Craig."

"Craig?" Toni looked suitably aghast. "Why?"

I told her what Edward said about Craig ignoring warnings about rising water temperatures to our detriment.

"What did Craig say about it?"

"I don't know. He's not answering my phone calls or calling me back."

Toni let out her breath. "Oh, Quinn. We're going to figure this out."

I picked up my glass. It was empty, and I didn't remember finishing it.

"Do you want another drink? Some water?" Toni asked.

"Sure. Water, please." Shoot, *was* our water fine? I hated having these doubts. I watched Toni fill water glasses in the kitchen.

When she sat back down, I told her what had been on my mind since I'd talked to Jade. "Remember I told you about that water filtration salesman, Brent Lange. He said Violet was the one who submitted the report, with what he claimed were falsified numbers, and then she was killed. He thought the two things were related. He also said Craig is part of some kind of a cover-up at the mine."

"That sounds a little dramatic, don't you think?"

I stared at the water for a few seconds. "That's exactly what I thought. It's just…"

"With what Jade said now, as well."

"Yes. And with Craig being evasive."

"Do you really think this has to do with Violet's death? What about Josie and Violet's ex-husband? Aren't they prime suspects?"

"I don't know. Maybe they did it, but I still want to know what's going on with the water quality reports. Maybe I'm worrying over nothing, but could you do me a favor?"

"Sure."

"I'd like you to come with me to get some answers. There's a place that may give us some insight into whether my brother is involved in some kind of cover-up or not."

Gaia Green was a grassroot environmental group that had a store on the other side of the river. As we walked in the door, I thought about how I wanted to be a more eco-friendly shopper, yet I often bought products that were convenient and cheap instead of those that embraced sustainability and purpose.

"I've never been in here," Toni said, holding a pair of recycled sterling silver earrings shaped like a whale. "My mom would love these. Seeing a blue whale in the St. Lawrence River was probably the highlight of her life."

"It would be cool to see a blue whale." I looked through a basket of utensils with "the future is bamboo" stamped on them. I could use a wooden spatula for Longfellow.

Toni picked up a package of produce bags. "I'm going to get these, too. Remember how Norman was against single-use plastic."

"I do. I'll take those as well," I said. It was a small step toward trying to do better. We took our purchases to the cashier.

"Is there a manager I could speak to, please?" I asked the young man.

"Yeah, sure. Hey, Lexi, can you go get Fran?" he called to an associate. By the time we'd paid for our goods, a thirty-something woman with pink hair introduced herself as the manager.

We stepped aside to speak to her. "I want to get some information on water quality and how it might relate to McCourt Mining," I said. "Do you know anything about this?"

"I sure do," she said. "We're in the process of filing a Clean Water Act citizen lawsuit against McCourt for discharging pollutants into the river."

Perspiration bubbled above my lip. I wiped it away and fanned myself. This was the news I'd feared. "I don't understand. McCourt is winning awards for environmental excellence."

She made a clicking noise with her tongue. "Right. They were one of the few sulfur mines to achieve this and may have deserved that award five years ago."

"I know nothing about sulfur mining," Toni said. "Have the standards changed?"

"Nope. They haven't, and that's the problem."

"I don't understand," I said, again.

Fran talked with her hands. In one, she held a pen and used it to point at the floor. "Nowadays, the metals that are still left in the ground are hard to remove. Sulfur is stuck in rock that needs to be crushed to get it out. Unfortunately, when large quantities of sulfur contact the air and water, there's a chemical reaction that creates sulfuric acid."

"Yikes," said Toni. "I know that's not good."

"No, it's one of the most serious threats to our water quality. Even if there's no acid rock drainage, toxic metals can still leach into the ground and poison the water."

"If this is a common hazard, then McCourt Mining must take steps to be sure they're not polluting the water," I said.

"There's never been a metallic sulfide mine that hasn't damaged its watershed. Sulfide mining has already polluted over twelve thousand miles of rivers and streams and one hundred and eighty thousand acres of our country's lakes."

I didn't know any of this. I recalled what Brent Lange said about the wild rice dying because it's sensitive to elevated sulfate levels.

"The mine *was* doing a decent job of it," said Fran. "It takes time for the water to reach dangerous levels of acidity. When that happens, we then have increased levels of bacteria, and this leaches even more metals from waste. Rainwater then carries acid from the mine into the river."

"Could climate change impact this?" I asked.

"Absolutely. It's part of the equation and the reason McCourt is failing. Increasing water and air temperatures cause metal discharges to become more toxic. Storms are increasing too, so there's greater runoff."

I was starting to feel sick. Why hadn't Craig mentioned any of this? "What does McCourt say about all this?"

"They say our tests are bogus, and we'll put the community into an economic crisis if the mine closes."

Their test was bogus, or was Violet's test bogus? Was she falsifying records, so the mine didn't have to spend the money it would cost to keep up with climate change? If so, why would she do this? For money? Could someone have paid her to do it?

"You believe our water is dangerous?" Toni asked.

"If we allow this to go unchecked, yes. Right now, the problems we're seeing in the wild rice and brook trout are south of the mine. With our lawsuit, we aim to expose the truth and get this problem fixed. You can help, you know."

"How's that?" I asked.

"Make sure you recycle your metals, and you can educate your elected officials and request stronger regulations." She pointed to the Gaia Green bags we held. "Buy products that contain recycled metals like ours do." She took a couple of business cards from the counter and handed one to Toni and me. "We have a newsletter on our website with more information."

"Fran, you've got a phone call." One of the staff called to her. "Do you want me to take a message?"

"No," I said. "We're done. Thank you very much."

"Thank you for asking. Have a good day."

I looked at Toni. "I feel like we've just opened a slimy can of worms."

Toni grimaced. "A non-recycled metal can full of greedy worms."

"Greedy, if the mine is putting their bottom line ahead of our water quality."

Fran appeared intelligent and credible. She wasn't pushing water filters. I couldn't think of a reason she would make up stuff like that. Did Craig know Gaia Green was filing a lawsuit against the mine?

I thought about how often Craig took credit for the environmental awards won by the mine. Those awards were his babies. I could easily imagine his shame if it should come out that their pristine record was a lie.

The knot in my stomach tightened. Was it possible Violet was murdered because she'd been fudging the water quality test results and someone found out? But why murder her? Why not report her to the police?

I couldn't get anywhere with this until I talked to Craig.

Chapter Twenty

THE NEXT MORNING, I woke to Oreo's paw batting my face. It took me a moment to realize I was still at the inn. I'd been dreaming I was at Break Thyme, back on opening day, sticky with night sweats, clad in pajamas, no makeup, bed head, everyone watching me. Dreams like this, where I was feeling unprepared and vulnerable, were a sign of stress. Go figure. I was unsure of the water, of Craig, of Violet's killer, and of the ghost twin who could pop in at any time.

"It's too much," I said to Oreo. "If I don't resolve these things, I'm never going to get a good night's sleep."

He jumped off the bed, moseyed over to his empty food dish, looked over his shoulder at me, and let go an annoyed meow. I'd gotten into the habit of giving him liver treats in the mornings to compete with the stellar cuisine he was growing used to.

"Okay, okay. It's coming." I got out of bed and sprinkled a few treats into his bowl. "Here you go."

While Oreo devoured his treats, I showered away my very real night sweats and the bed head that made me laugh out loud at my reflection every morning. How long were these hot flashes going to continue?

I had a full day at the café and then plans to meet Samantha at Longfellow, so I jumped into the shower right away, realizing mid-wash, I'd forgotten to check my phone for a message from Craig.

Showering fast, I left the bathroom and checked my phone. Craig's name was second in a queue of messages. I quickly opened his text. *We need to talk. Can you meet me at the lighthouse at noon?*

I swallowed hard. He'd never asked me to meet him across the bay, well outside of town. Did he not want to be seen? I'd better find the time to meet him. I sent back my response. *Yes, of course. See you then.*

I dried my hair, applied minimal makeup, and threw on a pair of capris and a blouse.

Oreo was waiting at the door. He knew the routine. I scooped him up and delivered him to Mrs. Carscadden who greeted us with a smile. "You go have a lovely day, Quinn, and don't worry about this furball. We've become fast friends, even though he thinks he's the boss."

I laughed and wished her a good day, too.

When I got to Break Thyme, things were bustling. Three of my staff were on duty today. I checked that the coffee pot was full. Since I was behind on paperwork, I grabbed a coffee and headed upstairs to my office.

An hour later, I came downstairs to see if the elderflowers had arrived. "Poppy, did a package come for me by courier?"

"It sure did. I thought you saw it last night. I put it on the counter in the kitchen."

"Great! Thank you." I went into the kitchen but didn't see a package. After looking high and low, I asked Poppy if she could have put it somewhere else?

She leaned closer to me. "Are you feeling okay, Quinn?"

"Yes. Why?"

"Weren't your elderberries in that package? There are four bottles of elderberry and rhubarb cordial in the fridge. Didn't you come in and make those last night?"

How serious was my peri-menopausal brain fog? I thought back to yesterday. After Toni and I visited Gaia Green, I'd met Samantha at the park, and we'd primed the walls at the trailer. It had been a finicky job because of the many nooks and crannies around the cupboards. At the inn, I'd fallen exhausted into bed. There was no way I'd had time or energy to make cordials.

I left Poppy wondering about my sanity and checked the fridge. Sure enough, four bottles sat on the top shelf, neatly labeled in what looked like my handwriting.

The phantom strikes again? Could Brielle have done this? If so, I wish she'd popped into Longfellow so I could ask her about the night of Violet's murder. I hoped she wasn't avoiding me. That thought made me laugh. Now that she was a helpful phantom, she was welcome to pop in.

I shook my head at the bizarre turn my life had taken. Surprised as well, because I felt more accepting of Brielle's presence. Maybe this was because Gloria had said my ghost twin wanted to help, evidenced by the cordials.

I removed a bottle from the fridge and poured about an ounce. It had the consistency of a light syrup. I took a sip. The perfect blend of sweet and tart with a subtle floral deliciousness tickled my taste buds. Delicious.

This could be the award-winning cordial. I downed the rest, savoring the sophistication of flavors, and felt a wave of happiness surge through me. Gosh, I needed this simple pleasure.

At noon, as I walked from the parking lot toward the lighthouse, shivers raced along my arms. I wished I'd brought a jacket. A cool breeze blew in from the lake, clouds darkened the horizon, and whitecaps roiled over the great expanse of Lake Superior. The temperature had dropped considerably in a day.

I saw Craig, looking solitary, as he gazed over the water, so I walked along the flagstone path to join him.

"Hey, you," I said, coming up behind him.

"Hi." He gave me a quick hug, his expression tense. I wondered if this was due to guilt or heroism.

Sibling relationships were often complicated. I loved my brother and envied him, but I'd never second-guessed his goodness. Even when his high-maintenance wife of nineteen years suddenly walked out the door, he never said a harsh word about her. He was strikingly good-looking, intelligent, and physically apt, but it had always been his integrity and kindness that set him apart. I was reminded of this as I looked into his worried eyes.

I told him what I'd learned from Fran at Gaia Green. "What's going on, Craig?"

"It's true," he said. "I had the water tested myself. The levels of sulfides have risen to where they should shut down the mine until they get this under control."

"What? Shut down?" This was a big deal. The mine was the primary driver of the economy in the county, employing nearly five hundred people. And on top of that, I didn't know how this might affect the small businesses in our town. "Violet was responsible for testing the water, right? Do you think it's possible she submitted false numbers?"

"Well, this kind of pollution happens over time. She'd only been around for about a year, so I don't know if she had a vested interest in falsifying reports, but I'd say yes, it's possible."

"On purpose?"

"The water is tested regularly. A few years ago, we got a report the sulfide levels were increasing, but then they went back down. We thought the increase was an anomaly, but I've been concerned about the rising water temperatures—"

"You've been concerned?" I interrupted. "Edward told Jade it was your fault the mine was falling behind on climate change protocol."

Craig cursed and shook his head. "He told Jade that? I recently learned he's been saying the same thing to the CEO. It's a lie. Edward was the one who ignored the protocol. I brought it to his attention two years ago.

I'm trying to prove it, Quinn, but someone hacked my emails. Every email with my concerns around the discharge of contaminated water is gone. The water is not being managed. As far as the worker's health and safety and the integrity of the mine, McCourt is getting on top of it, but it's expensive and they're not moving as fast as they should to stop acid rock drainage. I'm hoping it's not because the board doesn't want to see their annual bonuses diminished, but I don't know."

I hoped not, too. Understanding the intricacies of what McCourt should do to adapt to climate change was beyond my pay grade.

"You need to go to the police, Craig."

"I know, but I think I'm being set up to take the fall at the mine, and if Violet's murder is connected...?"

I felt sick. Panic tightened every muscle in my body. The more I learned, the worse this got. Murder, setups, water poisoning, these kinds of things, weren't supposed to happen in our small town, and certainly not in our family. I tried to still the panic and think. "What did Violet have to gain by allowing McCourt to pollute the water?"

"I don't know, Quinn. I can't figure that out."

I let out a heavy breath. "Okay, this is what we know about Violet. Her best friend, Josie, believed Violet wanted to have a baby with Derek. But forensics found sperm inside her that wasn't Derek's, so Violet was having sex with someone else."

"Really? How do *you* know that?"

I told him about Poppy's date with the deputy. "It's not clear why Violet would have sex with someone else if she wanted to reconcile with Derek. Unless she found out about Derek and Josie and did it to get back at him."

"Maybe," Craig said. "Did you ever meet Derek West?"

"No."

Craig took out his phone. "I was trying to learn more about Violet and found her on Facebook. There's a picture of Derek." Craig scrolled down the page.

I wasn't sure why I needed to see a picture of Violet's ex.

"Here." He passed me his phone showing a man with sandy-gray hair, clean-shaven, heavy-set.

"This is Derek?"

"Yep."

I examined the photo. "He looks a lot like Edward."

"I thought so, too."

My mind was racing. If Edward could go so far as to blame Craig for the mine's negligence, what else had he done? And how dare he! And why? A possibility flew through my mind—professional jealously? Now that I thought about it, I remembered times when Edward put Craig down professionally, and for no good reason. He'd made it sound like he was joking, but what if he wasn't? Maybe Edward was boiling inside at the way Craig excelled.

Another thought occurred to me. "My neighbor said she saw Derek at my house the night of the murder. Do you think she could have seen Edward—not Derek?"

"Sure, in the dark, it would be difficult to tell them apart."

A gust of wind whipped my hair into my eye. I freed the strand, feeling like my vision was cloudy from what I didn't want to see. We'd known Edward and Jade for a decade. It was surreal to consider Edward could have murdered anyone, and I still hadn't made that leap, but the possibility was now seeded in my mind. "Let's back up a second. I don't understand what Edward has to gain by letting McCourt pollute the water."

Craig looked up as a flash lit up the heavy clouds. It felt like our world was breaking up. "Back when we got the first report about the high sulfur levels, we were scrambling to understand it, putting in lots of long hours. One particularly long night, Edward and I went out for drinks. Just the two of us. And after the second drink, he got quiet, then he started unloading about how scared he was of losing the safety record. That everything he had was invested in this job, in this company. He said he couldn't let the mine shut down while things got cleaned up—it would hurt too many employees, but then he also hinted that he and Jade were overextended and could lose everything if he didn't keep his paycheck."

I stared at Craig. I was too shocked to speak. Jade had said nothing to me about them being in financial trouble. I was sorry she was going through stress like this, but I was also angry at them both. If Edward had coerced Violet to submit false water reports to keep the mine operating, well, that was horrible. But then he'd blamed Craig? And Jade had accepted that?

Craig cleared his throat. "I believe Edward is setting me up to take the fall at work, but I think it's even worse than that."

I found my voice. "What do mean?"

"We were at the conference together the night Violet was killed. You sent me a text to say she was off the rails and you were going to stay with Toni. Edward was standing beside me when I read your text. I told him about it."

I let out my breath. "What are you saying?"

"I'm saying, what if he left the hotel that night? It was only a ninety-minute drive to get back to Bookend Bay. We were at the bar until about midnight. I decided to pack it in. He'd just ordered a drink, but he left it unfinished to ride the elevator with me. It seemed odd—he isn't one to waste a drink, you know,—but I didn't give it much thought at the time."

"It did seem odd. Why order a drink and then leave it?"

"Maybe he thought I'd be his alibi if he needed one. I'd say he went to bed, although I couldn't confirm he stayed there. He could have driven back to Bookend Bay, killed Violet, and then been back to the hotel before morning."

"Wait. You think Edward killed Violet?" I still couldn't get my head around that. "Are we getting ahead of ourselves? Edward got what he wanted from Violet. Why kill her?"

"I don't know, Quinn. I'm not saying it happened. I realized later that Edward was nervous after I told him Violet was having some kind of breakdown. Now, he's spreading lies about me. He's up to something."

I thought so, too, but murder? This was a good friend we were talking about. And then there was my brother's reputation and possibly more at stake. My heart picked up. I might have the answer. What if Brielle saw Edward at my house that night? What if she saw him arguing with Violet? That would be enough for the sheriff to question Edward.

"We need to tell the sheriff about this," I said.

Wait. What was I thinking? The invisible woman as a witness? Even if Brielle saw Edward murder Violet, she couldn't tell the sheriff.

Craig shook his head. "I don't think we have enough to convince the sheriff to bring in Edward for questioning. I have no proof I sent emails to him about climate change. He'll deny it, and then it's his word against mine."

I drew in a breath, then released it in frustration. I remembered my last call to the sheriff's department, where I reported a disappearing woman in my trailer. I probably wouldn't add credibility to Craig's theory. "If Violet submitted a false report, that's a police matter."

"I know. But she's dead, and I have no proof Edward knew the numbers were false or even spoke to Violet about it."

He was right. I felt like kicking one of the stones on the beach into the turbulent waves crashing over the rocks. The explosive sound the waves made as they hit the shore accentuated my frustration.

We stood silent for a few moments. I tried to calm my nerves, so I could think. The rhythm of the waves gave me something to focus on, easing the pressure building in my head. I usually liked the power behind the wind, but today it felt more tumultuous than it ever had.

Every bone in my body screamed to protect my brother as if it was my job. But the mine had a job to do as well, and that was to protect our environment. It had to be held responsible. It had to clean up its mess. We had to find a way not to sacrifice Craig in the meantime.

If Violet and Edward were the true guilty ones, what did Violet want so desperately that she would allow the mine to pollute the water? I thought about this for a moment until a possibility occurred to me.

"If Violet did submit fake numbers, we need a good reason for this. I have an idea, although it's a bit out there. According to Josie, Violet was obsessed with having Derek's baby and saving their marriage. What if she considered the resemblance between Edward and Derek was close enough that Edward would make a good sperm donor? He's already fathered a child, so everything is in working order."

Craig grimaced. "Do you think she was that desperate to have a baby?"

I remembered what Josie said about Violet's behavior changing. She was already taking prenatal vitamins, and she'd bought baby clothes. Was this because she suddenly believed her chances of getting pregnant had improved? She was in her early forties, so she must have been feeling her biological clock ticking. "Yes, I think she was that desperate."

"I can't imagine Jade agreeing to something like that. Can you?"

I knew what he meant. I'd comforted Jade when she'd come home from the hospital after she'd had to have an emergency hysterectomy. The surgery had devastated her. She'd wanted siblings for her daughter, Maddie. "No. I think it would hurt her deeply to know Edward was making a baby with Violet."

Maybe I was grasping, but we needed something to prove Edward was in cahoots with Violet. If they were making a baby together, then Edward had skin in the game, so to speak. This could lead to the question of what else they'd done together? Falsified the water records, so Edward kept his job? I thought about taking this theory to the sheriff, and as I pictured myself laying it out, I saw a lack of evidence. It sounded far-fetched, and I didn't feel comfortable trying to sell this to the sheriff without proof—something to tie Violet to Edward. But what?

Wait. There was something. "If we could prove the sperm inside Violet belonged to Edward, then we could show their relationship was sexual. He's a married man. She's trying to reconcile her marriage with Derek. Wouldn't the police then consider Edward a suspect or at least a person of interest? Maybe they'd be able to find something that showed Edward knew the water records were false."

I couldn't read Craig's expression, couldn't tell if he thought I was out to lunch on this or not. "I don't know, but it's a moot point, Quinn. We can't prove it."

"We could if we had Edward's DNA. And then, as a favor to you, because this is a dire situation, I think we could convince Ian Urquhart to compare Edward's DNA to the sperm found in Violet." I didn't say it, but I knew we were both thinking of the medical examiner's sister, the toddler Craig rescued all those years ago. If anyone would do a favor for Craig, it would be Ian.

"As a favor, he likely would, but I don't think there'd be anything legal about it. Edward won't hand over a DNA sample if he's guilty. Even if he's not guilty, we can't ask him without accusing him. I doubt you can test someone's DNA without their consent."

This was one reason I knew Craig was innocent. He couldn't possibly be involved in the false reports because he was not a rule breaker. I, on the other hand, believed that in a situation like this, it was okay to break a rule for the greater good. "You know what they say about nice guys finishing last—we can't play by all the rules."

He hesitated. His jaw was tight. His expression was tight. Everything about him was tight. His disapproval was obvious, but this wasn't just his job and reputation at stake, it could get much worse.

The clap of thunder over the roiling water couldn't have sounded more ominous. A storm was imminent.

"Craig, there's another thing we could do—as a last resort. Could we ask Jordan if he can find the missing emails?" I mentioned this with reluctance because I wasn't sure if this would put my son at risk.

"Absolutely not," Craig shot back, his voice shaking with indignation. "I will not ask my nephew to hack into the mine's system. Jordan's business is just getting off the ground. If he got caught, it could destroy his reputation."

"Okay. You're right. We will not do that." Again, I was reminded of my brother's integrity and relieved for it. I had no idea what was involved in retrieving company emails, but he was right. We weren't going to risk Jordan to save his uncle.

"Besides, I already asked our tech guy to recover the emails, and he couldn't find them."

"Okay. So, we're back to trying to prove Edward and Violet had a personal connection, maybe a motive for working together to keep the mine running despite the polluting." I didn't know if this was the best course of action, but I couldn't think of anything else to do. I waited for Craig's acquiescence or opposition, but he said nothing.

"I'll take care of it," I finally said. I'd never had this feeling before. Me rescuing Craig. It was empowering. For the first time in my life, my brother didn't have all the answers. I could help him get out of this predicament, and I was going to do everything I could to make that happen. "You can count on me."

Chapter Twenty-One

As Craig drove away, I got onto my phone and googled DNA testing.

I knew nothing about DNA—well, I knew it was full of our genetic material and could be scraped from the inside of your cheek to determine ancestry. Edward would probably notice me inside his mouth with a scraper thingie, so that method was out.

On one site, I read DNA could be collected from a toothbrush. I tried to imagine how a conversation with Jade might go to determine which toothbrush Edward used. "I just love the way I was able to distinguish my toothbrush from Bryan's. My color was always yellow. What about you?" Considering what I planned to discuss with her, I couldn't imagine turning the conversation to toothbrushes.

DNA could also be taken from a razor, a licked envelope, chewing gum, or a hair sample with the root intact. Hair was my best bet, I thought. Edward had a full head of hair, so I'd need access to his hairbrush. I'd need a bag or something to safe keep my sample. Luckily, I'd been in their bedroom enough times to know he had a dresser, hopefully with a hairbrush on top.

First, I had to get Jade to invite me into her house. I didn't plan to call ahead. It was Friday afternoon, and if luck was with me, she'd be at home waiting for her daughter to come home from school. Jade didn't believe in leaving a twelve-year-old home alone.

I stopped at Break Thyme to check on things and grab a plastic baggie, which I stuffed into my pocket. As I came out of the kitchen, I saw Colleen at the counter talking to Poppy.

"He got his toothpaste muddled up with a tube of cortisone," Poppy said.

"At least he didn't muddle it up with fungicide!" Colleen said.

"Yikes! Who did that?" I asked.

"You mean, who made a muddle out of their mouth?" Poppy said.

Oh boy, this verb of the month thing was going strong.

I spoke over the whir of the frothing machine. "Never mind."

"Quinn, just the woman I was looking for. Do you have a minute?" said Colleen as she slipped off the stool.

I didn't want to delay my visit to Jade, but l also didn't want to tell Colleen I couldn't spare a minute. "Sure."

I followed her to chairs in the corner of the Cozy Nook out of earshot.

"I've been doing some research," she said when we'd sat down. "Have you heard of a double-walker or doppelgänger?"

"You mean someone who looks like you?"

"Yes, exactly. There's an old German folk belief that every living thing has a spirit double. This isn't a ghost, but it is supernatural. Sometimes they were seen as spiritual opposites or evil twins who'd give malicious advice or try to plant sinister ideas in their victim's head."

"Evil? I don't get the impression Brielle means any harm. By the way, she came back." I told her about my encounter with Brielle.

"Fascinating, especially that Poppy couldn't see her. I think you're right. I don't see why your double would be up to no good. Did you know Abraham Lincoln wrote he saw his double in the reflection of a mirror? Apparently, he saw two of himself and one of them was much paler than the other."

"I imagine Lincoln's double didn't say he was living the life Abraham was too afraid to live."

"I imagine not," Colleen said. "Let me do more research into this. If Brielle comes back, perhaps ask her what she's doing when she's not popping into your life. Get her to explain why she thinks she has the superior life."

"Oh, I certainly will." I was feeling pressure to get to Jade's house before her daughter got home from school. "I'm sorry, Colleen, I have to run. I appreciate you looking into this. Thank you."

"Och, don't mention it," Colleen said, getting up. "I'll call you when I know more."

I had one more question to ask Poppy before going through with my plan. Maybe the police already suspected Edward? I waited until she'd finished filling the citrus water dispenser.

"Poppy, have you seen the deputy again?"

She raised her eyebrows coquettishly. "I sure have."

I smiled, glad she appeared to be enjoying herself with Cody. "Have you talked any more about Violet's murder or Derek West? Since Derek wasn't the one having sex with Violet that night, are they looking at other suspects?"

"I think Cody would have told me if they'd found that guy. He likes to show off a little, and I think it's kinda sexy to hear him talk about the investigation."

No wonder he shares. "Did they find the murder weapon?"

"Nope, not yet. They're still looking."

So, it didn't sound like the police suspected Edward. "Okay. Thanks, Poppy. I have to run an errand, so I'll be gone for an hour or so. Do we need anything?"

"I don't think so, but I'll text you if we do."

As I dashed through the rain to my truck, my chest constricted. What if I was wrong about Edward, and I got caught snooping around his stuff? Would Jade tell the police? Would she understand I had to do it to protect my brother? If she did understand, how would she feel about my sneaking into her house to incriminate her husband? I didn't think it was possible to predict how a person would act under circumstances like these. At the same time, I was kind of looking out for her, too. Didn't Jade deserve to know if Edward was sleeping around with Violet, trying to get her pregnant?

What seemed like an electrical infusion in the surrounding air sent prickles across my skin. I shivered and rubbed my arms. My gut said it was vital to know if Edward was sleeping with Violet. He was the one who'd started this trouble by accusing Craig of wrongdoing, so I should stop dwelling on rationalizing my actions and remember I was trying to get to the truth.

Inside my truck, I looked at the sky and thought this feeling had nothing to do with the passing thunderstorm. It was a sensation like nothing I'd felt before. Like something was trying to get my attention. I scanned the street for Brielle.

She was nowhere to be seen. Surprisingly, disappointment washed through me. I'd love to be able to ask her if she'd seen Edward at my house that night, but that wasn't the only reason I was disappointed. I wasn't afraid of her any longer. My curiosity about my doppelgänger was as fully piqued as it had even been, and I wanted answers from her, too.

I drove onto Harmony Road behind the school bus, so I had to stop a couple of times and wait for the kids to exit. Just before I got to the Davis house, the bus stopped, and Maddie Davis hopped down the stairs. I powered down my window and waved to her before pulling into the driveway. Maddie was a beautiful girl with jet black hair like her mom's, and she had her dad's smile. Jade and Edward had started their family much later than I had, so

Maddie, at twelve years old, was a lot younger than my kids.

The chat with Colleen put me later than I wanted to be. It would have been better if Maddie wasn't home, but if I didn't do this now, I'd have to wait until after the weekend for another time when Edward wouldn't be home.

Maddie left the front door open behind her, so I gave it a cursory rap and walked in. Inside, she was tugging off her shoes. I heard feet approaching and Jade calling out.

"Hey, munchkin, how was your—" Her sentence stopped when she saw me. I could describe her expression as cautious. "Quinn. What's up?" Her tone wasn't unfriendly, and she gave me a soft smile.

"Hi. I'm sorry to barge in like this, but I was wondering if we could talk?"

Her fingers brushed Maddie's head as she scrambled past into the kitchen. "We're going out soon. Maybe another time." She looked apologetic, but I wasn't sure if she was still snubbing me. If I didn't do this now, I'd likely lose my nerve, so I needed to say something that she wouldn't dismiss. I closed the distance between us and lowered my voice. "It's about Craig. I think you were right, Jade. Something has happened. Please, I need to talk to someone about this. Is Edward home?" I was ninety-nine percent sure he'd still be at work.

Her eyebrows raised. "No. He won't be home for a couple of hours. What's wrong?"

Good. I swallowed hard, doing my best to look both worried and disappointed.

"You can talk to me," she said, giving me a quick hug.

Bingo. "If you can postpone your outing, I'd appreciate it. From what you said, the other day, Edward has some concerns about Craig, so perhaps you can relay what I tell you and get his opinion."

"Yes, of course. I'll make us a coffee, or would you like something stronger?"

I didn't want alcohol muddling my actions. Oh boy, now I was thinking in terms of muddle. "Coffee is perfect. I have to go back to Break Thyme."

The house was ranch style, with the living room in the center, bedrooms on the right side, and the kitchen and family room on the left. I followed her into the kitchen and took a seat at the island. Maddie was already in the family room with an iPad, earbuds plugged in.

"You can have thirty minutes of screen time, Maddie. Hello, Earth to Maddie." Jade waved her hand at her daughter who finally registered Mom was talking to her and removed an earbud.

"Thirty minutes and then it gets turned off. You can go outside and shoot some hoops or do your homework."

Maddie groaned and plugged back in; attention cemented to the screen.

Jade poured coffees. It seemed she always had a pot on, but it tended to be old. I wouldn't have noticed a thing like that before I had a café where coffee had a shelf life of thirty minutes. She came around the island, pulled out a stool, and sat beside me.

"What's going on with Craig?" she asked.

I told her what I'd learned from the Gaia Green people, being sure to mention the discrepancy in the water test results. "I didn't understand how climate change could make a difference in toxicity levels, but I do now. This is a big deal, Jade. When I asked Craig about it, he was evasive and that's not like him. Now, he's not returning my calls. I'm worried he's done something wrong or is in some sort of trouble."

Jade put her hand over mine and squeezed. "Edward said Craig hasn't been himself lately." She'd listened empathetically. It was uncomfortable to mislead her, so I reminded myself this was for the greater good.

I let go a sigh. "Did you know that Violet, my tenant, was a water quality technician and may have submitted false numbers?"

"I did know that. Edward said she was a friend of Craig's. Ed's concerned about that connection."

That was rich. If he was telling Jade this, he could be saying the same things to their colleagues. But did this mean Edward paid off Violet by being her sperm donor and then killed her? Sitting in Jade's kitchen made this seem far-fetched.

I'd sat on this stool many times over the years, sharing coffee, laughs, and tears. She'd been a good sounding board for me over the years, and I liked to think I'd helped her better manage her emotions. I thought of the time I'd reminded her to breathe instead of lashing out at Maddie's teacher when she'd questioned her reading level. And the time I'd talked her down when Edward's irritating sister criticized Jade's parenting. And the time she'd worried herself sick when someone burglarized a house miles away. Friends did that for each other, and I'd always been loyal to my friends and family.

But did that loyalty work both ways? Jade had not given Craig the benefit of doubt. She often teased him for being a demigod, yet she'd not questioned the veracity of Edward's accusations. How could Craig be a saint one minute and a traitor the next? She seemed willing to throw Craig under the bus.

I would not let that happen.

I slid back the stool. "Excuse me. I've had too much coffee today. I'll be right back." Heading toward the bedrooms, I stopped at the powder room and looked behind me. If Jade stayed sitting or wandered over to where Maddie was in the family room, she couldn't see me.

A second later, I closed the bathroom door and padded lightly down the hall to Jade's bedroom. The bedroom smelled faintly of Jade's perfume Obsession by Calvin Klein. I crossed the room to Edward's dresser. No hairbrush on top. I hated to have to open drawers. It was both noisy and nosy.

First, I went into their ensuite where there was a double sink. The counter had the usual adornments—a soap dispenser, toothbrushes, cotton balls, a folded washcloth. No hairbrush.

I pushed the door nearly closed and opened the vanity drawers, one by one, to no avail. The thump of my heart pounded in my ears.

I went back to the second drawer where I'd seen Edward's electric shaver. It looked pretty clean. Were these blades removable? I couldn't walk out of here with his entire shaver.

I left the bathroom and tiptoed past the bed, my nerves strung tight. It felt like I'd been in their bedroom for an hour.

What if Jade caught me with Edward's hair in my hand? I wouldn't be helping Craig then—he'd be in the same situation, but worse. I'd also be adding more fuel to Edward's campaign against Craig and earned his ire.

But what if my theory was correct, yet I backed out, and Craig suffered for it?

The angel side of my conscience reminded me that this was the ultimate invasion of privacy. The devil pushed me forward. *Sure, listen to the devil.*

I started to sweat as I hurried to the bedside table and slid open the top drawer. And there it was. Sitting in a small basket with a black comb and a pair of hair trimming scissors.

Please let there be a hair with a root. I removed the baggie from my pocket and tugged hairs from the brush. My fingers trembled. *Open the baggie!*

With the hairs dropped inside, I slid the zipper closed and stuffed it in my pocket.

I was closing the drawer of the bedside table when I heard a noise behind me. My heart stopped.

"Hi, Quinn." It was Maddie.

I turned, forcing my mouth into a smile. "You don't know where your mom keeps her nail clippers, do you? I have a horrible hangnail. It really hurts."

Maddie scooted over to Jade's vanity. "Probably over here."

"Oh? Right. You're so smart." I picked up the clippers and snapped them close to the side of my finger. "That's much better. Thank you. You're a lifesaver."

"You're welcome." She bounced into her bedroom and was already sliding past me as I reached the kitchen.

"Okay, Maddie, screen time is over," Jade said.

"But I just saved Quinn's life. I should get another fifteen minutes for that."

"Yeah, nice try." Jade looked at me questioningly. Would she believe my lame excuse or see right through me?

I swallowed, tried to sound natural. "Nope, she's right. I had a hangnail that needed a quick surgery. Maddie found your nail clippers." I wiped perspiration from my upper lip. *Please don't say I was suspiciously going through your bedside table.*

"See," Maddie said. "Told you."

"Very nice. Now, go outside and limber up. You've got gymnastics tonight."

Maddie scooted off.

I was going to get away with this. I expelled a long breath. Fanned myself with my hand.

The presence of the baggie burned in the back pocket of my Capris. Had I stuffed it down far enough or was part of it sticking up with Edward's hair follicles. I reached back and felt for it.

All good. I had to get out of there.

"Thank you for the coffee and for listening." I realized I was rubbing my arms and forced myself to stop. "I've got to get back to work."

"Don't worry, Quinn. There could be a reasonable explanation for this. Everyone makes mistakes, even Craig. Things get fixed, and we move on."

I nodded. She followed me to the front door and gave me a hug.

As I walked to my truck, I wondered what the next step would be if the DNA test proved positive. I'd have to tell Jade. She wouldn't forgive me for what I'd just done, and I didn't think I could forgive either of them for what they were doing to Craig. We'd chosen our loyalties. Sadness tightened my throat at the realization that our friendship would never be the same.

Chapter Twenty-Two

AFTER I LEFT JADE, I went to see Ian Urquhart and begged him to test Edward's hair sample against the DNA found in Violet. He wasn't easy to sway, but when I said Craig might be framed for murder, Ian agreed to do it. Craig was like family to Ian, and he understood I was asking for this favor on my brother's behalf because Craig wouldn't.

Back at the inn, I had another problem to face. The sheriff had left a message to say they'd finished with my house. I could move back in. This news didn't thrill me. I didn't think I was being unrealistic, feeling squeamish about living where a murder had been committed. Many people would. Yet, many people wouldn't also be concerned Violet was going to come back from the dead and accuse them of not taking her phantom seriously. As for that phantom, I had Brielle to deal with. I didn't want Violet's ghost in the mix, too.

But I couldn't afford to stay at the inn any longer. I was going to have to go home. Maybe I'd invite Toni to stay over the first night to help ease my jitters.

The next morning, Oreo was pacing at the door. To get my attention, in case I hadn't noticed his agitation, he jumped on my lap when I sat down to fasten my sandals. I gave his head a good scratch. "Hey, boy. You've become the king of the castle here, haven't you? I guess neither of us is in a hurry to go home."

Oreo was sure going to miss the inn. As I left, he was a cat on a mission and bee-lined it to Mrs. Carscadden, who welcomed him with a cat treat.

"He prefers the fish flavor over chicken," she said.

"No wonder he's scratching at the door to get out of my room." I praised Mrs. Carscadden for being Oreo's new favorite human and left the inn.

It was just past seven. I planned to spend the morning working on Longfellow and go into the café later.

Once I arrived at the park, I grabbed a package of rollers from my passenger seat. We'd finished the priming, and I wanted to get the first coat of paint on the walls. It was about seventy degrees. The perfect weather to paint. I unlocked the door and went in.

"Don't scream. It's just me," Brielle said, raising her arms as if I might shoot her.

I didn't scream, but she had given me a start. Brielle was holding a piece of sandpaper. Had she been sanding the cupboards?

"The next coat of paint will go on smoother if you give this coat a light sanding first," she said with an air of authority.

Okay then. Was I supposed to share my office and my trailer with her? "Do I have to get used to you showing up unexpectedly?"

"Yes. I think so. I have no control over where I appear." She stepped away from the cupboard and placed the sandpaper on the table. "I guess I'm not doing a good job of staying out of your way."

Colleen said Brielle may be up to no good. I wasn't convinced this was true, though, especially since I'd found her tidying my desk and sanding my cupboards. She seemed to be more of a helpful spirit than a harmful one. I wouldn't have sanded between coats.

"You don't have to sand my cupboards." I put the rollers on the table. "Or make my elderflower cordial and leave it in the fridge at Break Thyme. That was you, right?"

"Yes, I made the cordial. I'm sorry, but I can't sit idle. It drives me crazy to have nothing to do. I can cope better if I accomplish something while I'm here." She had a point. Sometimes I forgot I wasn't the only one trying to manage this.

It was strange for both of us. "I'd like to understand who you are and why you're suddenly in my life."

She sat on the bench. "Me, too. I've been doing some research, but it's hard to find any authority on what I'm experiencing. Can I ask you a few questions?"

Anything to sort this out. "Yes, of course."

"We have the same family as far as parents and sibling goes. But there are also differences between us."

Considering she'd been around for a while; she knew more about me than I did about her. I'd like to catch up. "Oh? How so?"

"Well, you have children."

"Yes. Jordan is twenty-nine and Samantha is twenty-five. Do you not have kids?"

"I don't, no. You married Bryan Delaney."

"Yes, I did. When I got pregnant with Jordan, we decided it was the best thing to do."

"It was a brave thing to do, a selfless thing. Do you remember when you decided to sleep with him? It wasn't done in haste. I know that. We spent days thinking about it."

It was eerie the way she said *we* spent days thinking about it. How did she know that? It was as she'd gotten inside my head, inside my memories. "How do you know that?"

"Because I remember it. From what I've determined, we were living one life then, Quinn, until that moment."

For a woman in a constant personal heatwave, I was suddenly cold. "What do you mean?"

"This is what I think happened. In everyone's life, there are times when we make pivotal, life-changing decisions. Like when you slept with Bryan, your life took a certain direction—the path that gave you your kids and roots in Bookend Bay.

"But what if you'd made a different choice? What if you'd not gotten pregnant, not married Bryan? You'd have lived an entirely different life—the one I've been living."

I was speechless, my mind hurtling back thirty years. Back to the week before Bryan and I checked into the motel in Marquette. We were nineteen. I was a virgin when most people I knew weren't. I was feeling left behind—not that I'd come to that decision lightly. I hadn't. I'd deliberated for nearly a month.

I could still see the condom with the tear in it, the one that changed everything.

We'd become parents at age twenty. Adjusting to a baby had been harder for Bryan. While our friends went to the pub, we changed diapers and managed toddler tantrums. Bryan didn't enjoy living with my parents, but this enabled us to finish college.

It took me six years to complete my degree in public relations—a degree I briefly used. By that time, we'd had Samantha. Bryan was climbing the ladder at the bank, and we'd bought a small bungalow. I stayed home, raised our kids, and made Bryan's life easy. Too easy, maybe.

Speaking of life-changing choices, at age forty-seven, he decided to live the life he'd missed in his twenties. I guess I had to give him credit for hanging in there until the kids were older.

When my marriage ended, I'd wondered how my life might have been different, maybe better, without Bryan. Not that I'd trade my kids for the world, but what if I'd married a different man? "Are you saying you're living the life I would have lived if I'd not gotten pregnant with Jordan?"

"I believe so, yes. I've been doing some reading on parallel lives. I think, by coming here into your life, I'm crossing over into a life choice I didn't make." She rolled her lip in the same way I did. Something I was hardly aware of, but I recognized the gesture.

I had so many questions about Brielle's life, I didn't know where to start. Had she married a better man?

"It's a theory," she said. "I seem to come into your life when I'm sleeping in mine. That's why I disappear suddenly. I wake up. Half the time, I don't remember I've been here—it's lost like a dream."

Disappear suddenly. I couldn't ask my questions yet. I needed to know if she'd seen Edward at my house the night Violet was killed. "Wait, stay here!" I couldn't ask that of her—she said she had no control. *Hurry.* I grabbed my purse and rifled through it to find my phone. "Please, look at this picture."

I scrolled through my phone to a photo of Edward and Jade. I enlarged it, so he filled the screen.

"Ten days ago, you were in my house on the river. I know this because you cleaned my kitchen."

She narrowed her gaze, thinking. "I remember that night. It was as if you'd left in a hurry. You never go to bed and leave things out of place."

"How long have you been snooping into my life? Nevermind." I passed her my phone. "Did you see this man in my house that night?"

She looked at the picture, hesitated, her gaze thoughtful. "No. I didn't see this man in your house."

I instantly deflated. Had I been wrong about Edward? Or had Brielle arrived before Violet was killed?

"Wait," she said. "I remember now. I saw him outside, in the woods by the river."

I let out my breath. Edward had an inboard/outboard boat for fishing. Had he come down the river from his house to mine? No. That didn't make sense if he planned to use the conference as his alibi. Jade could have noticed the boat engine start up and go missing.

Brielle continued. "I have difficulty remembering things that happen while I'm here. That man... I remember now. His behavior was odd."

"Why?"

"He was carrying a large salt lamp, a heavy one. I wondered why a man would run through the woods with it. I assumed it belonged to you since he was coming from the direction of your house. Did he steal your lamp?"

The potential murder weapon! Holy Hannah. I gripped the table and felt it jar under my hands.

"What did he do with it?"

Her laugh was softer than mine, but then we never recognize the sound of our own voice. Weird that I had that thought while I was freaking out.

Brielle hesitated. "It's funny you should ask because I followed—"

Poof! She was gone. "No! Come back here! What did he do with the lamp?"

I stared into the empty space, feeling my spine turn to ice.

Chapter Twenty-Three

Ack! "Followed who? Edward?" I cried into thin air. Predictably, I didn't get an answer.

I was shaking all over. I slumped down on the bench seat.

Could I be sure Brielle saw Edward? I supposed I could be as sure as my neighbor Sandy had been when she'd identified Derek. The two men looked alike.

I didn't know what to do. I wanted to call Craig, but was I going to tell him about Brielle? At the moment, I couldn't imagine that conversation. A cousin of ours once told Craig and me she'd seen a ghost in a military uniform sitting at her kitchen table. Craig gave her a neurological explanation for it that had to do with bottom-up brain processing or something like that. In other words, it was her brain screwing up, not a ghost because they didn't exist. At the time, I'd agreed, but I knew better now.

If Brielle's theory was correct that she came into my life when she was sleeping in hers, then she could be back in fifteen hours or so, depending on her sleep schedule. Or maybe she took naps like a few people I knew, and she'd be back sooner. If she'd found the lamp, and it had a fingerprint on it, then we might have evidence to clear Craig if Edward was trying to set him up.

In the meantime, I wanted to update Toni. She might have a thought or two that could be helpful. As I scrolled through my contacts, my phone rang. I nearly jumped through the aluminum roof.

It was Jordan. I took a deep breath and smiled since smiling was supposed to trick the brain and make you feel like roses.

"Hi, love," I said, my mind scrambling to remember the date and when I needed to get the dishes over to him.

"Hey, Mom, do you want me to pick up the dishes? You can tell me where they are."

They were packed with some crystal that I wanted to remove, so I'd rather do it myself. "It's okay, Jordan. I need to go through the boxes. I'll pick them up tonight and get them over to you. Are you going to be home?"

"Yes, I will. Okay, thanks a lot, Mom."

"You're welcome. I'll see you later."

I sent Toni a text to see if she was free later that day.

Life marched on around us. I still had a business to run and Longfellow to finish. Maybe I shouldn't have started tearing it apart, but I'd done it now. Summers flew, so I didn't want to put it off. I made a mental list of what I needed to get done that week.

Did Brielle use the bathroom when she was here? Don't ask me where that thought came from. The toilet was hooked up to the sewer, so I wouldn't need to dump the black water tank before leaving the park, but I wanted a lesson on how to hook up the electricity, water, and sewage for our trip. I wasn't looking forward to our first trip to the dump station, but it would have to be done.

Beach Meadows Park had a shortlist of handypersons who could give me a lesson and help me hook up the trailer to my truck for when it was time to leave. It would be nice if Samantha or Jordan were here for that, so I had another set of eyes.

I retrieved the list from my purse and called the first one, Alec Camden. I left a message, letting him know I was parked in spot 110, so he could check out Longfellow.

I had to put thoughts of Violet's murder aside for now and get a coat of paint on the cabinetry. The gray I'd chosen had undertones of aqua, a nice, cool tone. I opened the paint can, stirred it, and poured some into the small roller tray. I started with a brush on the upper cabinets to cut into the edges where they met the wall.

About an hour later, there was a knock on the door. Toni said she wouldn't be free until noon, but maybe her plans had changed. I put down the paintbrush and opened the door.

Standing there, looking up at me with deep blue eyes, was the hot guy I'd seen passing by the trailer last week. "Hello," I said, immediately aware of every drop of perspiration on my body.

"Hi, You're Quinn?"

Now that we were only four feet from each other, I could see he had a light smattering of freckles across his straight nose. He was tanned, but not leathery-looking, and his brown hair was just an inch longer than neatly trimmed. Long enough to look rugged, not scruffy.

"I am."

His smile, and the way his eyes lit up, could be taken as flirtatious. Yes, I quickly decided—in my fantasy, he was flirting. "I'm Alec Camden—park and recreation ranger and handyman on my days off. You left a message. I figured I may as well stop by and introduce myself."

"Great! I'm glad you did." I sounded a little too enthusiastic. I better dial it back a bit. "I'm new to trailer ownership, and I'm going to need help to disconnect the hoses and hook up to my truck. Can you walk me through it when you have time?"

"Yep. I'd be happy to. How long are you staying at Beach Meadows?"

"At the end of the summer, my kids and I are taking Longfellow to the east coast. I don't have a plan for the trailer when we get back. I guess I should think about that."

He raised an eyebrow. "Longfellow?"

The way he said it made me laugh. "Yes, we named the trailer after Henry Longfellow since his poem Evangeline reminds my kids of the east coast where their grandmother lives."

"Ah, the tale of the evicted Acadians."

"Yes," I said, impressed he knew the poem.

"You're right. It's a good idea to plan ahead. The park runs pretty much at capacity all season. Some spots here are nicer than others, some right on the lake with private beaches. I can keep a watch on availability if you like for when you get back?"

"That would be great. I'd appreciate that. A view of the lake would be awesome." I figured I could rent out Longfellow when I wasn't using it.

"You probably know about the hiking trail that begins at the west gate. It's a good loop, moderate difficulty, only seven miles."

"Oh, yeah. That's a good one, all right," I lied. I was not in good enough shape to walk seven miles. That morning, I'd dropped my facecloth and for a moment considered getting a new one, so I didn't have to bend over.

He smiled, and a brief pulse inside me sprung from the dead. "I've got your phone number," he said, "so I'll text you if a prime spot becomes available when you're away, or maybe before."

Did he promise everyone prime spots or was I special?

"Thank you. I'd appreciate that, Alec."

His phone chimed. He glanced at the screen. "I'll come and help you get your trailer ready to go. Can you send me a text with the date, so I get it on my calendar?"

"Yes. I'll do that."

"Take care, Quinn. Hope to see you again soon."

That pulse grew to a little thrill when he said my name. Holy cow, I was acting like a schoolgirl. I smiled at his back and unabashedly ogled his nice proportions as he walked away.

He looked back over his shoulder. I blushed, having been caught watching him. I gave a quick, awkward wave and went back inside, wishing I had a longer reprieve from the murder and mayhem going on in my life.

As I left the park, Ian Urquhart called to say he'd rushed the test and would email the results soon. I called Craig, and he agreed to meet me at my house at eight o'clock, so we could talk about what to do next.

I wasn't giving up on the Superior Taste contest. Before my life went cluster nuts, I'd planned to enter four cordials in the contest. I only had three—Blackberry and Star Anise, Elderflower, Mint and Rhubarb, and Lemon Rosemary—and I'd have to be okay with that since the deadline to enter was today. Technically, Brielle made the Elderflower cordial. But technically, Brielle and I were the same person, so I was following the rules. Besides, entries could be team efforts, and nowhere did it say the team had to live in the same universe.

I wanted to tell Colleen what I'd learned from Brielle, so I stopped by Mystic Garden before going to work. Colleen was in her backroom unpacking a box of crystals.

"Oh, dearie," she said when I'd finished telling her what Brielle said about parallel lives. "I'm jealous of you. 'Tis the most fascinating encounter I've ever heard tell of. Imagine, knowing how your life could have turned out differently."

I laughed. "You're jealous of this mayhem? I'd gladly pass it off to you if I could." As I said that, a part of me realized I didn't want to give up Brielle. Now that I knew she'd made a different choice all those years ago, I wanted to know how her life had turned out. Had I made the better choice? Was one life even better than the other or just different?

Colleen stroked the turquoise stone in her necklace. "Last year, a European customer came into the shop here. She told me she'd come to Bookend Bay to see her twin flame. They'd met five years before that."

"I don't know the term twin flame."

"Neither did I, so I read up on it. It's theorized that a soul can split in two and when born into a life, this split soul lands in two different bodies. Each of these souls is known as a twin flame."

The back of my neck tingled as Colleen continued.

"A twin flame could be someone to whom you feel deeply connected. This woman, and the man she'd met here in town, believed they were living a life together, but that other life was in a parallel universe. She said when they first met, they had a deep love for each other, instantly. They've only seen each other twice in five years, yet the love between them remained unrelenting."

Sometimes, when I spoke to Colleen, it was like lifting a curtain to another world. "I don't feel a connection like that with Brielle. There's nothing romantic or loving in our relationship."

"I didn't think so. But perhaps there are different twin flame experiences. She says she's living the life you didn't choose?"

"Yes." I told her when Brielle thought our lives had split.

"If that's the case, I suggest you consider how it might make you feel to learn about the path you didn't choose to live."

I let out a sigh. I'd just been thinking about this. "Weird, huh. You're right. It's something to consider, but at the same time, I can't imagine not knowing."

"Colleen," a voice called from the front. One of her staff poked his head in the storage room. "Can you come out and answer a question about incense?"

"Yes, lovie, I'll be right there."

I gave Colleen a hug. "Thanks…again. I don't know what I'd do without you."

"Oh, don't you mention it. This could be a wondrous gift, Quinn. I'm here whenever you need a sounding board."

She was much more than that. Colleen made me feel validated and supported in something that sounded like craziness in my own ears.

As I walked along Courtesy Boulevard to Break Thyme, my mind hardly registered the passing tourists and townsfolk. Then my phone pinged. An email from Ian jolted my attention away from twin flames. Three words that changed everything—*It's a match*.

I stopped and stared at the message as its meaning rang in my ears. Brielle was pretty sure she saw Edward with the murder weapon. Edward's DNA was inside the victim. To me, these two things meant there was a good chance Edward killed Violet. Jade might be living with a killer.

"Sure, just stop in the middle of the sidewalk like you own the place." A man with a bakery box said as he maneuvered around me.

"I'm sorry." *You impatient oaf.* I headed for a bench that faced the boulevard. I needed to sit down.

I owed it to Jade to deliver this news personally before telling the police. I had to convince her to come to my house tonight when Craig was there. I needed his support. I had the test results. If she saw the proof, knew that Edward had sex with Violet, she might come with us to the police. Of course, this could also go badly when I had to admit I'd stolen Edward's hair. Or maybe, considering the results, she'd understand why I had to do it. Maybe learning this would trigger something she'd overlooked—some behavior of Edward's, hopefully, something related to his accusations against Craig that could prove his innocence. At any rate, with shocking news like this, she'd need support.

I called Jade, praying she would answer. I let out my breath when the call connected.

"Hi, Quinn," she said. "I've been thinking about you."

"Hi. Jade, I have something vital to tell you. It concerns us both."

A pause. "What is it?"

"Not over the phone. Can you please meet me tonight at my house, at eight o'clock?"

"I suppose so. Is it about Craig?"

I didn't want to alarm her, so I said yes.

"I'm dropping Maddie off at dance class at seven-thirty. Is it okay if I come by after that? I'll be early."

Perfect. Maddie wouldn't alone at home with Edward. "Yes, that's fine."

"Shall I ask Edward to come too?"

"No! I mean, I'd rather you don't. I want to get your opinion first before telling Edward about this."

"Okay, then. I'll see you later."

I hoped I hadn't sounded panicky about her bringing Edward. Since I'd already spoken to her about my worries over Craig, I hoped she'd think it would be uncomfortable for me to talk to Edward about my brother.

I left the bench and hurried to Break Thyme. I wanted to lose myself at work, so my mind didn't race around in circles until that evening.

The first person I noticed when I walked in the door was Aubrey. She and Poppy were admiring Aubrey's artwork: Verb of the Month.

"Everyone loves it," Poppy said, glancing at me. "Don't they, Quinn?"

Aubrey was smiling wide. "Hi there. Yay! It's a hit. I wasn't sure how you were going to use verbs here at Break Thyme, but it sure is original. You could say I was in a *muddle* over it, although I guess in that context it's a noun."

Poppy laughed, and I managed a smile. "The sign is just perfect, Aubrey. Thank you again, and welcome back. Did you have a good holiday?"

"We had a fantastic holiday. Have you ever done the circle tour of Lake Superior?"

I'd lived on Lake Superior since I was twelve, but I'd never been to the north shore on the Canadian side. "I haven't, no. I didn't know there was a circle tour. Sounds like fun." Now that I had Longfellow, I might do something like this next year.

"The north shore is rugged, wild, and mountainous. Oh, the views. It was a great way to connect with the lake. We've already planned to do it again with our kids." Aubrey rubbed her belly.

"You're pregnant!" Poppy hugged her friend.

I congratulated Aubrey.

In the next hour, I got the cordials packaged to be delivered to the contest. I thought back to a couple of weeks ago when winning this contest meant everything to me. I wanted our customers to know we served award-winning artisan drinks here at Break Thyme. I wanted to see the winning plaque hanging in the Cozy Nook. I wanted someone to pat me on the back and say excellent job, Quinn.

Why? Because my husband didn't just leave me, he ran away to the other side of the world. He couldn't have put more distance between us. And one reason for his leaving was because I'd followed my dream to open Break Thyme. *Nearly seventy-five percent of independent coffee shops fail in the first five years!* Okay, but why couldn't my shop be one of the successful twenty-five percent? Why couldn't Bryan have believed in me? I remembered the raw whisper inside my head that had suggested I wasn't good enough to succeed. Maybe not even good enough to keep loving.

But I had succeeded. And time on my own, away from Bryan's constant doubts, allowed me to replace that raw whisper with a kinder, more loving voice, at least for the most part. No person was better than another. Everyone was good enough and worthy of love.

So, I'd let an award, an acknowledgment from people I'd never met, become the measure of myself as a success. I looked around my crowded café and registered the smiling faces and joyful sounds. I made a decent living and employed five staff. Did I need an award to feel like number one?

You bet I did. So, maybe my inferiority complex needed a little more work. I printed the shipping label and fixed it on the box of cordials.

Chapter Twenty-Four

I ARRIVED AT MY house around seven-fifteen that evening. Since my nerves were chewing up my stomach, I had no appetite for dinner.

At least, I'd not forgotten about the dishes for Jordan, so the first thing I did was head downstairs to my storage room.

The door to this room was next to the guest suite. An icy tingle chilled my spine as a gruesome memory tried to surface. *Don't think about it!* I looked away and opened the storage room.

The dishes were in a box on the bottom shelf. I also had glasses and cutlery—everything Jordan would need for Chelsea's party. I removed the crystal he didn't need and decided to put everything in my truck before Jade arrived.

By the time I'd carried the last box outside, Jade was pulling into the driveway. I put the box with the others and met Jade by her car. She looked nicely put together, as usual, shining black hair pulled back in a sleek tail, eye shadow blended expertly, and lipstick that complemented her rose-colored shirt. I hadn't bothered with makeup this morning and to not feel like such a bumpkin, I fluffed my hair.

"You look stressed," she said, hugging me. "What's happened?"

I couldn't remember a time when I'd felt inner turmoil like this. Then again, I'd never told a good friend I thought her husband was a killer. I let out a breath. For that revelation, I'd wait for Craig. He should arrive in about twenty minutes.

"Let's sit on the patio out back, and I'll explain," I said. "Do you want something to drink?"

She shook her head. "I'm fine. I just finished dinner."

We went around the side of the house, stopping at my herb garden. I cringed at the cracked soil and limp plants. On a normal day, Jade and I would tour the garden. With two green thumbs, she was always interested in the perennials that flowered with the changing seasons.

"Your herbs are usually thriving," she said, leaning over to pinch a flower from the top of a basil plant. The basil was next to one measly stalk of sage. "Oh man, Violet decimated your sage."

"She sure did. I'm going to need to raid your garden for Thanksgiving." I looked at my watch—fifteen more minutes until Craig arrived.

I carried on to the patio outside the guest suite. Jade stopped behind me. Her gaze fixed on the patio door. She grimaced. No doubt, thinking about Violet's murder—that it must have happened just inside these doors. Horror would now be a common reaction of the people who came to visit. How nice. My house of horror.

Jade's face paled.

"Let's sit on the other patio," I suggested, letting her walk ahead to the other side of the yard. As I followed, something inside my guest suite distracted me. It was sitting on the side table close to the door. I froze. *What the heck?* I moved closer to the patio door and cupped my eyes to see inside clearly.

It looked like the salt lamp was back on the table beside the couch.

Was I seeing things? How could this be?

Jade had stopped and turned to look at me. "Are you coming?"

"I have to check on something. I'll be there in a second. Please, just wait over there." I didn't want her thinking about Violet. At least not yet.

I ran to get the keys and was back at the door in less than a minute. I glanced at Jade, who was sitting about twenty-five feet away. She lifted her head from her phone as I unlocked the patio door.

"I just need a minute, Jade," I called and went inside.

Good grief! There it was, the pink salt lamp, sitting back in place as if it had always been there. I was stunned. Frozen. Staring at the surreal.

My thoughts kicked into hyper-drive. Only one person knew where this lamp had been hiding and that was the killer. I couldn't think of a reason the killer—if it was Edward—would have returned it to the crime scene, of all places. That made no sense.

Wait. Somebody else may have known about the lamp. Brielle. *It's funny you should ask because I found—*

The lamp? Was *that* what she'd found?

I leaned down. Without touching the salt rock, I looked it over. I'd seen these lamps at Mystic Garden. They usually sat on a wooden disc with an electrical cord clipped inside to illuminate the block of salt. The disc and cord were missing.

I looked closer, scanning all sides of the rock. There, within the crevices, were russet speckles. It looked like dried blood!

I needed to call the sheriff right away. I'd left my purse in the truck. I took a step toward the patio door and stopped as I caught the faint scent of sage. I looked down. I'd stepped on Violet's herb bundle. One she'd lit to exorcise Brielle.

Jade's comment came back to me. *Oh man, Violet decimated your sage.* I stood still, combing through my memory. I couldn't remember telling Jade about the sage. It hadn't been in the news. How did Jade know Violet had taken my sage?

"Quinn, what are you doing?" Jade said.

Her voice gave me a start. She was coming in the door toward me. Thoughts flew through my head. I willed myself not to look at the lamp as I hurried past it to stop her from coming in. I needed to get to my phone.

"I'm all done," I said. "I just need to grab my purse out of the truck. I'm sorry for getting sidetracked. You go sit. I'll be right there." Was my body blocking her view of the lamp? For the first time, I was thankful for my extra girth.

"What were you doing in here?" The only part of her that moved was her eyes.

"Jordan asked me to get dishes for his party, and I just realized I'd forgotten to put aside the big bowl for salad." I was rambling. The excuse was too lame.

Jade's eyes widened. I knew by the direction of her gaze and the look of shock on her face, she'd seen the lamp. If I'd had any doubt she'd been here in my house the night of the murder, it vanished.

My mind was racing. Had Edward confessed to Jade he'd killed Violet? He could have given her details of that night, which meant Jade was covering for him. Maybe, maybe not. Did Jade know he was having sex with Violet? I just couldn't imagine she'd let that ride.

If *my* mind was racing, Jade's had to be on warp speed. I didn't want to give her time to think. She didn't know I suspected her. "Let's go outside, Jade." My voice was shaky. I swallowed and steadied as best I could. "I have something to tell you about Craig. It's incriminating and I'm worried. I need your help."

She didn't move. Her gaze was still glued to the lamp. "Sure, Quinn, let's talk about Craig. But first, let's talk about you. Maddie said when she found you in my bedroom, you were using her father's hairbrush. What were you doing? Why did you really ask me here?"

She reached into her purse. And then it took me a mind-boggling moment for the gun in her hand to sink in.

I knew Jade and Edward owned guns. Their decision to bear arms was a choice we disagreed on. The gun in her hand was probably a birthday present from Edward. I remembered her talking about it. Other husbands bought jewelry.

"Me? What are *you* doing?" I managed to ask.

"Don't move. Just answer my question, Quinn."

"And if I don't? Are you going to shoot me, Jade?" Maybe I shouldn't be confrontational, but I couldn't help it. I'd thought the appearance of the salt lamp was surreal, but this...

She just stared at me.

"Jade, how is the gun going to help this situation? Don't let things get worse."

Had it been five minutes? Ten, since she'd arrived? Craig would be here soon. I needed to stall her.

"She was going to ruin our lives," Jade said. "Craig's too, you know. And everyone who works for McCourt."

The mine. "Because of the water quality report? Did Violet fudge the numbers to hide the toxicity levels?"

"She did something to the reports to hide the true level of contamination. And she intended to tell the truth about it. Just before Edward left for that conference, I saw the beginning of a message from Violet on his phone. *It can't wait until you're back. I need it right now or I'll tell...* was how it started. I asked Edward about the rest of the message. He said it was work-related and nothing to be concerned about. But he was hiding something. I could tell the message bothered him—a lot.

"I suspected something was going on between him and Violet. Twice over the last couple of months, she'd called him after hours. He'd dropped everything and left the house. When he'd said it was work-related, I let it go. But why the urgency? When I saw that last message, I wondered if he was having an affair. He was making excuses, so while he was away at the conference, I decided to get answers from Violet."

I said nothing. I just wanted her to keep talking. Where was my nosy neighbor Sandy when I could use her? Scared to take my gaze off Jade, I used my peripheral vision to find something to defend myself with.

"Did you know Violet was trying to get pregnant?" she asked abruptly.

It felt awkward to talk about it, so I wouldn't mention Edward's sperm inside the murder victim, but at the same time, I wanted Jade to know I wasn't alone in my suspicions. "Not until after she was killed. Jade, I had reasons to suspect Edward was involved with Violet. That's what I was doing with his hairbrush—getting a sample of his DNA. I had it tested. The medical examiner knows Edward's DNA is a match. He's going to tell the sheriff." Ian and the sheriff were good friends, but I didn't know if Ian would give this information to Sheriff Jansen.

I looked at the gun. "You don't want to make this worse than it is. Put the gun away, and I'll help you explain—"

"Stop! Edward wasn't having an affair. Violet extorted his sperm! That's what kind of person she was. Edward will fix the problems at the mine. He will not let it poison our water, but we can't have the mine shut down. We can't afford it, and neither can anyone else. Think about what it would do to all those families?"

What would it do to *her* family when McCourt learned what Edward had done? He'd used Violet's desperation for a baby to get the results he needed to protect his paycheck. "The mine may have been slowly polluting the water for years. When was Edward planning to fix it?"

Anger rose through my fear, but it wasn't smart to lash out at Jade while she had a gun in her hand. I forced myself to take a breath, and as I did, a better approach came to mind. At least I hoped it was.

Chapter Twenty-Five

I FORCED MYSELF TO feel compassion for Jade. It wasn't easy, but I believed she was a good person who'd done a horrible thing. I wanted to remind her of that. She must regret her part in the terrible chain of events that led to Violet's murder. Surely, she was as terrified as I was.

"You thought Edward was having an affair," I said. "But it must have felt even worse to learn Violet was trying to have Edward's baby. I'm sorry you had to go through something like that. You must have been devastated."

She swallowed and nodded. "I knew Violet was your tenant. I wanted to speak to her, get some answers. I planned to talk to you about it when I got here. I wanted your help, Quinn, but you weren't home."

Was she blaming me? Could I have saved Violet if I'd not gone to Toni's that night? Maybe I could have had more patience with Violet. Maybe I could have defused Jade. Hindsight sure provided clarity, but it couldn't change the past. I knew better than to feel guilty for something I couldn't control.

I needed to appear sympathetic. "I'm sorry I wasn't here for you," I said. "If I could change things, I would."

My heart pounded in my ears. I had my hands up, palms forward like a useless shield. "Put down the gun. You can't shoot me, Jade. It would make everything worse. You see that, right? Like my dead body to dispose of..." Was *that* real enough for her? "Please put down the gun and—"

She still aimed the gun at me. Sweat ran like a river down my back. How long had we been having this conversation? It felt like freaking hours. I wanted Craig to hurry, but it also scared me he could get hurt. I didn't dare look at my watch. She didn't know Craig was coming. How to use this to my advantage?

"No. I can't, Quinn." She held the gun steady. "Believe me, I've thought about how this would have turned out differently if you'd been home. Violet admitted she'd changed some water quality reports in exchange for Edward's sperm. She injected it inside her! She said it like it was no big deal, like it shouldn't matter to me because she wanted nothing from him. I was so freakishly mad at her. I've never experienced anger like that."

From the corner of my eye, I saw a marble candle holder. Could I reach it fast enough and then...throw it at her? What if the gun went off accidentally? "I agree with you, Jade. It was a ridiculous demand. She never should have asked." And Edward never should have agreed, but it wouldn't help to point that out.

"No. She shouldn't have asked. She was going to side with that company, Gaia Green, who is planning to sue McCourt. She was a mess that night, ranting, something about a phantom haunting her because she'd been submitting false reports. She said she'd burned through all your sage and the phantom was still hanging around, so maybe it wanted her to tell the truth." Jade looked as stupefied as she must have been that night.

"A phantom. She was crazy, Quinn. I didn't know what she might do. Come clean about the testing? Tell everyone Edward was going to father her child?"

I tried to be sympathetic as I could. "Right. Understandably, you'd be upset."

Jade was shaking with either anger or nerves, which was making me more nervous. "I was furious. I begged Violet to stop, to let us keep that ugly secret between us. If it got out, it would ruin our lives. I promised her I would make Edward retest the water, and I meant it. But she wouldn't listen. She seriously thought she was being haunted. She was going to tell the truth to appease a phantom. She was out of her mind."

"I know she was. I left the house that night and filed a complaint with the sheriff." Poor Violet. If only I'd seen Brielle before Violet did, maybe we could have talked about it, and she wouldn't have felt alone and desperate. It hardly mattered now. I wasn't going to tell Jade that Violet's phantom was real.

"You saw how crazy she was? She...she came after me. Out of the blue. I only hit her to save my life. I was defending myself."

That was a lie. Violet was hit on the back of the head. "I believe you, Jade. The police will too. It was self-defense." I took a step closer to her and put out my hand. "Give me the gun. You can't make this—"

Brielle appeared beside Jade. I startled. Brielle looked from me to the gun. Her eyes popped wide. "What's going on?"

Jade didn't react because she couldn't see my ghostly twin. "She's going to shoot me!" I cried to Brielle.

Brielle looked horrified. She took a cautious step toward Jade and stood for a second, looking at the gun trained on me.

Jade gave a clipped laugh. "You're seriously trying to fool me into thinking someone is standing behind me."

I locked my gaze on Brielle's. I knew what she was thinking. If she grabbed the gun, would it go off and hit me? I suddenly wondered if I died, would Brielle die, too? Was she thinking the same thing?

"Stop looking over there," said Jade.

"Be ready," Brielle said to me. She gripped her hands together, raised her arms, and brought her fist down hard on Jade's forearm.

Jade cried out. Her arm dropped, but she still held the gun.

I saw the mix of terror and confusion on her face just before I reached for the candle holder.

I threw it with all my strength. The candle holder hit her in the jaw. She jerked back. Correcting herself. But the gun went flying!

From the corner of my eye, I saw Brielle shove Jade, as I ran for the gun.

The gun had slid across the floor and hit the wall.

I dove after it with the speed of a twenty-year-old.

The gun was lighter than I expected. The metal warm. I fell back on my bum and pointed it at Jade, who was getting to her feet.

"Get back down on the floor," I said, impressed my voice was steady.

Jade went down on her knees. "What the hell was that?"

Brielle gave a shaky laugh. "Good question. What is going on here?"

"She killed my tenant," I said to Brielle as I got to my feet.

By the time the sheriff was on his way, Jade's face had paled too many shades to count.

"Did *you* put the salt lamp back?" I asked Brielle.

"Who are you talking to!" cried Jade.

Brielle glanced at her. "Yes, I'd forgotten about it until you showed me the picture of that man. I thought he was stealing your lamp, so I followed him."

Edward. I'd nearly forgotten Edward was here the night Violet was killed.

"Oh, gosh!" Brielle said as sirens sounded. "That's the police. I have to leave."

"Wait, a second. They searched all over for that lamp. Where was it all this time?"

"I can't stay. When I was here the last time, an officer saw me."

"What? Who?"

Brielle hurried out the patio door, turning to answer me. "I don't know his name. I'll find you later. I want to know what's been happening." She ran down the trail into the woods.

Jade moaned and shifted onto her butt. "Are you trying to make me go crazy?"

The doorbell rang. I didn't think the police would ring the bell after I'd told them I was holding a gun on a murderer. It must be Craig—finally. I yelled for him to come around the back. I wasn't sure if he heard me, but I wasn't taking my eyes off Jade.

"You were concerned Violet would ruin your lives, and now what will happen to Maddie, Jade? Did you think about that?"

"It was an accident. I was defending myself."

"Edward was here that night, wasn't he?"

Jade stared at the salt lamp, her expression confused, her spirit crushed. "No. He wasn't. I never told him what happened."

"You're lying. Edward took the lamp. Was he trying to make it look like someone else killed Violet?"

"I don't know what you're talking about. Why don't you ask your make-believe friend?"

Craig came through the back door as the sound of sirens wailed in the distance. His eyes widened as he saw me holding a gun.

"Jade killed Violet," I said to Craig. "Violet admitted she had a deal with Edward. His sperm, in exchange for her falsifying the water quality reports to keep the mine going. No one will believe this was your fault, Craig."

His face was a strange mix of horror and relief. A lot of horror was going around that night. I felt it too. My brother was safe, but Jade was living a nightmare.

"Not Edward? It was Jade?" He looked over at Jade, but her eyes were empty as she pulled up her knees and sat against the back of the couch. She dropped her head into her hands. Her body shook from her sobs, and for a moment, I felt sorry for her. I knew Edward played a part in Violet's murder, and I knew Jade was going to do everything she could to leave her daughter with one parent, even if she hated the man.

Chapter Twenty-Six

Toni and Poppy stood behind me as I opened the email from the Great Lake Superior Taste Awards. The pit of my stomach was heavy as I braced for the news.

When I saw that the first sentence started with the word Congratulations, I felt instant elation.

Toni read the first paragraph aloud and Poppy cheered. I'd won the Superior Taste contest with the Blackberry Star Anise cordial. Emotion filled my throat, and my eyes teared up.

I'd entered the contest to prove I was a winner, but I now realized that validation wasn't as meaningful as I'd thought it would be when I'd mailed in my cordials. My café was not a failure, as my ex had predicted. I was doing better than I could have imagined, and I didn't really need external validation to feel good about myself.

"Way to go, boss!" said Poppy.

"Son of a biscuit, I knew you'd win!" Toni hugged me. "And well-deserved, too. How many other contestants whipped up prize-winning cordials while solving a murder?"

True, but I felt a smidgen of guilt. How many other contestants had the help of an invisible twin? Without Brielle, I might not have been alive to read this email, but at least I'd won the contest with the cordial I'd made myself.

Winning was certainly validating, yet I was most proud of the fact I'd stuck my neck out and helped my brother when he'd needed me. Having done that meant more to me than receiving any certificate of excellence.

Poppy pulled a coffee cup from the dishwasher and put it on the shelf. "Yes, you sure did a good job *muddling* your way to an award-winning cordial. We're going to have to come up with a new verb for next month."

"Indeed we will," I said and poured Toni a coffee.

She took the mug. "I'm taking this outside. It's a beautiful day out there."

"I'll come and join you in a bit. I have a phone call to make first." I needed to call a realtor to list my home. I wasn't sure how hot the market was for murder houses, but I knew after moving back in, it no longer felt like my sanctuary. I didn't like going home at night, and I no longer cared to live in a house meant for Bryan and me to grow old together.

When I finished my call, I came downstairs and heard Poppy telling Edna Brooks it might help to take an Epsom salt bath.

Concerned, I came to stand beside Edna, who was in her mid-seventies. "Don't tell me you've been climbing up on chairs again." Last year, she'd fallen and wrenched her rotator cuff.

"No, no. I overdid it at my new exercises class. I'm trying to improve my strength and balance."

"Oh, dear," I said. "But good for you. I should think about an exercise regime."

"Yes, you should," she said. "Use 'em or lose 'em, they say. I noticed a loss in my strength after menopause—and oh, the weight gain. It's not enough to be running around here all day, Quinn. You need to get your heart rate up, keep your bones strong, and stay flexible. Clive and I walk thirty minutes every day, good and brisk, and you should, too. Look at doing some weight-bearing exercises as well."

I tugged on my apron. "You're right." I couldn't remember the last time I'd exercised on purpose. I didn't enjoy seeing myself in the mirror, yet I wasn't doing anything about it. I could see that my spirit double wasn't letting herself go.

"If you don't like exercise classes, there are great yoga routines online," said Poppy. "I do one every morning."

"I used to like yoga." I thought for a moment. "I'm going to suggest a yoga challenge to Toni. We can keep each other accountable. You are an inspiration, Edna."

I said goodbye to Edna, and while I poured myself a glass of citrus water, I watched Poppy work with ease and efficiency. I had to give credit where it was due. Poppy ran Break Thyme as skillfully and thoughtfully as I did. Leaving her in charge while I took a holiday was a sensible plan.

Now that I didn't have a murder to solve, it would give me time to think about Brielle's accusation that I'd somehow been afraid to live my life. Had living in my brother's shadow made me afraid to even try to compete? My father and then my ex's constant criticism sure hadn't boosted my confidence.

It had been a year now since Bryan left. With some distance and as I began to build a life on my own terms, I'd started to recognize disturbing patterns in my marriage. He'd always put me down. Not in big, noticeable ways, but with subtle digs and gestures that slowly chipped away at my self-esteem. Given my sense of inferiority to Craig, it was a wonder I'd had the confidence to open Break Thyme.

But I'd done it. The café was a success, and I felt like a success, too. I smiled at the sound of laughing customers and headed outside to find Toni.

With no breeze, the great lake was as smooth as a blueberry, and the air was a comfortable temperature now that the heatwave was over. The beach, with its wet footprints and grassy shoreline, floppy hats and fishing poles, sun sleepers, and food coolers, always relaxed me. It had the same effect on Toni. She'd turned her chair to face the lake. With her gaze on the water, a soft smile lifted and brightened her face.

"I got an update on the case from Poppy via Cody," I said, pulling a chair beside hers and sitting down.

"It's Cody now, is it? No more teen-deputy?"

"No," I conceded. "He's been coming around off-duty to pick up Poppy. Turns out, he's not a bad guy. I asked him if we were going to be friends now."

"And?"

"He didn't know why I'd think otherwise. I guess I read more into his dislike of me. I have to remember that sometimes a person is just having a bad day, and it has nothing to do with me."

Toni slipped her feet out of her sandals. "Good point. So, what's the update."

"For one, the police exposed Edward's nefarious role in the run-off water management at the mine. He'll likely go to jail for that and then there's the small matter of accessory to murder."

"You're kidding. I thought Jade said he had nothing to do with it."

"She did, but that changed when forensics found both of their fingerprints on the murder weapon. Cody said Edward confessed that after Jade killed Violet, she'd called him. She blamed him for what she'd done and said he better come and clean up her mess. He drove home from the conference and came down the river by boat."

Toni gave me a sideways look. "It was a mess all right. I feel bad for Maddie."

I didn't want to think about how hard this would be on Maddie. "Me, too. She's probably staying with her grandparents."

"It'll be difficult for all of them." Toni shooed a gull that was getting close to her feet. "I guess they proved Violet submitted false reports."

This still made me angry at Violet—compromising our water quality for her gain. "Can you believe she did that? And she wasn't the only one. The guy who preceded her at the Department of Health had been submitting samples of water from his own faucet and labeling them as if they'd come from the river. Edward bribed Violet into doing the same thing by giving her what she wanted."

"It's crazy, isn't it? Makes you want to ring all their necks. Did Edward admit to sleeping with Violet or did he just deliver sperm in a cup?"

I grimaced. "Ew, gross. I don't know if they slept together or not. It's hardly debatable which is worse. Anyway, she wanted a baby with her ex-husband's features. She was trying to win Derek back with a baby who looked like him, and that insanity got her killed."

Toni made a sound of agreement and stretched her legs out. "I'm looking forward to *not* talking about murder every time we get together. Have you decided what to do about your house?"

I was tired of talking about murder, too. "I imagine I'll take a substantial hit, but I'm going to try to sell it. In the meantime, I'll stay in Longfellow since we finished renovating."

"It turned out beautifully, but I'm surprised you'd live there. You said you couldn't live in a space as small as mine. I've got a few hundred square feet on Longfellow."

"I know, but this isn't forever. I spend most of the day at Break Thyme, anyway. So, I'm thinking I can adjust in the short term with most of my stuff in storage. There's a lot available in Beach Meadows Park with a lake view. I've already paid for it. I just have to move the trailer."

"You may end up loving a smaller footprint. I sure do. Having less stuff means less to look after. It's freeing in ways I couldn't have imagined."

I liked the prospect of simplifying my life. Violet's murder and Brielle's appearance were two life-changing events that left me both shaken and retrospective. And I'd thought turning fifty in a few months was hard to process. I was about to enter a new decade, and now that my marriage was over, I'd have to rewrite how I'd once envisioned my fifties. I wouldn't be growing old with Bryan in our riverside home. My kids lived their own lives. I owned a successful café, a travel trailer, and a twin from a parallel universe. None of which I'd seen coming a few years ago, so who knew what the next decade would bring.

"What's happening with Brielle?" Toni said. "You've not mentioned her in the last few days."

The reference to my twin phantom gave me a ping of angst. "I don't know. She said she'd be back, but it's been a week."

"Weird, huh? Maybe she's been showing up at your house or trailer when you're not there?"

I supposed she could be popping in anywhere, or maybe it wasn't something that happened to her every night. "That could be. She said she has no control over where she appears, so who knows."

"Since we're on the topic of appearing out of nowhere, the reappearance of the salt lamp must be driving the sheriff crazy." Toni laughed. "I can't imagine how that will ever be explained if Brielle put it back."

That made me chuckle, too. A loose end that would never be tied. "I know, but what I don't know is why it took her so long. She didn't seem to know about Violet's murder, but she also said something to suggest otherwise."

"Oh, yeah? What?"

"She thinks a police officer saw her."

Toni shook her head in dismay. "Really? So, some people can see her. I wonder if I can see her?"

I wasn't sure how I felt about that. It seemed things could get rather stressful if some people were seeing two of me and some weren't. How would we manage that? "I guess we should test that out the next time we can."

"Do you know which officer saw her?"

"No, she hasn't cleared that up either."

"Isn't it strange she wouldn't ask why the police had been at your house?"

"Yes, it is, but everything is strange when it comes to Brielle."

I had to get back to work and Toni had an appointment, so we said goodbye.

Later that day, I left Break Thyme to my trusted employees and drove to Beach Meadows to move the trailer to the lakeside spot. As attractive as he was, I decided not to ask Alec Camden for help. I wanted to accomplish this task with my son. He'd gone to the trouble of sending me how-to videos on YouTube and felt confident we could do it. I'd watched the videos, too, and made a checklist. This was a reason to spend time together, and that was more important to me.

Jordan's blue T-shirt emphasized the blue in his eyes. When he was little, he loved it when I told him his eyes were the color of cookie monster—his father's eyes. He still wore his sandy brown hair long, just like his dad's had been thirty years ago. Today, he'd tied it back. For a second, I thought about Violet wanting a baby that looked like Derek. There was a subtle reward in seeing your family's lineage in your children, but I doubted I would long for it if it wasn't there.

I did notice Jordan had shaved off his beard. "It's nice to see your face again," I teased, pinching his jaw.

"Enjoy it while you can. I'll let it grow in the winter."

Last weekend, Chelsea's party had been a success, with the dishes I'd laid out. She'd even sent me a text thanking me for my help. All had been forgiven between us and he seemed to be in good spirits.

I let Jordan take charge while I unhooked the electrical cable, water supply, and sewage hose. With everything in Longfellow secure, I shouted directions for Jordan to line up the truck hitch to the trailer coupler.

Soon, we were latched, locked, and had the safety chains and wiring hooked up. "All the lights work!" I verified.

Without mishap, Jordan drove the trailer to the new site. It only took a couple of tries to get it backed into the place where I wanted it. The warmth of our accomplishment spread through me and for once wasn't instigated by a hot flash.

Jordan helped level the trailer and get everything hooked up and working. Inside, we admired the cloud-white walls and slate gray cupboards.

"It looks good, Mom, but it's a little bare-boned in here, no?"

"It's empty because we were painting. I've got things in the truck to make it homey."

Jordan sat on the edge of the bed and gave it a bounce. "The mattress is good, and that's what matters. Okay then, I'll give you a hand unloading your truck and putting things away."

Over the next hour, we unpacked boxes and had Longfellow looking livable. I'd only brought necessities. It would take time to make it truly cozy and homelike.

"You're sure you'd rather live here? Chelsea and I could make room—"

I gave him a look. "I'd like Chelsea and me to be friends, Jordan, so let's not push it."

He laughed. "Okay, never mind. And, Mom, I do appreciate the effort." He slung an arm around my shoulders and kissed the top of my head the way he'd done since he'd grown taller than me. Goodness, I loved this boy. He glanced at his watch. "I gotta go. We'll bring dinner over next week, okay?"

"That sounds great." I hugged him tightly, then said goodbye, grateful we were back to our old selves. I hated to think it, but things were always easier between us without Chelsea.

But I swore I'd keep trying.

It was nearly dark, and I'd bought firewood. I was going to treat myself to a campfire and watch the stars come out over the lake. This was a beautiful spot and exactly what I needed. My mind was often a busy place, and I wanted to unwind and quiet my thoughts, especially after the stressful weeks I just had.

I tried not to think about it too much, but staring down the barrel of a gun in the hand of a friend had left me feeling like a different person in some ways. I wanted to hug my kids more often and my friends, too, even my customers. I'd found myself thinking life was precious, and many times during the day, I appreciated how fortunate I was. Like, this view, for instance, as the sinking sun painted the western sky in crimson and golds, then faded to black.

A little while later, I was dodging smoke, unsuccessfully. It cut into my eyes, so I had them shut tight when I heard footsteps.

"Hi there, Quinn. I see you got yourself set up. I would have been happy to help."

I blinked tears away. It was him. The hot guy. And he remembered my name!

Chapter Twenty-Seven

I STOOD UP STRAIGHT, sucked in my belly, and ran my fingers through my hair. "Thank you, Alec." *I remembered your name too.* "My son wanted to do it. It was good for us to have some mother/son bonding time over the hitching and sewage hose."

He laughed and looked out over the dark expanse of Lake Superior. "This is one of my favorite sites at Beach Meadows. There's nothing like falling asleep to the sound of waves rolling across the pebbles. I think of that sound as the breath of the earth."

I smiled at that, feeling a pleasant intimacy in talking about bedtime. Imagine that.

"I'm glad you're here, Quinn."

"Me too, and thank you again for holding this spot for me. I appreciate it." I liked this guy and if I was reading him right, he liked me too. I felt a sneeze coming on from the smoke I'd inhaled and wiggled my nose. I sniffled, wishing I had a Kleenex. I didn't want to run for toilet paper. He glanced at the trailer and then at the fire.

I had an extra chair leaning against the trailer. Oh. He was waiting for an invitation to join me. I was new to this kind of thing, and surprisingly, I liked looking into his eyes a lot more than I would have guessed. Maybe it was time to open myself up to romance. I couldn't think of a nicer way to spend my first night at Beach Meadows—the crackling fire, the rolling waves, the moon rising, and Alec and I getting to know each other over a glass of wine or two.

"Well, I just stopped by to see you got set up alright and to let you know, there's a fire ban. Sorry, but you'll have to put it out."

My dream bubble burst. "Shoot, I forgot to check that. I'm sorry, I'll extinguish it right away." I reached for the bucket of water sitting beside the fire pit.

"Have a good night. Enjoy the waves." And he was gone.

I felt ridiculous as my fire hissed and turned to soggy, charred wood. With everything put away, I went inside the trailer. The temperature had dropped, and I was only wearing a plaid shirt over my jeans. I decided not to turn on the furnace, though. I had a warm quilt and an extra blanket if I needed it.

In the bathroom, I cringed when I saw my face. A dark streak of soot ran from my nose to jaw, making me look like I had a lopsided jowl.

By the time I finished washing up, I'd decided Alec Camden didn't know what he was missing. Sure, I was a little overweight, but I used to be hot stuff. I would be hot stuff again—and not because of internal combustion. Edna had been right. I wasn't being kind to myself or practical by dreading my fiftieth birthday next year. And who was I kidding—not Father Time. Instead of bemoaning my age, I should celebrate the good grace that got me through fifty years. And keep myself healthy and strong. How I treated my body now would dictate how I felt when I reached the next milestone.

"Don't scream. I've popped in behind you."

I didn't scream, but she'd given me a jolt. I turned to face Brielle. "Finally. Where have you been?"

She looked worse for wear. "For one, I've had a bout of insomnia. And I think I've been popping in at your house lately, but it's hard to remember." She turned around to take in my new abode. "Are you living here now?"

"Yep, just until I buy something else. I'm selling my house on the river." I had a thought. "I wonder if you'll still pop in there when I no longer own it. So far, it seems you're drawn to places connected to me."

"I suppose I am. That's too bad you're selling. It's a nice house." She walked over to the small counter and turned the bottle of hand soap so the label faced the back.

I followed, checking to be sure I'd drawn all the blinds. I didn't want to be seen talking to the cupboards on my first night. At least if someone heard me, they'd think I was talking on the phone.

"It doesn't feel nice to me any longer," I said. "The space feels tainted and not just with the violence of the murder. I don't want to be reminded of the place where Jade pointed a gun at me."

"I'm sorry it happened, Quinn. I imagine it will take some time to get over."

No doubt. I felt the pressure of using this time with Brielle to get a better understanding of her life, but I also wanted to know what happened with the lamp. "Do you remember telling me you saw Edward with a salt lamp in the woods? Can you tell me what happened after that?"

"I've been trying to remember because it seemed important to you. Do you know when you wake up in the morning, and if you don't think about it right away, you can't remember what you dreamed?"

I wasn't sure what this had to do with the lamp, but I agreed.

"It's like that for me when I wake up in my life. I only remember fragments of what happened in your world. It's only when I return that I remember some of what happened the last time I was here, but not everything. It's like I have some pieces of a puzzle, but not all."

"I think I can relate. Sometimes, I feel like I have brain fog, which I hope is related to peri-menopause. And trying to figure out why Violet was murdered and how Craig was involved was like having just a few puzzle pieces. Try to remember, Brielle. You also said a cop saw you. It would be good to know who."

She picked up the dishcloth and wiped down the faucet. It was something I would do when I needed time to think. I stood a few feet away, quietly, to not rush her. She folded the cloth neatly and turned, resting her back against the counter. "Okay. This is what I remember. I followed the man who stole your lamp. He put it in his boat, and I rode with him down the river to a house."

I pictured Brielle sitting in the boat with Edward and wondered if people could walk through her.

"I forgot about the lamp until you mentioned it, and even after that, it was hard to remember what he did with it."

"But you did remember. You found the lamp and returned it."

"Yes, that's right. I did! I finally remembered he buried the lamp in the woods behind his house. It was nothing short of a miracle that I found it."

Well, that explained the lamp. I moved closer and touched her shoulder. To me, she was solid.

She looked at my hand. "I can feel that. I don't feel people who can't see me. I guess it's the same for them."

That answered that I supposed, but I thought we better test Brielle's solidity theory to know for sure. Toni would be a good subject.

Moving on. "When did the officer see you? Do you know who it was?"

She looked upward as if she could pluck the answer from above. "No, I don't know exactly when it was. I appeared on your patio one day. There was a young police officer outside poking around. He yelled at me. When I realized he could see me, I panicked and ran."

I remembered Deputy Wilson's comment the day he was on goat removal. *Do you think I didn't see you back at your house?* It must have been Brielle he'd seen. He'd thought I'd come back after he'd caught Toni and me. No wonder he'd been hostile that day.

"Well, this isn't good. Three people have seen you—Violet, Deputy Wilson, and maybe Gloria, the psychic."

"But most people don't see me. Believe me, I can tell."

This inconsistency was going to be a problem. "Speaking of Gloria, did you toss that cordial recipe onto the table at Mystic Garden?"

She thought for a moment, then her eyes lit up. "Yes, I did. You were ignoring it, so I wanted to be sure you saw it."

I supposed she'd been right on that. The cordial was delicious, and I planned to incorporate it into a new drink at Break Thyme. My thoughts were starting to run wild again. There was so much I wanted to know about Brielle's life. "I think I'd like a glass of wine to take the edge off. Another glass, that is. Can you join me?"

"Sure. I love that Shiraz you always buy."

Had she been drinking my wine?

"I have a clear memory of that cordial recipe," she said, sitting on the bench seat while I opened the Shiraz. "Did you know it came from Grammy MacQuinn? I make it all the time."

Weird that I didn't know that. "I miss Grammy. Did you write out that recipe for me? For the contest?"

"I did, yes."

I took two glasses from the cupboard and poured the wine. "*Slàinte*," I said, clinking my glass against Brielle's and sitting down. While I appreciated Brielle's input with Grammy's cordial, I was uncomfortable about her making decisions that affected my life. "We're going to have to put down some rules around your visits."

She scoffed. "Rules? I don't see how. I can't control where I appear or when I disappear. I can't know ahead of time who will see me and who won't. We're going to have to figure out a way to manage both of us living your life."

I let out a heavy sigh. Life with a spirit twin was going to be complicated. If I didn't become the queen of diplomacy, Brielle could cause all sorts of trouble for me.

I stared into those eyes, the color of stormy waters, just like mine, and recognized the stubborn streak I often denied. I feared I was about to see more sides of my personality than I'd like.

Speaking of fear... "You said you were living the life I was afraid to live. What did you mean by that?"

"I did? I'm sorry. That wasn't fair. You're rather fearless, Quinn. I suppose what I meant was that you've not embraced our...well, our psychic nature, for one thing."

"Our what?" And then a flicker of a memory surfaced. Decades ago, when Jordan was a baby, I'd had a sudden vision pop into my head of a woman driving off a bridge into the water. The vision had startled me, but I'd been too busy with the baby to dwell on it. It terrified me to read the news the next day and learn the vision was accurate. I prayed to never see a thing like that again and kept my mind as busy as I could. Maybe my fear was heightened by the fact I'd become a mother. Fortunately, it hadn't happened again.

"You are psychic?" I asked.

"A little, yes. I've tried to develop this ability, but I think it might be my fascination with astral projection that brought me here."

Astral projection? Why would anyone want to leave their body? "Good grief. We have certainly taken separate paths." So, she'd not been living the life I was afraid to live. In this case, I believed fear was the sensible option. I'd made rational choices that kept me safe and sound in my own little world. Whereas she was projecting herself all over the universe. Had she made other reckless choices?

I was about to ask when she vanished. Poof! Again.

Would I ever find out which one of us had the superior life? Was there even such a thing?

I picked up both our glasses, took them to the sink, and dumped them. I was suddenly weary and didn't really need the alcohol. It would just disturb my sleep and give me night sweats.

Besides, I had to protect every one of my brain cells since I had to figure out how to manage this mostly invisible, disappearing twin.

The only thing that was crystal clear at the moment was that I couldn't let fear and worry decide my future. If I wanted to look back one day and feel grateful for the decisions I'd made, I'd best find a way to prevent my life from becoming a catastrophic muddle.

Because I'd thought midlife was murder *before* Brielle showed up.

If you enjoyed A *Spirited Double*, join Quinn and Toni in their next crime-solving adventure in *Spirited Vengeance*, Book 3 in the Midlife is Murder series. Available here.

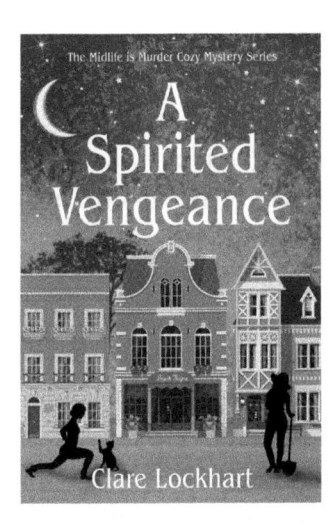

An OCD twin from a parallel universe. A meddling ghost. A desperate plea for help. Is it time for Quinn to accept her role as an apron-wearing crusader for justice?

With her new café bustling, Quinn is trying everything to understand the bizarre turn her life has taken, even visiting a haunted house to find answers.

But when her best friend Toni's cousin shows up with a suitcase, a mysterious man, and a vow to leave her abhorrent husband, Quinn must now decide how far she'll go to help.

Is breaking into a safe too far?

Things take a drastic turn when the police arrest Toni's cousin for murder.

Faced with a slack sheriff, a growing list of suspects, and a missing fortune, the two midlife friends band together while Quinn grapples with the ethics of using her invisible, parallel-life twin to get to the truth.

Will Quinn's connections with entities from other dimensions help or hinder her?

If you like fast-paced, fun, light-hearted stories that keep you guessing, you'll love A Spirited Vengeance, book 3 in the Midlife is Murder paranormal cozy mystery series. Get it on Amazon here.

If you haven't already joined Clare Lockhart's newsletter for a FREE book, goodies, and exclusive news please join here.

Also by Clare Lockhart

Midlife is Murder
Paranormal Cozy Mystery Series
A *Spirited Swindler* (Book 1)
A *Spirited Debacle (Novella)* (Book 1.5)
A *Spirited Double* (Book 2)
A *Spirited Vengeance* (Book 3)
A *Spirited Betrayal* (Book 4)
A *Spirited Delusion* (Book 5)
A Spirited Accusation (Book 6)
A Spirited Reckoning (Book 7)

Midlife is Magic
Paranormal Cozy Mystery Series
Visions and Villainy (Novella) (Book 1)
Curses and Consequences (Book 2)
Potions and Plunder (Book 3)
Scandals and Snafus (Short Story in A *Witch of a Scandal* anthology)
Sorcery and Suspects (Book 4)

Magical Matchmaker Romance
(writing as Sharon Clare)
Love of Her Lives
Trick Me Once
In For a Spell

Acknowledgements

I want to thank my editor Wanda Ottewell for your enthusiasm for this series and for improving the stories I strive to tell.

And a big thank you to my critique group: Carole Ann Vance, Linda Farmer, Sheila Tucker and Norma Meldrum, for your ongoing insightful edits and for sticking with me and my endeavors for many years.

I also want to thank Irene Jorgensen for your helpful suggestions and for all the brainstorming sessions we do.

A special thank you to Megan Bernas, chef extraordinaire, who is always available to provide food and café details. And to Ashley Christian, a meticulous beta reader, who finds little details that make a big difference.

And to John Burrows for being my champion, for helping me plot (fictional) murder, and for climbing marketing mountains. I will be forever grateful for your rabbit-hole searches and never-ending encouragement.

About the Author

CLARE LOCKHART WRITES PARANORMAL cozy mysteries set in the fictional small town of Bookend Bay about best friends in midlife who find themselves in the odd pickle, unravelling murders while dodging cheeky, paranormal visitors.

She would love to hear from you, so please send an email to clare@clarelockhart.com and visit https://clarelockhart.com to learn more about Clare and her books.

If you'd like to receive free content, hear the latest news, and stay in touch, please join Clare Lockhart's Mailing List on her website.

Milton Keynes UK
Ingram Content Group UK Ltd.
UKHW021904151124
451262UK00014B/1356